ROLLER-COASTER

ROLLER-COASTER

Michael Gilbert

Carroll & Graf Publishers, Inc.
New York

Published by arrangement with the author.

First published in Great Britain by Hodder and Stoughton in 1993.

First Carroll & Graf edition 1994

First Carroll & Graf mass market edition 1995

Carroll & Graf Publishers, Inc.
260 Fifth Avenue
New York, NY 10001

ISBN 0-7867-0220-6

Manufactured in the United States of America

1

"I declare the court to be in session," said the judge. He settled himself comfortably in his chair and lit a cigar. "Bring in the prisoner."

"Right away, Farmer."

"Really, Goat. You're forgetting your manners. When addressing me in this tribunal you call me Your Honour."

"Beg pardon, I'm sure," said Goat. He showed his yellow teeth in an apologetic smirk. His wizened face and tuft of beard made it clear how he had acquired his name. "Lend us a hand, Buller."

Buller the Bull heaved up from his chair the bulk which had been admired in many an all-in wrestling ring and padded behind Goat to the door which led into an ante-room.

The court was the ground floor of the Packstone Building, a defunct chandlery enterprise in Cubitt Town. When its owners departed it had been tightly locked and bolted; but not too tightly for the Farm Boys who had found a way in through a goods hatch in Packstone Passage. This had given them access to the big central room on the ground floor. Such light as reached it was filtered through the dirt-encrusted windows, set high enough in the walls to be out of reach of the boys, who would otherwise have enjoyed poking sticks through the bars to break the glass.

Considered as a court room, it had a certain dignity. It rose to the full height of the building and was topped by an overhead lantern. Galleries on the north and east sides served the doors of a number of upstairs rooms.

1

Up from the cellar came Buller the Bull and Dog Henty. They represented the muscle of the quintet. They were carrying the prisoner, who certainly could not have made the ascent under his own power. His top half had been forced into a canvas strait-jacket of the type used in lunatic asylums. His ankles had been strapped and his legs roped together. His mouth had been covered with a broad strip of sticking plaster, wound twice round his head, leaving his eyes and ears clear. It was fouled at the back by the blood, now dark brown, which had run from a slash in his scalp.

Only the eyes of this bundle were alive.

"Put him where we can see him," said the judge genially. "Learned counsel for the prosecution, pray open your case."

Since no one accepted the invitation the judge said, "That means you, Dog. Wake up."

"Oh, is that me? OK. Pleased, I'm sure." The opening of his mouth exposed the over-developed canine teeth which had earned him his name. "Shouldn't I have a wig, Farmer?"

"We've only got one. You'll have to share it with counsel for the defence. Hand it over, Piggy."

The wig, which was white and fluffy, had formed part of a Father Christmas outfit. Dog adjusted it over his oiled black hair and said, "Well, Your Honour, this lump of shit which we see in front of us – "

"Hold it. It would be more in accordance with the dignity of the proceedings if counsel were to use the word excrement."

"If that's what you want, Your Honour, I'm willing to oblige. Well, this lump of ex-cement had wormed his way into our confederation by claiming to be one of the boys and wanting a share of the action."

"Well put," said Piggy. He was fat and white and had a thick projecting nose not unlike the snout of a boar. "I think that was well expressed, don't you, Your Honour?"

"In view of the fact," said the judge coldly, "that you are charged with the prisoner's defence, it might be as well if you cut out your compliments to counsel on the other side."

"So I am," said Piggy. "In the heat of the moment I'd quite forgotten." He was the only one of the five who was showing any open excitement. "I withdraw the last statement. What I intended to say was that I object to the foul insinuations of my learned friend." His voice demonstrated that he was an educated man.

"Objection overruled," said the judge. "Carry on, counsel."

"Well, what I've got to say is that this lump of ex-cement, called Ernie Flower, didn't turn out to be no sweet-smelling flower, but a lump of dirty grass. He took part in our operations and was beginning to be a trusted member of our community when, by chance – "

Anyone looking down might have seen the eyes of the man on the floor flicker, with the first sign of animation he had shown.

" – quite by chance we discovered that he was in communication with the Old Bill and was receiving regular payments from them. He had become, in other words, a tool of that arch lump of ex-cement called Morrissey."

. The mention of the redoubtable gang-buster and thief-taker caused a momentary drop in the temperature.

The judge said, "Morrissey may have planted him, but he won't be getting no more fruit off this particular tree, however hard he shakes it."

This earned a murmur of approval from the court.

"If that concludes the case for the prosecution," said the judge, "I will now call on counsel for the defence."

"Well, really and truly, there isn't much I can say, in the circumstances."

"What about the prisoner's background?"

"Oh, his background. Yes, of course. The court must give consideration to the prisoner's background. We understand

3

that he came originally from Newcastle, a part of the country where children are notoriously subject to abuse. He is also the product of a broken home, deprived of the benefit of a two-parent family and therefore only too easily led into bad ways."

This produced a round of applause from the members of the court, suppressed by the judge, who added, "Has the prisoner anything to say in his defence?"

Not surprisingly the prisoner had nothing to say.

"Then it only remains for me to pass sentence. Prisoner at the bar – "

"Hold it," said Dog. "When you pass sentence, shouldn't the prisoner be standing up? They always made me stand up when they did it."

"Must do the thing properly," agreed the judge. "Stand him up."

Bull and Goat heaved the bundle onto its feet and held it swaying there.

"Prisoner at the bar," the judge resumed, "after a full and fair hearing you have been found guilty of the foul crime of treason. Treason to your fellows. For such an offence there is only one possible sentence." He took a black silk handkerchief out of his pocket and spread it over his bald and sun-burnt head. "The sentence is death. It only remains to decide how you shall depart this life. I am open to suggestions from the court."

"Really, we ought to hang him," said Dog. "We've got plenty of rope."

"Hanging's for murder," said Buller. "This is treason. The proper thing for treason is he should be hung, drawn and quartered. I could fetch a cleaver and a saw from the shop" – Bull was a part-time butcher – "and we'd have his guts out and chop him into four bits in no time at all."

"Too messy," said the judge.

"Nothing we couldn't clear up."

"I think," said Piggy, "that both those ways are what you might call crude. I think it should be something that takes longer. Give him time to think over his evil ways."

Goat said, "There was a piece I read in the papers about the French soldiers in Algiers – "

"I didn't know you could read, Goat."

"Silence," said the judge. "This is a serious discussion. Proceed, Goat."

"Well, when they caught one of the rebels, they used to hang him up by his heels and leave him there."

"And how long did that take to kill him?"

"Sometimes twenty-four hours, or more."

"We can't have him hanging round here for days," said the judge. "It's got to be quicker than that."

"Then might I make a suggestion," said Piggy. "I can get a compressed air cylinder from our garage. If we attached it to the prisoner's exhaust pipe we could blow him up so tight he'd float up to the ceiling. Of course, it'd kill him too, but not as quickly as cutting his head off or hanging him."

During this discussion no one had been looking at the prisoner. He called attention to himself by giving an energetic wriggle and a heave, which turned him over onto his face where he lay, jack-knifing like a fresh-landed salmon. A further frenzied movement brought him over again onto his back and they saw that his face, as much of it as was visible behind the plaster gag, was dark red and purpling and that his eyes were almost starting from his head.

They watched him curiously as his struggles grew even more frantic and he rolled, with a final convulsive effort, onto one side. Then he lay still.

"Seems to be trying to escape," said Dog.

"I'm not sure," said Piggy. He bent down to look, then stood up slowly. "Do you know, I think he's done the job for us."

He took out a lighter, clicked it on and held the flame against the prisoner's wide open eye. There was no reaction. He took hold of one end of the adhesive tape and jerked it clear.

"What I thought," he said, standing back to avoid the mess that came with the tape. "He was trying to be sick and he couldn't and it choked him. That stopped his heart. Drunks often go that way."

"Well," said Dog with a sigh, "that's it, isn't it? What do we do now, Farmer?"

The judge inhaled generously on his cigar and then loosed the smoke in a series of neat circles. He was collecting his thoughts.

"We get rid of him," he said.

There was no dispute about that.

"How?" said Goat.

"In the river, of course, stupid," said Bull.

That was the natural destination; the river Thames, depository of so many embarrassing secrets. It ran not twenty yards from where they were sitting.

"Got to be careful, though," said Farmer. "I've known too many things what was put in come out again. You brought that stuff I told you, Goat?"

Goat went out into the lobby and came back, first with a roll of sacking and some cord, then with a battered suitcase which, from the way he handled it, was clearly heavy. When it was tipped up a number of iron objects and large flint stones tumbled out onto the floor.

"Right," said Farmer. He spoke as a man who knew what had to be done and had made his preparations for doing it. "First we strip him naked. Put his clothes and shoes in that suitcase. They'll go into my furnace tonight. Right? Now we roll him up in this sacking."

It had been carefully cut. It was long enough to swathe the body, with an open pocket at each end.

"That's where the heavy stuff goes, Goat. Fasten them with that cord. Twice round and knot it good. Don't want the weights slipping out. Now, Piggy, did you bring those pliers with you?"

"Bloody hell, I went and forgot all about them."

"Being certain you would forget, I brought a pair of my

own. There you are, Piggy. Out with his gnashers, every one of them."

Whilst this grisly extraction was going on Dog was looking at the sack-enshrouded body of Ernie Flower.

"Something worrying you?" said Farmer.

"What I was thinking was, even without his teeth, if he did happen to surface – I'm not saying he will, but bodies do, however careful you are – "

"It's possible," agreed Farmer. "When he gets really blown up. So what?"

"Well, mightn't he be identified by his face or his prints? To be quite safe, shouldn't we get Buller to take off his head and his hands?"

"Thus making an unnecessary mess," said Farmer. "Which has been the ruin of many a promising career. What really excites the Old Bill? I'll tell you. Blood. That's what gets them and their scientific pals worked into a lather. A drop of blood. That's all they need. Even a stain on the floor. Difficult to get out, however hard you scrub."

Piggy looked up from his dentistry for a moment and said, "Scotsman called Macbeth had the same idea."

"Get on with it and less backchat," said Farmer. "I understand what you're getting at, Dog. But there's a better way. That's why we've left those holes in the sack. Little doorways, you might say, to allow the fish to get in. Particularly the eels. Wonderful eaters, the Thames eels. In three or four days, or maybe even less, there won't be anything on his face or his fingers to identify him.

"I'll bear that in mind," said Bull thoughtfully, "next time I'm offered a dish of stoodles. When he's all packed up, what do we do with him?"

"We put him in my van. Two of you go out first to see there's no one in the passage. Then stand at either end, to give the all-clear. Can you manage him, Bull?"

"With one hand," said Bull.

"You clear up in here, Goat."

Goat sniffed. It seemed to him that he did most of the dirty work.

"What are you planning to do with these?" said Piggy. The teeth he had extracted had gone into a plastic shopping bag.

"You're going to get rid of them. They can go down the storm drains in the street. Take them out tonight. One tooth down each drain."

Piggy grinned. It seemed an odd thing to do, but dropping tooth after tooth down different drain holes was somehow a satisfactory way of rounding out the day's work.

"And what about him?" said Bull, indicating the bundle which he had slung over one shoulder.

"I'll get rid of him tonight. Best place will be the jetty at the south end of Barking Creek. You can come with me. There's a track down past the sewage works. Won't be anyone around. Not at night. OK?"

"OK," said Bull. Like the others he had great confidence in Farmer.

When the last of the men had gone silence descended on the place. At first a complete silence. Then a silence broken by a scuffling noise, as though of some small creature in the woodwork.

The maker of this noise was a boy called Arnold. He was in the north gallery which overlooked the central room and was squeezing himself into as inconspicuous a bundle as possible. He was appalled by what he had seen and heard and had moved neither hand nor foot as it went on. He had scarcely even dared to breathe. His overriding idea now was to get out; but he realised that, for absolute safety, it would be better to wait until dark and by an effort of will, remarkable in such a young boy, he stayed where he was, only moving backwards into a more natural position to ease his aching limbs.

He was a solitary boy and a known thief. He had unusual ability in two fields. The first was a photographic memory, which enabled him to remember useful things, like lock-combination numbers, and also to remember and repeat, verbatim, things which people said about other people. This was not always a popular performance. His other talent was an extraordinary ability to insert himself into rooms which were, apparently, securely fastened.

No part of his neighbours' possessions was safe from his agile fingers. He was only saved from massacre by the fact that his older brother was a formidable bruiser. He organised the sale of Arnold's plunder and kept most of the proceeds for himself.

At long last, when dusk had deepened into night, Arnold slipped out through a gap where the bars on the basement air tunnel were slightly bent apart; an opening which no one who was not as thin and as agile as he was would have dared to attempt.

Packstone Passage seemed to be clear, but he was taking no chances. He slipped along, under the shadow of the wall, a shadow among shadows. As he went he was making up his mind. It had been a tremendous event, but he dared not tell anyone about it. No one, that was, except his best friend, Winston, a West Indian boy. And him only under the most rigid vows of silence. The thought of what those men would do to him if he talked about them and they heard about it, sent cold shivers down from his stomach and into his thin legs.

2

"Glad to have you back, Skipper," said Chief Inspector Gwilliam.

"Glad to be back," said Petrella. He was deeply tanned and thin and stringy as a bunch of seaweed.

"Do I hear you went out looking for trouble again?"

An edited version of Petrella's doings during the last five months had evidently reached east London. In the early spring of that year he had completed an assignment for Deputy Commissioner Lovell which had left him with a cracked skull, a collar bone broken in two places and a badly damaged left hand. Lovell, visiting him in hospital, had cheered him by telling him of his pending promotion to superintendent and then dampened his spirits by repeating the verdict of the doctors. 'Three months off duty, relax and try not to do anything stupid.'

Petrella had taken himself, his wife Jane and their two children to Morocco where his father, Colonel of Police Gregorio Petrella, now retired, was running his own fruit farm on the Oum er Rbia river, inland from El Jadida. Here he had lain about in the sun for ten weeks, lending a hand with the bookkeeping side of what was clearly becoming a highly profitable business. Then, feeling fully recovered and disregarding Lovell's injunction, he had taken a Land-Rover, with some spare cans of petrol and water, and had driven through Marrakesh, over the High Atlas and the Lesser Atlas and out into the desert. He was making for Chenachèn, of which he had heard an enthusiastic account from an archaeologist friend of his father's.

He had got there all right, had lost his way coming back and had finished the last of his water and petrol in the middle of the Hamada Tounassine, where he would have finished his life as well if he had not been sensible enough to tell his father where he was going.

The colonel had sent a flight of army helicopters to look for him. One of them had picked him up, three-quarters dead of hunger, thirst and general dehydration. This had added two months to his enforced leave and it was early in August before he surfaced at Maplin Road.

No question he was glad to be back and to start exploring the marches of his new kingdom. As a superintendent he was now the lord of No. 2 Area East, the old H Division bounded on the south by the Thames, on the east by the river Lea, on the north by a line running along the south edge of Victoria Park – but exclusive, he was glad to note, of that notorious trouble spot – and on the west by the underground line from Shoreditch Station southwards; an area full of tough people and criminal possibilities.

Since Maplin Road was both the head station of HA and his own headquarters he was forced, like an admiral, to reside in a battleship under command of a captain and might have been uncomfortable if he had not known Gwilliam since Highside days when Taffy had been a sergeant and he had been the newest thing in detective constables; young, inexperienced and happy. The reversal of their positions had caused neither of them any embarrassment.

It was very hot. The start of an August which was to break records.

"Sergeant Blencowe," said Petrella, "used to maintain that crime was seasonal. In summer, arson, wife-beating and indecent exposure. At Christmas, shop-lifting and cruelty to children."

"We've certainly had two fires that didn't look like accidents. Big insurance on both. You'd better have a look at the reports."

11

Petrella eyed his in-tray without enthusiasm. There was a mound of letters and dockets in it. Some of them looked like official bumph from Area and from Scotland Yard. The weight of administrative responsibility on top of routine was already beginning to make itself felt.

"And shop-lifting's not just at Christmas," said Gwilliam, "it's an all-the-year-round growth industry now. And there's another thing." He indicated a file in a dark blue cover with a red star in the corner. Petrella had already noted the title: 'Drug-Related Offences'.

"It's the kids mostly. They get high on glue and do the daftest things. Kill themselves sometimes. And other people too. Boy on a motor-bike the other day – it was much too powerful for him anyway – ran straight into a bus queue and sat on the pavement with a stupid grin on his face, like as if he'd done something clever. What he had done was kill a nice old lady, break a man's arm and a small girl's leg. I'd better leave you to do some reading. A quiet morning and you could get through most of it."

When he had gone Petrella looked again at his in-tray. A morning might enable him to read it, but whether he could do anything useful about it was another question.

His hand was on the dark blue docket when the intercom sounded. It was the efficient Inspector Ambrose. As a sergeant he had practically run Petrella's previous station. Now promoted to inspector he ran the present one even more efficiently. If you wanted to see the man in charge you had to see Ambrose first and often you got no further.

He said, "It's Sergeant Kortwright, sir. From the Docks Road Station. He's been landed with the job of West Indian community officer – " He didn't say, 'Poor chap', but it was clear from his tone of voice that that was what he meant.

"Can you deal with it?"

"I've been trying for ten minutes to do just that. But he says the complaints he wants to discuss with you are an inter-divisional problem and he'll have to see you."

"All right. Send him up," said Petrella.

Sergeant Kortwright had a pale face which contrasted with his jet black hair. He was not a cheerful man. His gloom stemmed equally from resentment at not achieving promotion and apprehension over the additional responsibilities if he did achieve it. Petrella offered him a chair, on which he perched, and a cigarette which he refused.

"Well, now," he said, "what can I do for you?"

"It's not easy," said Kortwright. "Not at all easy. I'm sure you'll appreciate that, sir. One policeman being put into a position where he has to complain about another."

"I understand that. But I assure you that nothing you say here will go outside this room."

"It's not what you might *say*, sir. It's what you might feel bound to do. Then people will guess – "

"If I'm forced to act," said Petrella, "you may be sure I shall do it on my own initiative. It won't appear as the result of anything anyone else has told me. OK?"

Kortwright looked a little relieved, but not much, squared his shoulders and started to talk. It was a story which was not uncommon at that time, but it had lurid highlights of its own.

The heart of the problem was a group of West Indians who lodged in four blocks of flats in Limehouse Fields.

"If they were only on the other side of Commercial Road," said Kortwright, "they'd be in D. Much better if they were."

"Oh, why's that?" said Petrella. He had spent some time memorising the sub-divisional boundaries. "Why should it be better if they came under Trench, at D, rather than – " the name had escaped him for a moment, " – rather than the head of C?"

"It isn't Chief Inspector Ramsbottom I'm worried about, sir – "

Ramsbottom. Of course. He had already heard rumours about him. Some favourable, some not. Kortwright was evidently one of his admirers.

"I'm not worried about him. Not in the least. A very nice

13

man, easy to work with. It's that sergeant of his. Sergeant Stark."

"Dod Stark?" Recollections of something he had heard came back to him. "Didn't he come to us from the army?"

"From the SAS. That lot. A core of the ayleet, they call themselves."

"I've heard them called less polite things than that," said Petrella. "Tell me. Do you happen to know why he left them?"

"He was a bit quick on the draw on one of their jobs. In Northern Ireland, that was. Shot an IRA man. At least he thought he was, only it turned out that he wasn't. He was behaving suspiciously, but he wasn't armed."

"Yes, I remember now. I read about it."

A court of enquiry had exonerated Stark, but it had clearly been thought prudent to get him out of Ireland and to organise a change of jobs for him.

"It's unusual, you see," said Kortwright. "Because mostly it's the youngsters, just out of Hendon, who act antagonistic. And even with them it's mostly verbal. They call them coons and sambos and such. There's not much physical action. With Stark, it's different. Nine-tenths of the time he's dead normal. Rather quiet, really. But one piece of backchat and he hits out."

"Hits? What with?"

"His fist, mostly. He knocked more than one man out cold. Now he doesn't have much occasion for that sort of thing. When they see him coming, they get out of his way. Any trouble he has now is with the kids. They hang around the streets and rubbish him. He can't chase after them. Lowering to his dignity."

"I don't suppose he'd catch them if he did."

"That's right. Little monkeys. Plenty of bolt holes."

"Don't they go to school?"

"When the schools can catch 'em. After school hours they sometimes go to one of the clubs."

14

"Clubs?"

"Church clubs, mission clubs. There's a big one in Commercial Road. The Athletic, they call it. Father Freeling from St Barnabas Church, Cable Street, runs it."

Father Freeling. Note him as someone to look up.

"Right," he said. "That's the general picture. Now, which particular lot are people complaining about?"

"It's not people complaining about other people. It's complaints about the police. That's nothing new. Just normal grousing. But lately it seems to be – well – a sort of campaign."

"So who are the campaigners?"

"It was the newspapers started it. A man from the *Sentinel*. Name of Carver. He started to hang round asking questions. Stark threw a scare into him and the paper called him off and put in another man, name of Poston-Pirrie."

"Come again."

"It's hyphened, Poston-Pirrie. I believe he's quite well known. Signs his own articles. There've been a couple in the *Sentinel* lately, sort of aimed at this part of the world."

"Naming names?"

"Not yet. But not far off it. 'A certain detective sergeant well known for his brutality.' That sort of thing and it wasn't just articles. When Stark chased their man Carver off they really got busy. First they talked to the community council. Then to our local MP. He must have said something to the Home Secretary, who got onto Central and through them it came down – gathering speed as you might say – to Area. And then a lot of the shit landed on me."

If it hadn't been so serious Petrella might have been tempted to laugh at this Heath Robinson conception of a long pipe with numerous bends and junctions, starting in a lavatory somewhere and finally emptying its contents on the unhappy Kortwright. Instead of laughing, he said, "All right, Sergeant. I'll look into it. And in future see that all complaints come to me."

Kortwright departed, looking not much happier than he had when he came in, and Petrella's hand had hardly closed on the top document in his in-tray when the telephone rang again. This time it was Gwilliam.

"Sorry to disturb your reading," he said. "But I've got Detective Hoyland here. He's brought in an odd story and I think you ought to hear it."

"And so I will," said Petrella. "But come up yourself first and tell me about Hoyland. Is he the long streak, badly in need of a hair cut, that I spotted in the detectives' room? Looks about fifteen years old."

"That's him."

"He can come up here in five minutes. That should give you time to tell me about him."

Gwilliam was not surprised at the suggestion. Petrella had always seemed to be more interested in people than in things.

When Gwilliam arrived he said, "I've got his c.v. here. Gives you all the details." Petrella waved the document away. He said, "Come on, Taffy. One of your well-known character sketches."

"Well," said Gwilliam, "if you want it in shorthand I'd put it this way – " Then he stopped, clearly embarrassed.

"Go on," said Petrella.

"I've changed my mind," said Gwilliam. "I realise what I was going to say would have been out of place."

"Never change your mind. First impressions are always best." He had an idea of what was coming.

"Right, then. What I was going to say was he's a lot like you were when you first turned up at Highside. Only not so crafty."

Petrella laughed. "He hadn't the good fortune to have my early upbringing. I was a street boy in three different countries before I was a schoolboy."

"Well, Hoyland's just a big schoolboy. Lots of brains. You're a bit surprised he isn't wearing a big pair of glasses on the end of his nose. Not that there's anything wrong with his eyesight. Nor his guts. He proved that more than once on the beat. But, just like you, his mind somehow seems to be somewhere different from where his body is. If you follow me."

"I follow you exactly. An excellent thumb-nail sketch. And here he is. Stick around, Taffy."

Gwilliam parked himself in the corner. He seemed to be subduing a grin. There were two chairs in front of the desk. Petrella waved the newcomer to sit down. Hoyland picked his way across the room with the care of a soldier entering a minefield; knocked over one of the chairs, picked it up with an apologetic smile and parked himself on the other one.

"All right," said Petrella, "let's have it."

"We were driving along Roman Road, sir. In one of our Pandas. We saw two men fighting on the pavement. The bigger one had got the smaller one down and seemed to be trying to bang his head on the pavement. I got out and pulled him off. I said, 'Stop that. You'll damage him.' The bigger man said, 'That's what he wants. Damaging. In fact he ought to be pulled in and charged and if the police were doing their duty he would be.' There were a few swear words mixed in, but that was the gist of it."

Educated voice. Straight-forward statement. Petrella was glad to note that he had been driving along Roman Road. Not proceeding along it. He said, "All right. Leave out the four-letter words. Did you gather what it was all about?"

"The small man was a newsagent, a Mr Chipping. We were just outside his shop. The big man's name was Jackson. I've got his address and particulars if they're needed. He'd gone round, he said, to teach Chipping a lesson. It seems Jackson's son had been in the shop the day before to get a copy of his usual comic. When he got it home and started to read it, he found, stuck in the middle of it, a page of what his father called 'filthy muck'. It seems to have been photographs of naked girls and young boys."

"Doing what?" said Petrella.

Hoyland hesitated and suddenly looked even younger. He said, "They were performing."

"No call for paraphrase," said Petrella. "Let's see the exhibit."

"Exhibit, sir?"

"The page of dirty pictures."

This produced an uncomfortable silence. Then Hoyland said, "It didn't occur to me that you'd want to see that."

"Listen, son. If you want to be a success in the detective branch you'd better remember two things. The first is, never leave a job half done. The second is, don't leave important exhibits behind when you come in to report."

"No, sir."

"Then go and get it. And bring it back here. As quick as you can."

When Hoyland had departed, looking as though he was glad to get out of the room, Petrella said to Gwilliam, "Well, what do you think?"

"It was stupid of him not to latch onto that page of pictures, but I think he was embarrassed by the whole business and lost his head. He'll improve."

"You mean we all have to live and learn."

"That's right."

"Like I did."

"That's right," said Gwilliam again, without the glimmer of a smile.

After he had gone Petrella looked, with no enthusiasm, at his piled in-tray. The act of putting his hand out towards it seemed to be an unfailing cue for the telephone to ring.

This time it was Ambrose. He said, "Sorry to interrupt you, but I've got a Mr Pirrie here. He wants to have a word with you. It's important, he says."

"Pirrie? Oh, you mean Poston-Pirrie. That newspaper man."

"That's right, sir. A reporter on the *Sentinel*. He's the one who got Hood into trouble. I expect you remember that."

"Yes," said Petrella, "I remember that. Well, I can't see

him now. I've got a lot of stuff to look at and then I'm going to get some lunch. Tell him I'll see him this afternoon. No. On second thoughts, make it tomorrow afternoon. Three o'clock."

"Right, sir."

Ambrose sounded so delighted at the idea of sending Mr Poston-Pirrie about his business that Petrella concluded that he was not a popular figure at Maplin Road.

"I talked to Hoyland like a Dutch uncle," said Petrella.

"Poor Perry," said Jane.

"Is his name Perry?"

"It's Peregrine. But everyone calls him Perry."

"I don't, I call him 'Detective Hoyland' and he calls me 'sir'."

"I hope you're not turning into a Barstow."

Superintendent Barstow had been head of District when Petrella was a junior detective at Highside.

"Barstow was a damned good policeman."

"You didn't say so at the time. You said he had the mentality of a middle-aged rhinoceros."

"I can see things in better perspective now," said Petrella complacently. He was leaning back in his chair in front of the wide-open window. It was a second-storey flat in a modern building in Grove Road, just round the corner from Maplin Road police station. It had come on the market whilst Petrella was in Morocco and fearing he might lose it he had installed his cousin, Casimir, to keep it warm for them. Jane had come back from Morocco, with the baby, a few days ahead of Petrella and his nine-year-old son, Donald, who had been most reluctant to give up the freedom of his grandfather's fruit farm for the constraints of London and school.

The first of Jane's jobs, which she had carried out with her usual efficiency, had been to get rid of Casimir. The next had been to set right the disorder which his bachelor existence had left behind. He seemed to have entertained a lot of friends.

"What gossip did you pick up? Apart from Detective Hoyland's Christian name."

"I wasn't after gossip," said Jane austerely. "I was looking for information which might help to put you in the picture."

"Of course."

"I had dinner with Gwilliam. He's a good man."

"The best," said Petrella. "What did he tell you?"

"It was rather a sad story. You heard about Lampier?"

It had all been in the first docket he had opened that afternoon.

"Do you know," he said, "I was half afraid something like that might happen. It's the difficulty about under-cover work. When does cover turn into reality? I remember when he was talking about that YMCA hostel we got him into. 'I soon found out,' he said, 'that half the young Christians were juvenile delinquents and the other half were working hard to qualify.' All right, I laughed when he said it. But I ought to have seen the red light and got him out."

"Gwilliam said that when you left he seemed to go to pieces. Then those horrible Farm Boys got hold of him – "

Petrella had no wish to discuss it further. It was all in the docket. He would have to talk to someone at Central about Lampier. Morrissey, possibly.

Jane said, "I had your father on the telephone this morning. It seems he's planning to come over to England."

"For any particular reason?"

"You know how cagey he is. He said something about business, but he didn't explain what it was."

"Probably wanted to see his grandson. He and Donald got very friendly indeed."

"There," said Jane, "Lucy heard you say that. She doesn't approve of favouritism." A wail had sounded from the bedroom. Jane departed to deal with it.

Lucinda was only nine months old. The reason for the long space between her and Donald was a miscarriage. Petrella thought back to that desperate time when Donald had been kidnapped by Augie the Pole and the shock had deprived them of their expected second child.

He leaned back in his chair and the sounds and smells of London in summer came up to him through the open window: a man at the far end of the street who was getting the worst of an argument with a taxi driver; two girls tittupping along the pavement in their high-heeled shoes, chattering; the hoot of a distant steamer and a smell compounded of petrol, hot tar and a faint tang of fresh salt air blowing up from the river on the evening wind.

3

Next morning Petrella called on Chief Inspector Ramsbottom, head of HC Sub-Division, at his Harford Street Station. He found a large amiable man with a mop of woolly grey hair and a warm smile.

"Glad to see you, Chief," he said. "Very glad. Whilst you were away I found myself acting head of the area. Quite a responsibility, I assure you."

He didn't look as though the responsibility had worn him down. Possibly, thought Petrella, his carefree temperament allowed him to skim over rough waters which would have swamped a more conscientious man.

Petrella came straight to the point. He said, "I wanted to talk to you about one of your sergeants. Sergeant Stark."

"An excellent man."

"I'm glad to hear you say so."

"Before he came, we were having a lot of trouble with a crowd of West Indians in the Globe Road area. They used to hang about in Limehouse Fields and annoy passers-by with their comments. Not now. Stark attended to them. Now they're quiet as mice."

"When you say he attended to them?"

"Ask no questions," said Ramsbottom, with a smile so wide that it unveiled the whole of a noble upper set of false teeth, "and you'll be told no lies."

"Unfortunately, the press *has* been asking questions."

"Surely we don't worry about what the papers say."

"Maybe not. But when the Home Secretary says it and it comes down through Central – "

"Our shoulders are broad."

"It's not the breadth of your shoulders that concerns me," said Petrella, keeping his temper. "What I want to find out is whether the things that this man Poston-Pirrie is saying are true or not."

"I'm afraid I haven't time to read all the nonsense these journalists cook up." Conscious, from the silence which followed, that this was not an entirely adequate answer, he added, "Was there anything in particular?"

"One of the things he mentioned was a complaint by a West Indian that when he and some of his friends were driving along in a car they were stopped and asked for their documents. A lot of white people had been driving along the road at the same time. Why weren't they treated in the same way? It seemed they were being picked on because they were black."

"I don't think you could describe it as being picked on," said Ramsbottom tolerantly. "There was probably some reason for it. They may have assumed that the car had been stolen."

"On what grounds?"

"Well, those West Indian boys don't often have enough money to buy their own cars. And another thing, as often as not, when people like that are stopped and searched they're found to have drugs on them."

"But, surely, we only stop people and search them if they are acting suspiciously."

"Exactly."

"Then for a West Indian to drive a car *is* a suspicious act."

"Not in itself, perhaps. No. But there may have been other reasons."

"Such as?"

"Well, for instance, they might recognise one or other of the men in the car as men with records."

"I see," said Petrella. What he did see was that he and Ramsbottom were not on the same net. He said, "There

23

were other complaints. Specific acts of violence. Might that have been the sort of thing that happened when Stark was 'attending to' the West Indians in the Arbour Street area?"

"That might be so," said Ramsbottom. He leaned back comfortably in his chair. "But what you have to bear in mind is that I've received no official complaints. None at all. It beats me. If these characters think they've got something to complain about, why don't they come to me? Wouldn't that be more sensible than running off to people like Poston – what's his name? And even he didn't come here to see me. No. He preferred to talk to our local MP, who's as left-wing as all come and well known to be anti-police, as I've no doubt you'll discover when you encounter him. If you want the short and long of this thing, it's a case of harassment of the police by the media."

By this time Petrella understood why nothing had got through the chief inspector's defences. His vast, amiable, amorphous nature could suck up complaints like a huge bath-sponge and squeeze them away down the drain.

He said, "Well, thank you for telling me this."

"Not a bit of it. It's been a pleasure to talk to you. I was sure you'd understand."

'I think, if you don't mind, I'd better have a word with Sergeant Stark myself. I don't want you to think that I'm going behind your back, but it seems that he's probably got a lot of first-hand information."

"Of course, of course."

"I expect he's pretty busy, but if you could find a moment when he's not on duty."

"I'll do that. You'll find him a most interesting man."

"I'm sure I shall," said Petrella.

He left Harford Street, driving himself in the aged station runabout which was on loan to him until he could buy a car of his own. His conscience was nagging him about the pile of work which awaited him at Maplin Road. He ignored his conscience, turned north and made his way through the maze of small streets behind Commercial Road. In most of them the boys, revelling in the heat and the weeks of freedom from school, had turned the pavements into cricket pitches or the roadways into football grounds.

He drove carefully until he reached the open stretch of Hackney Road. He was heading for Shepherdess Walk, where Chief Superintendent Liversedge had his headquarters. This was not a police station. It was the administrative centre of No. 2 Area.

He had met Jim Liversedge before and even on short acquaintance had had no difficulty in understanding why he was known as BTB, which stood for By The Book. It was not, perhaps, an entirely admirable characteristic, but at least you knew where you were with him. Also he had detected, deeply hidden under an iron exterior, an unexpected vein of humour.

He listened in silence to what Petrella had to say. Then, still without speaking, he took down from the shelf behind him the volume, containing 800 closely printed pages, which is entitled *Police Orders*. It specified every detail of police organisation, down to such important points as when officers on street duty are permitted to appear in shirt sleeves rather than tunics, and how the sleeves should be rolled – a matter of some importance that month.

Finally he closed the book, remained for a few seconds in what seemed to be silent prayer and said, "*If* Ramsbottom is correct in saying that he has received no official complaint about Sergeant Stark, then he is in a strong position. Therefore, the next time that anyone reports any irregularity of any sort by the sergeant, or anyone else, it will be up to you to forward an official complaint. It will be on Form PCD 6. There should be four copies. One goes to Ramsbottom, for action; one to me for information, with a spare copy in case I wish to forward it to Central and, of course, one for your own files."

"Of course," said Petrella. "One for my files."

"Does that deal with your point?"

"Fully," said Petrella.

It seemed that this was all that Liversedge had to say, so Petrella stood up. He had reached the door when Liversedge added, "You can't reach high rank in the police without attracting a nickname. I am well aware of mine. I regard it as a compliment. Ramsbottom got *his* nickname at recruit school. He's been known as Sheep's Arse for the past twenty-five years. I'll look forward to hearing from you how this matter develops."

Petrella left feeling oddly comforted. It was the confidence of a nervous full back who suddenly realises that he can trust the goal-keeper.

At Maplin Road the detectives' room was on the ground floor, opposite the public office. Passing the door on his way upstairs Petrella paused for a moment. He heard the voice of Sergeant Wilmot saying, "Tell us, Perry. Suppose you're giving evidence and counsel says to you, 'You're very young. Tell us, do you still have wet dreams?'"

A strange voice said, "Can counsel say things like that?"

"When he's got a policeman in the box, counsel can say anything he bloody well likes. Well?"

"I think," said Hoyland deliberately, "that I should say, 'Only on Sunday night.' And when he asked why, I'd say, 'I've often wondered. I think it must be something to do with the sermon at evensong.' "

The guffaw which this produced was cut short when Petrella opened the door. He said to Hoyland, "If you've got that paper, I'd like to see it."

When it was spread on the table he examined it curiously. It was half of a double sheet. He could see the jagged end where the other half had been torn off. What interested him most was the condition of the paper. It was shabby. Its edges were crumpled and the area round the photographs, which had once been white, was now grey. Also there were spots on it which looked like chocolate.

"An odd thing to find tucked into a brand new comic, isn't it?"

"That's what Mr Chipping said. He swore he'd never set eyes on it before. He produced a dozen copies of the same comic and there was nothing in them. I got the impression he was telling the truth."

"If he didn't put it in, who did?"

"Someone wanting to get him into trouble, perhaps."

Petrella had returned to inspecting the exhibit. He said, "How did it come to light?"

"The boy's mother found it in his sock drawer. She showed it to her husband, who blew his top. It was a double spread, so he tore it in half and then tore the first half into about fifty pieces so small that no one could see what was on them. He was planning to treat the other half in the same way when his wife came in and stopped him. She said, 'You'll need that if there's going to be any trouble about that man you hit.' So he thought he'd better keep it. He told me, 'The half I tore up was worse than this bit.' All I can say is, if it was worse, it must have been pretty hot."

When he stopped he became aware that Petrella was looking at him. It was not an agreeable look. When the silence had become uncomfortable Petrella said, "Just what did you mean by that?"

"Mean – ?"

"You described this production as 'pretty hot'. Well?"

"I suppose I should have said that it must have been obscene. Filthy. That sort of thing."

"Let me give you some advice. If you think a thing is obscene, call it that. Don't make it sound like something you think is funny – or half-way acceptable on a man-to-man basis."

"No, sir."

The colour which had started to mount in Hoyland's face had now spread from his cheeks to his hair line.

"That may seem unimportant to you. But once the police

start adopting that line about pornography, we're heading for a precipice. The one the Gadarene swine went over. Do you understand?"

"Yes, sir."

Embarrassed though he was, Hoyland managed to stand his ground. He said, "There was something I meant to mention about this paper."

"Go on."

"It looks to me as though it had originally been the back sheet of a magazine. I mean, the double spread inside the actual covers. If that's so it's a great pity Jackson tore off the left-hand half. If that was the first page, it might have had some useful details on it. I asked Mr Jackson about that, but he couldn't remember and didn't want to discuss it. On the other hand, if the bit he did keep is the last page, there ought to be some printer's mark on the back."

"Very likely. The printer is supposed to identify himself. In a case like this, no doubt he does it as inconspicuously as possible."

"Just what I thought, sir. And if you hold the page up to the light you can see – it's more like a water mark – it looked to me like I.P."

Petrella got a magnifying glass out of the drawer of his desk. Hoyland watched him anxiously.

Finally he said, "Yes. I think you're right. The Yard has got a very good index of printers' monograms. Always supposing this one has been registered. I'll find out when I'm up at Central tomorrow. Meanwhile, have another word with that newsagent. Find out if he's got any enemies: trade rivals; people who'd like to do him a bad turn. At the same time you could find out if he wants to pursue a charge of assault against Jackson."

After Hoyland had departed he took up his glass again and stared through it at the monogram. Was it a tiny peephole, through which a little piece of truth might eventually be seen?

Philip Poston-Pirrie arrived at ten past three, the ten

minutes having been added to show that he was not impressed by the police. When he had rejected the first chair offered and settled himself to one side of the desk, so that the light from the window behind Petrella did not shine directly on him, he further asserted his independence by refusing the offer of a cigarette and producing his own case. He then opened the conversation with a well-thought-out preamble. It was based on one of his own articles.

"It will clear the air," he said, "if I make my own position in this matter quite clear. It is also, incidentally, the position of the paper which I represent – "

"I hadn't understood that you were on the staff of the *Sentinel*."

"Nor am I. I am a freelance journalist. Of some repute, if I may say so."

"Certainly," said Petrella. "You may say anything you wish – in this room."

"Are you implying that I should not repeat it outside the room? Because if so – "

"All I was suggesting was that there must be a difference between the things you say in private and the things you say in public. You would agree with that, surely."

These interruptions had thrown Poston-Pirrie off his track. He hoisted himself back onto it.

"Perhaps I might be allowed to explain my point of view, which is also, as I mentioned, the *Sentinel*'s point of view. It is this. That the police are a public service and answerable to the public – "

"Not correct, surely. The police are responsible to the Home Secretary who is, in turn, answerable to Parliament."

"That may be the constitutional position, but since Parliament is often busy with other important affairs, it has to be left to the press to act as the watch dog of the public. To bring to its notice, by barking, any cases in which the police exceed or misuse their powers – "

"You mean, I think, cases in which it is *alleged* that they have done so."

There was nothing offensive about what Petrella was saying. But it was unexpected. His experiences as an investigative journalist had often taken Poston-Pirrie into difficult, sometimes even dangerous, situations. He was by no means lacking in courage. He was well prepared for police officers who gave him a cold brush-off and the occasional lion who could be provoked into roaring. What was unusual was to encounter someone who was prepared to tackle him in his own dialectic.

Before he could climb back onto his high horse, Petrella said, "Wasn't it you who was responsible for the disgrace – and, incidentally, the death, of Superintendent Hood?"

A month after his dismissal he had been found in his exhaust-filled garage. The coroner had accepted the rather unlikely theory of an accident.

"I brought certain facts to the attention of the authorities, yes."

"Such as?"

"Such as that he was in close and friendly contact with some of the known heads of the pornographic trade."

"Did it occur to you that it might have been his duty to keep in touch with them? Policemen often have to go into dubious company if they are to obtain the conviction of villains."

"Ingenious," said Poston-Pirrie with a kindly smile. "Very ingenious. But if there had been the slightest suggestion that he was setting a trap for them, surely there would have been some mention of this in the report of the investigating officers from MS 15?"

If he had not been off balance he would not have said this and he realised his mistake as soon as he had spoken.

"You saw this report, then?" said Petrella.

"Certainly not."

"Then how do you know what was, and wasn't, in it?"

"I didn't need to see any report. Both the police and the

public had long made their minds up about Hood. To start with, he was a known homosexual."

Petrella said nothing. He was watching his visitor's face.

"No longer always an offence, I agree. But highly undesirable in the case of a senior police officer, laying him open to every sort of blackmail and bribery."

He had compressed his lips into a prim line of distaste. Yet it was not entirely distaste. There was something else. Hardly definite enough to be classed as gloating, but a suggestion of enjoyment; enjoyment of the power which such knowledge would have given him.

When Petrella still said nothing, he seemed to realise that he had been drawn some way out of his planned path. He said, "However, I did not come here to discuss Superintendent Hood. The complaints that I have had are from coloured people."

"West Indians?"

"Many of them."

"And the complaints?"

"They are, in short, that the police, in their dealings with them, have shown themselves both prejudiced and brutal. That they are liable to be arrested on suspicion when no grounds for suspicion exist. That in this area a point has been reached where they scarcely dare to walk abroad at night. And if they are driving a car this is automatically regarded as evidence that they have either committed, or are about to commit, a criminal offence of some sort."

"I see," said Petrella. "Might we, for a moment, abandon the general and come down to the particular?"

"The particular?"

"Particular instances of prejudice and brutality."

"One of the men I was speaking to specifically told me that he had been struck, without provocation, by Sergeant Stark."

"Without provocation?"

"So he said."

31

"And he complained."

"In this instance, apparently not."

"Why not?"

"I imagine that he was afraid to do so."

"Tell me, Mr Pirrie, have *you* ever been struck by a police officer?"

"Certainly not."

"But you have been in places where these West Indians live. You have walked the streets at night and no doubt driven the car which I observe parked outside. How is it that *you* have totally escaped the attention of the police?"

"I imagine that my white skin has protected me."

"Possibly. But you see what a difficult position it puts me in. The complaints you are making are second-hand. They are things which have happened to other people, not to you. I can only take action on a complaint when it is made by the person who has suffered."

"Red tape."

"Oh, certainly. But I have no objection to red tape as such. It serves a useful purpose by keeping a bundle of documents in some sort of order. There is a well-tried procedure for complaints. If made to me, I should forward it on – er – the appropriate form, to District and through them to Scotland Yard."

"I will see if I can oblige you."

Petrella stood up. Accepting the hint, Poston-Pirrie rose also. He was aware that he had not achieved his main objectives, which were to provoke Petrella to indiscretion and to acquire material for the article which the *Sentinel* was expecting.

When he had left, Petrella turned to his slightly diminished in-tray and started to read a report on drug-related offences and juvenile delinquency.

Two shadows slipped along among the other shadows in Packstone Passage and disappeared through a hole in the ground. Arnold, who had been that way before, negotiated the grid at the bottom of the air tunnel without difficulty. Winston, the West Indian boy who was with him, needed help, but squeezed through at last after removing his jacket and pullover.

Both boys were excited. Winston was frightened, too. He asked questions in a hoarse whisper.

"What's this room?" "Is it the place?" "Is this where it happened?" "The men won't come back, will they?"

"Of course they won't," said Arnold. He qualified this comforting assurance by adding, "Not unless they've got someone else they want to do."

Winston was beginning to wish he hadn't come.

The door which led from the spacious lobby into the even more spacious central room was unlocked. A full moon was playing among the clouds, throwing alternate washes of light and shadow through the dust-caked windows.

"I can't see nothing," said Winston, who had gone down on his knees.

"What are you looking for? You won't see any blood. Like I told you, they were careful about that."

"Where were you, then?"

"Up there." Arnold pointed to the gallery looming above them. As he did so they heard the noise. Difficult to say what it was or where it came from. The boys froze. After a long minute Arnold said, "It's all right. It's rats. They're in the wall. Hundreds of them."

"I don't like it," said Winston. "Let's get out."

Arnold agreed. He was not feeling all that happy himself.

When they were outside Winston felt braver again. He said, "That was great. I mean, seeing it like that I could believe just what you said happened."

"Remember. You're not to tell anyone."

"I've promised, haven't I?"

As Winston said this he made one mental reservation. He would tell his greatest friend, Delroy. No one else.

4

"If you want my opinion," said Commander Morrissey, "I think Lampier's behaved like a berk. A snot-nosed berk."

Morrissey had headed the Metropolitan Serious Crimes Squad for four years and was now in charge of the squads nationally. While promotion made some policemen pompous, it seemed only to have made Morrissey more foul-mouthed.

"If we'd taken the trouble to look into his background, we might have guessed that he'd go off the rails. Did you know that his old man was a cat burglar?"

"Yes," said Petrella. "I knew that."

"And had taught his son some of his tricks?"

"He certainly had," said Petrella. He remembered watching Lampier go up a drainpipe as though it was a ladder.

"And that two of his uncles and his older brother all had form?"

"No. I didn't know that."

"Shouldn't you have found out?"

Before Petrella could answer this unanswerable question he added, "I suppose you're going to say it's easy to be wise after the event."

"No. It hadn't occurred to me to say that."

"Then let me tell you this. It's never easy to be wise. Before or during or after the event. But it is possible to be careful."

"Yes, I ought to have looked into his background more closely. Could you tell me, what did he actually do?"

"What he did was to get in with those turds who call themselves the Farm Boys." Morrissey was silent for a moment, while his jaw moved as though he had swallowed the Farm Boys and was about to spit them out. "It's not as if Gwilliam hadn't warned him more than once to leave them alone. They're filth. And in case you've got ideas of going after them yourself, I warn you: you won't find it easy to pin anything onto them. Because they're crafty. They operate through stringers. Half a dozen minor villains, who do the dirty work. They're well paid and if they make themselves too conspicuous, they're laid off and another lot are recruited."

"And Lampier had joined the string?"

"It seems he did one or two minor jobs for them: driver, or look-out man, something of that sort. His first real scam was a lorry snatch, organised by Dog Henty. He'd told Lampier it was a doddle. Because the driver was an old army pal of Henty's. He'd agreed to stop at this café in Chingford – "

"What was in the lorry?"

"Whisky."

"And just the one driver?"

"Yerrs. But the lorry had a hidden switch. Controlled all the electrics. So when the driver got out for a char and wad with his old army mucker, he naturally switched it off."

"And Lampier, who'd been told about it, switched it on again and drove away."

"That's just what he did," said Morrissey with a savage grin. "But what he *didn't* know was that the lorry ran on a system of a main petrol tank and a reserve one. Just a couple of gallons to take him to the nearest pump if the driver miscalculated. He'd been told about the electric switch, but he hadn't been told about the spare tank. Or that the main tank was almost empty. After he'd driven the lorry a few hundred yards it began to die on him. He just managed to turn it into a quiet side street, where it rolled to a halt."

"Awkward," said Petrella.

"He was up shit creek without a paddle, the stupid little sod. All he could do was abandon the lorry and make off. Unfortunately for him, a postman saw him getting out of the lorry. And a shopkeeper had seen him getting in. Both unshakeable witnesses. He had to be charged."

"And was convicted."

"After a fight. Counsel tried to make out that Lampier was really on our side. Acting as a stooge. The question he couldn't answer was, if that was so, *why hadn't he told us where the lorry was?* Actually, it stood where he'd left it for two days, with five thousand pounds' worth of booze in the back, asking to be looted. And then it was only reported because it was blocking someone's front gate. The jury didn't like that. In the end they said 'Not guilty' to theft, but 'Guilty' to attempted theft, which meant a piddling little sentence of six months. Four months with full remission."

"And discharge from the police."

"Of course. Ignominious discharge. I insisted on that."

There was something behind this that Petrella did not understand. There was a hidden anger in Morrissey. A personal anger, which was odd in a man who rarely allowed his feelings to colour his professional outlook.

To probe a little further, Petrella said, "You told me just now that it wouldn't be easy to pin these people. Then the only possible line would be to infiltrate them. To get someone right among them. He'd have to be prepared to stand up in court and give evidence – "

"We're not daft," said Morrissey. "Naturally we'd thought of that. Even if Lampier had been prepared to play ball with us, after what had happened, we didn't need him. We'd got just the man for the job. A minor character, called Flower. Ernie Flower. He'd been involved in one or two of the capers the boys set up and was beginning to get cold feet. He saw that if anything did go wrong, he and his friends would get the stick, while the Farm Boys were sitting pretty. He saw it was time to get out and make a bit for himself on the side. There are two big bank rewards still not collected. I didn't underrate the opposition. Their intelligence system is remarkably good. So, when Flower approached us, I took every precaution I could think of. A four-man committee here handled it all. The Deputy Commissioner and Watterson – you remember him at Q – ?"

Petrella nodded. He certainly remembered Watterson.

"He's Lovell's number two now. And tipped to take his job when he goes up. The others were me and my number two, Charlie Kay. I grabbed him when the Porn Squad was disbanded. After the Robin Hood episode – "

"Yes, I know about Hood."

"I told Flower that any reports he made should come from a different call box – a different one each time – to a direct line in my office which would be manned from seven to ten every evening. My daughter, who was working at Central, took on that job. She shared it with me."

"Sounds watertight."

"It sounds that way, but somehow or other the finger started to point at Flower. Nothing definite. But he began to get nervous. He'd got news of a smash and grab on a Securicor van the boys were setting up. He said, if he gave us the full details, could that be the signal for out? I took that call myself. No exaggeration, I could hear his teeth chattering. I said, OK, we'll collect you from your pad late tomorrow night. We'll set it up as a normal arrest."

Morrissey stopped. He was making an effort to restrain the anger that was boiling inside him. He said, "Perhaps you can guess the rest. No sign of Flower in his one room bed-sit. No papers, either. Someone had been through the drawers and cupboards, not forgetting the pockets of his best suit hanging behind the door. Careful, you see."

"And Flower?"

"Gone. I suppose he may turn up. In whole or in part. But I doubt it."

"Well, thank you for bringing me up to date," said Petrella. "I've taken up enough of your time. There was one other thing." He laid the half-sheet of photographs on the table. Morrissey examined it in silence. Then he said, "Paedo-porn. It's the latest disease. I'm told that a lot of this stuff is shot in Holland. Sometimes we catch it on the way in. It's worrying the DC. Anything you can do, he'll certainly support. If you want an expert view on this, have a word with Charlie – "

Petrella found Superintendent Kay in his office across the passage. In appearance, he reminded him of photographs he had seen of First World War infantry officers; the stubbly moustache, the weather-reddened face, the look of someone who had been through a lot and was glad to have come out on the far side. He said, "Watcher, Patrick. Back from a lovely mike on the Mediterranean beaches."

"That's right," said Petrella. "Back on the job, bursting with enthusiasm and full of questions."

"I was afraid of it."

"First, could you find out for me what magazine this unpleasant exhibit came from. There's what might be a printer's mark on the back."

"Very helpful. If it's registered." Kay took the page, looked at it briefly, folded it up and put it into an envelope. He said, "It was a diet of stuff like that that made me glad to leave the Porn Squad. What's next on the menu?"

"I was talking to Morrissey about Lampier. I wondered if you had any ideas about it."

"When I first heard the story, I just thought, one more lump of shit down the hole. When I thought about it a bit more, there *was* one thing that did strike me as odd. Look – you're driving a lorry with one of these main tank–spare tank arrangements. Right? Do you let the main tank run down to the last perishing drop of gas before you switch on the spare?"

"Certainly not. It would probably cause an air lock."

"Then why in this case?"

"You think the main tank may have been drained on purpose?"

"I think it's possible."

"But why?"

"Your guess is as good as mine. But you can see the result of doing it. Suppose the boys weren't quite sure about Lampier. Suppose he wasn't even quite sure himself. Fixing it this way would force him to make his mind up, wouldn't it? If he's really doing the job as a decoy for the police, he reports it. Job done. End of story. If he isn't, he lies low and hopes he hadn't been spotted."

"You mean it was an experiment?"

"Something like that."

"Rather a dangerous one for the boys."

"Why? They'd got nothing to lose, except a lorry full of booze. That was poetry. Did you notice?"

"Yes," said Petrella patiently. "I noticed. But didn't it mean that if Lampier was a police spy he could put Dog Henty on the spot?"

"How? *He* hadn't done anything wrong. Just arranged to meet a pal – they really had been in the army together – and chat about old times over a cup of char. Whilst they're doing it someone comes along and nicks the lorry. No one more surprised than them."

Petrella thought about it. He could see the logic in it. It could have been fixed that way. It didn't make Lampier much better; or, for that matter, much worse. He said, "What I did find odd was the way the old man had taken it. I've never known him like that before. You'd have thought that Lampier had done him a personal injury."

"In a way, perhaps he had."

"In what way?"

Kay seemed undecided whether to go on or not. Petrella

39

said, "Come on, Charlie. Let's have it. You can't leave it like that."

"All right. Here it is. You know that young Lee Morrissey was on the phone here for this operation?"

"Yes. He told me."

"And did you know that she was Lampier's girlfriend?"

Petrella stared at him. A cold wave of possibilities rendered him speechless.

"When I say girlfriend – well – you know what young people are these days. At one time they'd been close. Very close. After he ran into that bit of trouble it seems to have cooled off. But they were still meeting from time to time. Behind dad's back, no doubt."

"Are you telling me," said Petrella – speaking as though the words choked him – "that Morrissey's own daughter gave the game away to Lampier and that he passed it on – "

"Hold your horses," said Kay. "It needn't have been as bad as you're thinking. Suppose one evening Lampier says to Lee, 'I've got two tickets for a show.' Something like that. Or maybe suggests they went out dancing. Lee says, 'Can't manage tonight. I'm on the phone, seven to ten. In fact, I'm on most evenings. Special job.' Lampier knows she's working at the Yard, doing odd jobs for her father. He wonders what this seven to ten lark is all about. Hurries round to report it to the Boys – part of his effort to prove himself useful after his spell inside, no doubt. The Boys think there may be something in it, so they have *all* their stringers watched. They notice that Flower is on the blower most evenings between seven and ten, from a different call box each time. Quite enough to set their nasty little minds working."

Petrella had heard him out in silence. He said, "Have you explained your ideas to Morrissey?"

"I haven't, because I thought that if I raised the subject at all he'd blow his top. He isn't very easy to work with these days."

"If he's thinking what I think he's thinking," said Petrella, "you can't blame him really, can you?"

That same afternoon Poston-Pirrie was summoned to the office of the *Sentinel*'s news editor, a sardonic Scotsman. He had the pages of PP's latest contribution spread on his desk. Looking at them upside down he saw that they were liberally slashed with the green ink which was the news editor's speciality. 'Green for Danger' as one of his predecessors had put it before leaving the *Sentinel* and starting to write scurrilous novels about Fleet Street.

"It won't do," said the news editor. "I'm sorry, but really it won't. I mean – it's well written and all that sort of thing, but this is a newspaper. What its readers want is news."

"Topical stuff, surely," murmured Poston-Pirrie.

"That's my point. Is it really topical? Is it new? Ever since the Policy Studies people did that thing – you remember? – *Police and People in London*, and that was nearly ten years ago – people have known about the police slanging West Indians and subjecting them to unnecessary stops and checks – the last volume was full of it."

If Poston-Pirrie had been the sort of man who was easily embarrassed, he might have blushed since a substantial amount of his latest piece had been taken, almost verbatim, out of that useful volume. Instead of blushing he decided to attack.

He said, "I went down there, none too willingly, when your last man was scared out by the police. So what did you expect me to do? Write a piece saying they were all angels with harps and wings?"

The news editor softened his approach. Poston-Pirrie was, after all, a well-known name and it had been a feather in their cap to get hold of him. He said, "There are two lines you might hunt. To start with, we'd like to find out more about this new Superintendent Petrella. Odd name, odd man. Seems his father was a top Spanish cop, with a European reputation. His mother was an English lady. And I mean lady. He's come up from the ranks and come up pretty fast. If he's starting to throw his weight around, we could do a story on that, running it along with our views on this bullying sergeant of his."

"Dod Stark? Now he *is* a tough customer."

"When you put it like that you seem to be suggesting that Petrella *isn't* a tough customer. Our records department has turned up one or two things that might change your mind. For instance, when he was in Q Division he nailed the younger brother of a very unpleasant character called Augie the Pole. Augie badly wanted his kid brother out, so he lifted Petrella's six-year-old son and told him that unless he played ball he'd get his son back without his skin."

"For God's sake – "

"So Petrella went after Augie. The next bit's a trifle obscure, but our medical editor managed to get a sight of the pathologist's report on Augie."

"Then Petrella killed him?"

"No. Actually he was killed by two Irishmen, who were after his blood that same night. They opened up at short range with two shot-guns. But the point is that immediately *before* this happened Petrella had taken Augie away, to somewhere quiet, and persuaded him to tell him where he'd put the kid."

"Persuaded him?"

"The pathologist's report mentioned extensive cutting and burning which might, of course, have been part of the shot-gun damage. Or might have been Petrella's Spanish side coming out. I'm telling you this so you won't imagine you're dealing with a boy scout."

"I'll bear it in mind," said Poston-Pirrie thoughtfully. "You had another suggestion?"

"Go after the youngsters. Children are always news."

Petrella meanwhile was pursuing a line of enquiry he had decided on some days before. He declined Gwilliam's offer of the station runabout. He said, "I'll go on foot. Get my legs out from under this desk."

"Please yourself," said Gwilliam. "It's not my idea of walking weather."

Although it was not yet nine o'clock the heat was already building up. Relief only came when the evening breeze began to blow up river. Until then the stew-pot of east London simmered around boiling point.

He made his way south, down Harford Street, passing the headquarters of C Division (Sheep's Arse! Really!) down White Horse Road, across Commercial Road and into Cable Street. Here the church of St Barnabas looked down on the river; no product this of Hawksmoor or Wren, but a modern building, in square white blocks, with its rectory alongside.

He had seen, as he went past, that there had been a service that morning; an unusual feature on a weekday in a church in this area, which suggested that Father Freeling was an enthusiastic and successful evangelist. He found him finishing his breakfast.

"Have a cup of coffee, Superintendent. It is Superintendent Petrella, isn't it? I thought as much. Only instant coffee, I fear, but drinkable."

"I'm not a coffee snob," said Petrella. "I'd love a cup."

The rector bellowed, "Martha," and a wizened old woman with a hook nose appeared. She was carrying a broom in one hand. Petrella wondered if she had just alighted from it. She was clearly deafish, but able to understand, or lip-read, the rector. She deposited her broomstick in one corner and disappeared.

"Stabling her horse," murmured Petrella.

The rector laughed. He said, "Not much more than a hundred years ago old women round here were credited with all sorts of powers. It's a very primitive part of London."

"Full of primitive people."

"Certainly. That's its attraction. My first job was in Putney. Respectable folk. First-class citizens. But goodness, how dull! Different here. Lots to do."

"Our community officer tells me that you run a club for the youngsters."

The light of enthusiasm kindled in Father Freeling's eye. "The Athletic Club," he said. "I didn't found it, but I run it and get a lot of pleasure out of it. Boys are the same anywhere, you know. White, brown, black or yellow. Equal proportions of saintliness and devilry."

"It seems you manage to keep them happy."

"A lot of the time, yes. It's mostly darts and table-tennis. And swimming in the summer and football matches, when we can arrange them."

"Easy enough with the good kids. Do you have any trouble with the lunatic fringe?"

"The real bad lads." The rector smiled. "When I first came, yes. Not now. I was lucky. They had an all-comers boxing night at the local stadium. It started with some sparring exhibitions. After that, they threw it open to the audience. You know the sort of thing: 'Is any gentleman prepared to oblige us and see if he can stay on his feet for one round?' I was waiting for that. I'd boxed for Cambridge and I'd come along in my lightweight boxing boots, so all I had to do was take off my coat and roll up my sleeves. My opponent was a professional. Much too clever for me to put down, but I landed one or two good punches and at the end of a brisk two minutes I believe he was more uncomfortable than I was."

"The perfect way of making friends and influencing people," agreed Petrella.

At this moment the coffee arrived. When the old crone had hobbled off, Petrella said, "Tell me about the trips you organise for the boys. If you go to places like Rome and Paris they must cost money. I don't suppose the boys' families can foot the bill."

"I don't ask them to." Father Freeling went across to his

44

desk and took out a folder. It was a glossy production with a three-colour picture of the Cnidian Venus on the front. It was entitled 'Educating Our Children for a Better Life'.

"You can skip the verbiage," said the rector. "It's the list on the back I wanted you to see. They are our patrons. Keep it. I've got plenty of copies."

It was an impressive list. Petrella recognised, among others, the names of the vice-chairman of an oil company and the head of a nationally known hotel chain. There were accountants and solicitors, whose names had been in the papers in connection with the unending guerilla of take-overs which had enlivened the City in the past few years; a merchant banker, George Granlund of Granlund Brothers and Ray Glenister of Angus, Hardy and Glenister who had held the English ring in the computer fight against the Japanese.

"With backers like these," he said, "you must be able to lead some interesting expeditions."

"I have, in the past," said the rector unhappily. "But I'm far from sure that I shall be able to continue them."

"Oh? Any particular snag?"

"Last time, I couldn't go myself. So I sent the party off in charge of two ladies from our Dorcas Society. Don't misunderstand me. Excellent people in every way. But this particular party got out of hand. Some of the boys went off one evening and didn't get back until the early hours. Four o'clock in the morning. And they wouldn't say what they'd been up to."

"Where was this?"

"Amsterdam. A pity. As a cultural centre it's got a lot going for it."

The mention of Amsterdam touched off a spark of memory. Petrella tried to fix it, but, for the moment, it eluded him.

"If I could go myself," said the rector, "I'd do it. I went there once, as a boy, and I remember the Rijksmuseum – not only its paintings, but its wonderful collection of model ships, which pleased me even more than the pictures. The trouble is that as my congregation here increases – which, I'm glad to say, it is doing quite fast – I'm finding it more and more difficult to get the time off. What I really need is a strong-minded, strong-armed escort who'd guarantee to keep the boys in line."

"Someone like Sergeant Stark?"

"Yes," said the rector with a smile, "the sergeant's reputation has reached my ears. But I fear he's even busier than I am."

That evening Poston-Pirrie, in search of the sort of copy his editor had wanted, set out to look for the Athletic Club. The Telephone Directory gave its address as Commercial Road, a lengthy thoroughfare which stretches from Aldgate Pump to Limehouse Broadway. He planned to strike it at its mid-point and with this in mind left the tube train at Aldgate East and set off towards Commercial Road, confident that he must hit it somewhere.

By the time he reached White Horse Road he was beginning to wonder if he had overshot the mark. He was also extremely warm and the doors of the White Horse public house looked inviting. He decided to deal with his thirst and to ask for directions.

The saloon bar, which opened onto the road, was empty and there was no one behind the counter, but he could hear laughter and voices from an inner room which he took to be some sort of private bar. He opened the door and went in.

If he had realised that this particular room, although theoretically open to the public, had become, through long usage, a sort of private club for HC Division, whose station was a few yards away, up Harford Street, he might have hesitated. Not knowing it, he advanced confidently to the bar and demanded a pint of ginger-beer shandy.

The landlord served the drink, but said, as he pushed it

across the counter, "I think, sir, you'd be more comfortable in the other room."

Poston-Pirrie, who had lowered half the pint in one grateful gulp, said, "I'm quite comfortable here, thank you. And anyway, I wasn't planning to stop. All I wanted to do was to ask the way to a place called the Athletic Club."

The men who were in the room had stopped talking and before the landlord could say anything one of them, a large character with a white face and brownish-red hair clipped short, said, in a surprisingly gentle voice, "Aren't you a bit old for juvenile athletics?"

This produced a rumble of laughter.

Poston-Pirrie, realising that the atmosphere was unfriendly, reacted by saying stiffly, "It was not my intention to join in the activities of the club. It is simply that I was interested in the boys."

"Interested in boys, eh?" said the large man. "Well, that's a frank admission, wouldn't you say, Lofty?" This was to the tall thin character standing beside him.

"Practically a statement of intention," said Lofty. "In my experience men who are interested in boys keep quiet about it."

"And hope the boys will keep quiet, too," said a third man.

Poston-Pirrie was beginning to lose his temper. He said to the big man, "You wouldn't be Sergeant Stark by any chance?"

"Your fame has gone ahead of you," said Lofty. "Next thing, he'll be asking you for your autograph."

"And the rest of you? All policemen, I suppose. Or, in the vulgar language of the neighbourhood, pigs."

"That's right," said Stark, unruffled. "You've fallen among a herd of swine."

"I see. Then you may be interested to know that what I'm looking for is information. Information about how you treat the youngsters – particularly the coloured boys – in this neck of the woods."

"Are we to take it, then, that you're a reporter?"

"A newspaper man."

"We had one of them here before. But he got the impression that he wasn't popular. Right, Lofty?"

"He seemed to get that impression somehow. A sensitive sort of man, I should have said."

"I see," said Poston-Pirrie. "I suppose that means that being six to one you were bold enough to threaten him."

"No threats were offered," said Stark. "Someone might have pointed out that the river could be dangerous. Particularly on a dark night. Muddy verges, slippery steps. That sort of thing."

"Being sensitive, you see," said Lofty, "he might have taken it in the wrong way."

"That's how bullies always talk," said Poston-Pirrie. Temper and discretion had gone together. "I hope the time is coming when you'll be shown up for what you are."

"Why not?" said Stark. "Let's have all the cards on the table. You say what you think of us. We say what we think of you. Right?"

There was a growl of agreement. What had started as banter was developing into something more dangerous.

"Gentlemen," said the landlord. "Really, now – "

No one took any notice of him. Stark said, "Tell us. What do you really come down here for? To make a bit of easy money by rubbishing the police, who are trying, as best they can, to keep you and your sort safe? What would you do if we all marched out and took cushy jobs on a building site?"

"Or cleaning out the sewers," said Lofty. "It'd be a nice change to dispose of the shit instead of having it chucked at us."

Stark brushed this aside. The full force of his personality was concentrated on the newspaper man. He said, "It's not such a wild idea, either. Less than two hundred years ago there were no police. Most men carried weapons and looked after their own skins. Would you like to go back to that?"

"I don't think – "

"Of course you don't think. Your sort never think. They just spit and run away."

By this time Poston-Pirrie was at the door, which the landlord was urgently holding open. He said, "What I was going to say when you interrupted me, was that no one in their senses attacks the police as a body. But they reserve the right to point out the occasional people who defame it by their actions. Men who have got so little control of themselves that they'll shoot an unarmed and innocent man."

By this time the landlord had managed to get him out of the room and the door shut. Poston-Pirrie realised that he wasn't only upset. He was frightened.

"You shouldn't have said that, sir. That thing that happened in Ireland. The sergeant doesn't like being reminded of it."

"So what?" said Poston-Pirrie. He was in the street by now. "I'm not afraid of that big ape. If he doesn't like what I say, he must lump it."

He was annoyed to find that he was shaking. Partly it was anger, but there was a small, uncomfortable deposit of fear in it. He became aware that a policeman in uniform was coming up the road towards him.

"Is there something I can do for you, sir?"

"No," said Poston-Pirrie. "I'm quite all right – I mean, yes. There is something. You could tell me how to find the Athletic Club."

"Go on to the end of the road and turn left. It's a few hundred yards along, on the left."

As he walked away he was aware that the policeman was looking after him thoughtfully.

5

"Two ladies to see you," said Inspector Ambrose. "I told them you were busy, but I guess it would take an armoured division to keep them out."

"Then you'd better let them in," said Petrella. He consigned to the wastepaper-basket a memorandum on road safety. It was full of windy exhortation and devoid of constructive suggestions.

When Mrs Millington and Mrs Broad arrived in his room he could see what Ambrose meant. There was nothing offensive about them. They were both substantially built and well dressed. Both were armed with the implacable force of women firmly established on the rock of middle-aged, middle-class stability.

Mrs Broad said, "We won't waste your time, Superintendent. Mrs Millington and I are members of the East London branch of the Dorcas Society. Our normal function is making and distributing clothes to people in need. But on occasions we are able to help in other directions and our rector, Father Freeling, asked us recently to take charge of a party of boys on an educational trip to Amsterdam."

"How large a party and how was it made up?"

"Forty boys, from eight different schools in this area. There was a fairly wide age spread, eleven to sixteen, which was one of the difficulties. However, we saw no reason to suppose that we couldn't cope with them."

"None at all," said Mrs Millington, "if the hotel had been chosen a little more carefully."

"In what respect?"

"It was a smallish place called the Witte Raaf – that is the White Crow – in the Ortelius Straat, behind the Orteliuskade, the main street which runs along the frontage of Rembrandt Park. It seemed to be a favourite place for school parties. One was leaving as we came and another took over our accommodation when we left. They may have been attracted by the prices, which were certainly on the moderate side."

"So what did you find objectionable about it?"

"Two things. It had no night porter and since the boys had keys to their own rooms, this meant that on nights when there was nothing organised for them they could come and go as they liked. Provided, of course, that they got back before the hotel was locked for the night. The other thing was the presence of a man who seemed to be a friend of the proprietor. He offered to take the boys on a sight-seeing trip round the red-light district – an offer which we naturally vetoed. This didn't stop him hanging round and talking to them, when he could get hold of them."

"What sort of man?"

"He looked like a crow himself," said Mrs Millington. "A black one, not a white one."

Mrs Broad said, "It's never easy to be sure about people – foreigners particularly – when you don't really speak their language. But one of the boys told me that he had also offered to take them to a strip-tease show. And when they said that they hadn't got the money for that sort of thing, he said that he'd pay for them. We managed to stop that, too."

"Had this man got a name?"

"The proprietor called him Hendrik. We never found out his surname."

"Can you give me a little more description?"

Mrs Millington said, "I called him a black crow and that's the most appropriate description I can think of. Always dressed in black, with smarmed down black hair and a way of looking at you out of a sharp pair of eyes."

"Turning his head quickly from side to side," said Mrs Broad. "Just like a bird, really."

Petrella said, "Thank you." He had his tape recorder running. "Now, I gather you ran into trouble."

"It was the last night. We were booked out next morning and the boys had been busy packing and had gone to bed early. I'd hoped for a quiet night. And so it was, until about four o'clock in the morning when I heard a car stop and someone at the front door. Also boys' voices. That got me out of bed fast. I looked out of my window. A big, closed car was drawing away – I couldn't get the number – and there were four boys on the pavement, all in a state of high excitement, saying things like 'Hush' and 'Hurry up' to one of them who had a key and was having some difficulty with the front door. By the time they got it open I was in the hall to meet them. As I'd half suspected, they were four boys from the Old Ford Chantry School. Twelve- and thirteen-year-olds. As a group they'd been a nuisance from the start. There was an older boy with them, who'd tried to keep them in some sort of order. A decent kid. I was glad to see he hadn't been out with them. I said, 'What in the world have you been up to?' But I soon saw I wasn't going to get any sense out of them."

"Oh, why?"

"Because they were all drunk. Or half-way there. I said, 'You'd better go to bed. I'll talk to you in the morning.' Which I did. All I could get out of them was that Hendrik had produced a car and driven them round the town. The smallest boy, who was still a bit muzzy, kept saying, 'Sights. He said we'd see sights. We certainly did see sights,' and they all giggled."

"Dead-end," said Petrella. "I take it you spoke to the proprietor."

"We certainly did. And he told us nothing. He didn't know this intrusive character personally. Always called him Hendrik. Didn't know his surname. He couldn't stop people dropping in from time to time to have a drink at the bar. It was open to the public. And if he talked to the boys and the boys talked to him, what of that? We pointed out that they seemed, somehow or other, to have got hold of the front-door key. 'Probably lifted it from the desk,' said the proprietor. He didn't actually say 'Boys will be boys', but his greasy smile said it for him."

Mrs Millington said, "We were on a bad wicket, because we knew, and he knew, that the bus was waiting outside to take us to the airport. So we had to leave it there."

"And that was the end of the matter?"

"Not quite. When we got to the airport I noticed one of the boys who had been out seemed to be very flush with cash."

"English money?"

"Five-pound and ten-pound notes. And he had a lot of them. Fifty pounds at least. It was hardly something I could enquire about. What money he brought with him was his own business. But I couldn't help wondering. Then the whispering and giggling started. It was impossible not to hear bits of it. It was clear that they had been photographed, or filmed. Something like that."

"And paid for their services."

"So it seemed. When we got back we made a point of seeing the parents of the boys concerned. One of them said he'd already heard rumours of what had happened and had questioned his son, who had shut his mouth tight. Not a word. No more giggling. One of the other fathers said the same thing. His boy seemed scared to open his mouth."

"Although they'd talked about it freely to their friends on the plane on the way home."

"Never stopped talking. In fact, at that point, they were boasting about whatever it was had happened."

"And now they were scared to talk. Were all the boys like that?"

"All four of them. Just the same."

"Well, thank you for telling me," said Petrella. "Though it's difficult to see what we can do about it from this end."

"It's some sort of racket. It wasn't just these boys. There'll be other parties there, too. Surely it ought to be stopped?"

"Yes," said Petrella. "It ought to be stopped."

It was while he was thinking about this that a name occurred to him.

Wilfred Wetherall.

When he had first met him, Mr Wetherall had been head-master of the South Borough Secondary School. Though he had long passed the compulsory retirement age his services to education had been considered too valuable to be dispensed with entirely and he had been given the job of 'adviser' to the new and inexperienced head of East London District. Those who knew Mr Wetherall were not surprised to be told that he was soon running the whole outfit.

Petrella knew him well, from the days when, as a detective inspector at Gabriel Street, he had lodged below Mr Wetherall's flat in Brinkman Road. When he was not otherwise engaged there was nothing he had enjoyed more than an after-dinner gossip. Mr Wetherall's knowledge of London schools and London schoolboys had been extensive and entertaining.

A telephone call brought him round to Petrella's flat that evening.

"Of course, I'd heard about it," he said. "The story was all over east London. At least, to be precise" – Mr Wetherall was noted for his precision – "what was quickly spread was the fact that there *was* a story. Not the details. It seems that on the plane coming home the boys let drop a number of hints – more about the money in their pockets than about what they had done to earn it. This, no doubt, was being saved up for recounting later, in less public circumstances, to their particular friends. But it didn't happen. Not a word. They went dumb."

"I suppose their parents had told them not to talk about it."

"If you really suppose that would stop them," said Mr

Wetherall acidly, "you display an astonishing ignorance of boys of that age and class. Advice from their parents is seldom listened to and even more rarely followed. What had happened was that they had been visited. By men who were able to frighten them into silence. I imagine you've heard of the Farm Boys?"

Petrella nodded. His dislike of that band of agricultural thugs was growing stronger every day. It was no surprise that they should be acting as protection to a filthy racket. Interesting, all the same. The promptness of their action demonstrated a fairly close tie-up between Amsterdam and London.

"I would surmise," said Mr Wetherall, "that they explained to the boys, in detail, exactly what would happen to them if they opened their mouths. Dave Cusins, who was with them at the hotel, is my godson. He comes from the same school and, as an older boy, he'd been more or less put in charge of them and I imagine he felt some responsibility for what had happened, though I don't see how he could have stopped them."

"I suppose he'd be the boy the Dorcas lady told me about. She said he was a decent kid, who'd refused to join the jaunt."

"I doubt whether it was moral scruples that held him back. The fact is that he's a very promising athlete. Football and boxing. He probably calculated that if he was going to get anywhere he had to keep his nose clean."

"Cusins? That wouldn't be Franky Cusins' son?"

"He'd be flattered to hear you suggest it. Franky's well over eighty. No, he's Lefty Cusins' grandson."

To Petrella the Cusins were names, remembered dimly. Both of them had been world-class boxers. He said, "Have you got any idea at all of what actually happened that night?"

Mr Wetherall's leathery and wrinkled face settled into a mask of distaste. He said, "I'm sure you don't want second-hand evidence."

"Second-hand, third-hand, any evidence at all," said Petrella.

"Very well. It was repeated by one boy – not himself concerned – that one of the four, not named, had said to him, 'Lovely money for being photographed with your trousers down.' "

"I see," said Petrella. "Much what I thought." He produced the page of photographs that Hoyland had given him. "I imagine that these are stills from a film made on an earlier occasion. As you see, the focus has been quite skilfully adjusted. The faces of the boys are unidentifiable. They haven't been so careful about the girls, from which I assume that they may have been prostitutes. Or maybe girls brought in off the street, who weren't too fussy about being recognised."

Whilst he was speaking Mr Wetherall had settled his spectacles on his prominent nose and was subjecting the photographs to the sort of attention he might have accorded to an essay given to him for correction. Petrella waited for his verdict. In the end he said, "Incredible," and handed the page of photographs back. "I thought I knew boys of that age and type fairly well. It seems quite incredible to me that twelve- and thirteen-year-old boys could have been persuaded to perform like that with girls of that type."

"They were drunk. Or so Mrs Millington said, when she saw them at four o'clock next morning."

"Mrs Millington?"

"A member of our local Dorcas Society. I've got everything she told me on tape. Perhaps you'd like to hear it."

When he had heard it, Mr Wetherall said, "One thing is quite clear. I have enough influence in educational circles to ensure that no party of schoolboys goes to the Witte Raaf Hotel again."

"I've no doubt you could. And I shall shortly be asking you to do just that. At the moment, however, I'd prefer you to hold off. This character, Hendrik, could operate just as easily from any other hotel, once he'd fixed the proprietor."

"Block one hole," agreed Mr Wetherall, "and the rats will soon find another. So what do you propose to do?"

"I might be able to get in touch with a senior Dutch policeman. I'd do it through my father. Before he retired he had a lot of European contacts. But the Dutch police can only move if we give them detailed information. The essential point is to find out where the boys were taken that night. If we promised him to keep his name right out of it, surely one of the boys would be prepared to come across?"

"Maybe," said Mr Wetherall. "But I'm not sure that any of the boys could help you, even if they were persuaded to talk. I got a pretty full account of the earlier part of the evening from young Cusins, who'd had it all from the boys, whilst they were still talking, on the plane coming home. The transport was a big saloon, with blinds over the rear windows. The boys travelled in the back of it. First stop was a Braunen café. There's one in almost every street. They're fully licensed and it was here that the boys were introduced to the pleasures of Dutch beer and geneva. When they were well primed they moved off again, cruised around for a bit – no doubt to confuse the boys' sense of direction – and ended up at a place which they described as a mixture between a warehouse and an office block. They were hustled out of the car without having any opportunity to see the name of the street. Same routine on the way back."

"A careful crowd," said Petrella.

"One of the boys who seems to have kept his head better than the others – or maybe drank less – says he remembers crossing a stretch of water on the way out. It was near the zoo in the Artis Garden, because he heard one of the lions roaring. After touring about a bit they re-crossed the same water, but not, he thought, by the same bridge."

"How could he tell?"

"He said it sounded different."

"Leaves a lot of options open," said Petrella, who had furnished himself with a map of Amsterdam. "There's only one way of tackling the problem. Next time Hendrik operates he's got to be followed. It's not going to be easy to fix it. But I've got the outlines of a scheme in mind and I shall need your co-operation."

"You shall have it," said Mr Wetherall. Petrella noted the frosty gleam in his eye and smiled.

"It won't be very active, I'm afraid. I'll tell you about it when I've sorted it out a bit."

That evening he put the whole problem to his wife.

He said, "One thing's clear. On the information which I have at the moment, second-hand from the Dorcas Ladies and third-hand from Mr Wetherall via Dave Cusins, I can't possibly initiate official action. And yet – "

"And yet," said his wife, suspending repairs to one of Lucinda's undergarments, "you want to do something because you think – as I do – that it's a foul and dangerous racket."

"Certainly. But there's more to it than that. The speed with which the heavy mob got on to those boys suggests to me that the whole thing may be organised from here."

"Filming in Amsterdam. Distribution in London."

"That could well be right. And if it is, it's my job to do something about it. But there's no chance of getting Central to move unless I can give them some facts. Where the filming's done, who does it and, more important, how they organise the import of the finished product into this country."

His wife said coldly, "You're circling round the problem like a cat round a suspect dish of meat. It's quite clear what's got to be done. Someone's got to go to Amsterdam and ferret out the answers to all those questions. If he can't go officially, he'll have to go unofficially. Right?"

"Your logic is impeccable. The only point you have evaded is the vital one. Who is to go? And don't suggest me for the job. I've got far too much to do here. Anyway, it would be inappropriate. It's a job for a junior officer. He could be given a week's leave – on compassionate grounds

– there's a police fund which assists with things like that. It would help if he could make himself understood in Holland – most of them speak French or German – "

"Someone with a degree in foreign languages?"

Petrella looked at her suspiciously. "That would certainly be useful," he said. "Have you anyone in mind?"

"You know perfectly well who you want to send. Perry Hoyland's cut out for the job."

"His name had occurred to me."

"Then why are you dithering?"

"I'm not dithering. I'm thinking. The choice is between sending someone like Hoyland, who doesn't look much like a policeman and who might therefore be able to pick up the information we want. Or sending, say, Sergeant Stark, who'd be recognised as a policeman on sight. He'd be perfectly well able to look after himself and would learn nothing."

"Then the choice seems obvious."

"It may seem obvious to you. But don't forget. The men behind a racket like this will be well organised and dangerous. And Hoyland is young and inexperienced. He's been a detective constable for less than six months."

His wife thought about this, whilst her needle performed a number of arabesques, then she said, "Just how old and how experienced were you when they sent you to Bordeaux to look into that drug-smuggling racket?"

Petrella made the gesture of a fencer acknowledging a hit.

He said, "When I was given that particular assignment – with considerable reluctance on the part of my superior officers – I was as young as Hoyland and even more recently qualified. And I was so damned stupid that I came within an inch of getting myself killed. And should have been if I hadn't happened to know how to construct a pick-lock out of a broken section of a wine rack and how to use it when I'd made it. Those were some of the things I'd learned at that rather peculiar college of further education in Cairo, but

I'm quite certain it was *not* something which was taught at Wellington."

"Then Hoyland must take great care not to get himself locked up. Tell me, if you do decide to send him, how do you suggest he should set about finding this studio, or whatever it is?"

"He'd have to keep an eye on Hendrik. According to the Dorcas ladies there's another party of schoolboys there now. If Hendrik tries the same game with them, he'd have to follow him."

"And just how is he going to do that? As soon as he goes anywhere near Hendrik or the boys he's bound to be spotted."

"Difficult. But not impossible."

"I can think of one way of making it a bit easier. You said that Mr Wetherall was willing to help."

"More than willing. Anxious. I saw him visualising himself in Amsterdam, in disguise, trailing Hendrik to his lair. Not, I fear, a very plausible scenario."

"Then let me suggest a better one. Get him to give Hoyland an official assignment, a letter on Education District paper, asking him to check up on the available accommodation for school parties in Amsterdam, Paris and Rome. Coupled with an undertaking to defray all reasonable expenses, but insisting on second-class travel – he'll know just what touches to put in. Armed with that he can march into that hotel – "

"The Witte Raaf."

"Right. And ask to see the proprietor. He'll be able to question him about the arrangements he makes for school parties and might comment unfavourably on being told that there is no night porter. With any luck he'll spot Hendrik talking to the boys and ask who he is and what he thinks he's up to. The more suspicious he is about Hendrik, the less suspicious Hendrik will be of him."

"Brilliant," said Petrella and meant it.

As soon as he got to his office on the following morning

he sent for Hoyland and was irritated to find that he was unavailable. Ambrose, appealed to, inspected the day book and said, "He seems to have gone out on a job suggested by you. He's seeing that newsagent, Chipping, to ask if he's preferring charges and to find out if there was anyone who had a down on him and might have tried to frame him."

"Yes," said Petrella. He remembered making the suggestion. He had not thought it would come to very much.

"I've got Inspector Trench here. He'd like a word with you."

"Send him up."

Inspector Trench was the youngest of Petrella's subdivisional heads. He was in charge of CD, otherwise the Isle of Dogs, which was not, in fact, an island, but a peninsula, surrounded on three sides by a loop of the Thames.

He said, "I'm afraid it's another boat theft, sir."

"Yes, I saw your last report. How many does that make?"

"Fifteen from my manor alone in the past year. This was one of the worst. More open and more violent. The others were mostly sneak-thieves, lifting boats which had been left unguarded or badly secured. Not this one. It was a very well-equipped motor-cruiser, lying at Millwall Pier. The details are in my report."

"Left unattended?"

"Far from it. The skipper and a crew of three men were on board, ready to take her across next morning to St Malo, where the owner was going to pick her up. There were at least ten men involved. Six of them scrambled onto the ship. They knocked the skipper out, after which the other three didn't seem to have shown a lot of fight. They soon had them all off the boat and locked up in a shed opposite the pier. I don't think the owner of the shed was involved. They simply wrenched off the padlock he'd put on the door and substituted their own."

"You said ten men?"

"Yes. The other four took no part in the actual theft. But they held the ring. Two men happened to come past and seemed to be interested in what was going on. They were told to bugger off."

"And buggered off?"

"Rapidly. But one of them did stop at the first phone box they came to and reported the theft."

"Five out of ten for public spirit," said Petrella. "Could he give any description of the four men?"

"Yes. But not a very useful one. They were all wearing animal masks."

"What animals?"

"A bull, a goat, a pig and a dog."

"Did that suggest anything to you?"

"Certainly. It suggested two possibilities. Either they were the Farm Boys or – which seemed more likely – people pretending to be them."

"Not easy. Better check them anyway. No doubt they'll have carefully interlocking alibis. But see if you can shake them down."

"Do what I can," said Trench. "It seems to me those lads are getting too big for their boots."

After he had gone Petrella sat for a few minutes thinking. Trench had put his finger on the point that hurt. It wasn't the theft itself. Thieving had become a fact of life to be dealt with as expeditiously as possible, but with a strong probability that neither the stealers nor the stolen goods would be identified and that the only sufferers would be the insurance company. No. What stung was the openness and violence of the operation. It argued a contempt for the police which was insulting and dangerous.

He was thinking about this when his internal telephone rang. Ambrose said, "I've got a call here from Seymour Street. Chief Superintendent Spice."

Seymour Street was the headquarters station of DM, a sub-division which ran up from Oxford Street to the

Marylebone Road. Petrella knew Spice by name, but had never met him.

He said, "Sorry to trouble you. I expect you've got a heap of things on your plate. It's just that a newspaper man's gone missing and his people are getting worried."

"Is it Poston-Pirrie you're talking about?"

"That's right. I was told that he was doing some investigation down in your area and wondered if he had holed up there."

"How long's he been missing?"

"Since Saturday. To start with it was assumed that he'd gone off for the weekend. Then he failed to turn up at a meeting which had been fixed for Monday morning at the *Sentinel*. The paper had got hold of some people he particularly wanted to meet and he'd definitely promised to be there. So they started ringing round."

Petrella thought back. He said, "It must have been a week or more since I last saw him. He didn't make any mention of coming to live down here."

"I don't suppose he would. He had a very comfortable pad in New Cavendish Street."

"Are you putting Missing Persons on to it?"

"A bit early for that. But I'd be obliged if you could keep your eyes open."

Petrella promised to keep his eyes open. And his ears. If Poston-Pirrie was lurking anywhere in the neighbourhood he reckoned he'd hear about it soon enough.

At that point Hoyland arrived. He said, "I think I've got to the bottom of that sheet of photographs. Mr Jackson got the truth out of his son – in the end. The story that he'd found it in his comic was something the kid had made up. It wasn't true. The page of photographs was being handed round at his school. On a strictly commercial basis. You paid a pound and could keep it for a week."

"I guessed from its condition it was something like that. Did he tell his father who he got it from?"

"No. He wouldn't do that. But he said it must have been through a dozen pairs of hands before it reached him."

Petrella thought about this. Then he said, "I don't think we can trace it back. None of the boys will want to talk. But we might be able to short-circuit it. If this thing" – he held the crumpled sheet of paper by its corner, as though closer contact would dirty his hands – "has been in circulation for twelve weeks, we could find out from the school whether a party of their boys has been on one of these foreign tours within, say, the last six months. If they have, we could get the names of the boys who went and might be able to shake one of them down. I'll put Wilmot on to it." Noting the disappointment in Hoyland's face he said, "I'd have given you the job, but I've got something more important for you. Do you speak Dutch?"

"Enough to make myself understood. Not enough to pass as a Dutchman."

"You're not going to pass as a Dutchman. You're going to be an inspector from the East London Education Department. Here's what I want you to do."

He talked for ten minutes and Hoyland listened. When he got out a pencil and started to make notes Petrella stopped him. "Better not put anything on paper. What you must remember are these two telephone numbers. The first is Wilfred Wetherall's office number. If you've got any urgent information to pass to us, contact him, from a public call box, at any time in normal business hours. The second number is Police Commissioner Spaan, of the Amsterdam force. Commissioner in their set-up is equivalent to Commander in ours, so only use it if you need help badly. I hope you won't have to, because this is strictly on an unofficial level."

"Understood," said Hoyland. He sounded cheerful. The only thing he was worried about was that he might forget those two telephone numbers. As soon as he was out of the room he would write them down and learn them properly.

"If you can't strike a line in seven days, come home. That gives you a week to produce some return for the public money that's being spent on you."

Hadn't someone said that to him once? A long time ago.

6

When his plane touched down at Schiphol Airport, Detective Peregrine Hoyland had no settled plan of campaign, which was just as well since the situation was fluid.

An early visit to the Witte Raaf was called for and he had considered the advisability of actually putting up at this hotel, but had rejected it. By staying there he might pick up further useful information, but, when it came to the crunch, it would limit his freedom of movement.

Studying a map of Amsterdam he had seen that there were three parallel streets. The Orteliuskade, which fronted Rembrandt Park and called itself a quay, though the only water near it was the ornamental lake in the park. Behind that ran Ortelius Straat, with the Witte Raaf about two-thirds of the way along it. Behind that again was Spilbergen Straat, in which his guide-book had mentioned a number of hotels classified as 'medium range'. The Reizigerhof seemed a suitable one and it was to this that he directed his taxi.

Mid-August was not, it seemed, high season in Amsterdam and he was quickly fixed up with a small, clean bedroom on the second floor overlooking the street. He dumped his bag, washed away some of the grime of his journey and descended into the blazing sunshine. It was hotter than in London. He had dressed, in the manner which he thought would be appropriate to an inspector in the Department of Education, in a dark suit, white shirt and old school tie, with a handkerchief peeping out of his breast pocket. He was beginning to regret this. Most of the men he passed wore open-necked shirts and light linen trousers; in one or

66

two cases even Bermuda shorts. His respectable suit felt hot and heavy.

Turning down one of the narrow passages which separated the two main streets he found himself almost directly in front of the Witte Raaf. It seemed a popular place. A party of American tourists, armed with cameras and guide-books, was coming out as he went in and most of the tables in the reception area were occupied. He could see no sign of any schoolboys.

A man with a flat brown face and a fringe of white beard was standing behind the counter talking to the receptionist. Hoyland guessed that this would be the proprietor and marched up to him.

"Herr Sturmann?"

"I am indeed he."

"Might I have a word with you? In private." He produced Mr Wetherall's letter. The proprietor read it quickly, smiled and said, "Certainly. Follow me, please." He led the way through a door behind the counter, across an outer office where a middle-aged lady with a moustache was pounding a typewriter, and into his inner sanctum.

"Please to sit, Mr Hoyland. A cigar? A drink? No. Then what can I do for you?"

Though accented, his English was quick and fluent. Not a fool, Hoyland guessed. He moved straight over to the attack.

"We received a number of complaints from the organisers of a recent party of boys who were accommodated here. The East London schools party."

Sturmann was turning the pages of a ledger. He said, "Yes. I remember that the ladies in charge did speak to me. A little rash, I thought, to put high-spirited boys in charge of females – however, that was the business of the organisers."

"The business of the organisers was to see that the boys came to no harm."

"Harm? Surely you are exaggerating. There was an

incident when three or four of them stayed out late on the last day of their visit – "

"Four o'clock in the morning could certainly be described as late, for boys of that age."

"Was it as late as that? The ladies did not make the point clear to me."

"Certainly it was four o'clock in the morning. And the boys were drunk."

"Really, Mr Hoyland. You shock me. Are you sure of your facts?"

"We regard the women as totally reliable. But there was more to it than that."

Up to this point Sturmann had been leaning back easily in his chair, his right hand fiddling with the glass paper-weight on the desk, his left hand coming up to scratch the back of his sun-reddened neck. Now all movement ceased. He said, softly, "Yes?"

"There is a man who, I am told, comes here so frequently that he seems to make it his second home. I have only been told his first name, which is Hendrik. You know the man I mean?"

"It is a common name in Holland."

If he had not noticed Sturmann's sudden immobility, Hoyland might have been deceived. But he was sure, now, that he was on to something. He repeated, in the flat tones of someone who is speaking a self-evident truth, "You know the man, I believe."

"It might be Hendrik Winkel you speak of. He is a regular customer at the bar here. Sometimes he dines. Has some complaint been made of him?"

"He is said to make himself very friendly with the boys. Nothing wrong with that, I agree. Boys are friendly creatures. But in two cases his conduct was certainly open to criticism. On one occasion he offered to take the boys round the red-light district and on another to a strip-tease performance."

"When you put it like that," said Sturmann, "it sounds

terrible." Hoyland noted that he was easy again. "But in fact neither invitation was as unreasonable as it sounds. The red-light district, the Walletjes, is a famous Amsterdam sight. Groups of tourists visit it regularly, treating it as a sight, you understand, an exhibition. In such visits there is only curiosity, no thought of immorality. The strip-tease, so called, would be one of several turns at the Concert Gebouw. What you might call a smoking concert. The boys would not understand the jokes and exchanges, but would certainly enjoy the spectacle."

"I can't agree that either entertainment is suitable for twelve- and thirteen-year-old boys. We will leave that for the moment as a matter of opinion. But now tell me this. To what entertainment was he driving them on their last night here?"

Stillness again. A dangerous stillness, with anger behind it.

"I don't understand you."

"I am sure you understand. I am referring to the occasion on which he took a party of boys out by car and brought them back at four in the morning."

"That is a serious accusation, Mr Hoyland. Will you tell me upon what it is based?"

"The information came from the boys themselves."

"Indeed? Then clearly it calls for investigation. I will question Hendrik Winkel myself and ascertain whether he has some explanation."

"I hope it will be a satisfactory one."

"I hope so, too. For the good reputation of my hotel. Leave the matter with me. Tell me, what are your plans? How long do you stay here?"

"That depends on how quickly I can carry out my programme. You will understand that I have to speak to the owners of other hotels, to find out what terms they can offer. Half a dozen names have been given me."

"And if the terms they offer are not so good as ours, you will not, I trust, be prejudiced by the matter we have been discussing. I am sure that the explanation will demonstrate, as we say, *van een mug een olifant maken*! Making an elephant out of a fly."

The proprietor was smiling now. Hoyland thought that it made his pear-shaped face even less attractive. He said, "Today is Tuesday. I should be finished with my investigation by Thursday. On Friday morning I go on to Paris. And, yes, if your terms are the best, *and* Mr Winkel can explain his curious conduct, I will not allow it to prejudice me."

"Excellent. Let us not part on bad terms. I invite you to sample our luncheon. That will, I am sure, enable you at least to report favourably on our catering. Allow me to conduct you."

The dining-room was crowded.

Apart from three tables, which had been pushed together and looked as though they were waiting for a party, the only one left was in the window embrasures looking out over the Rembrandt Park. Since the proprietor swept Hoyland straight up to it, he assumed that it was one he kept for his special guests.

The waiter was taking Hoyland's order when a quiet voice from behind him said, "Would you think it an intrusion if I shared your table?"

"Of course not." Hoyland said it the more readily since the newcomer was not only English but, as evidenced by his voice and his clothing, was clearly a gentleman.

"I wouldn't have butted in, but this seemed to be the only place left. I understand that the tables in the middle are held for a party of schoolboys."

He turned his attention to the waiter and gave him his own order in reasonably fluent Dutch.

He said, "Thom Sturmann is making a good thing out of this caravanserai. It's getting almost uncomfortably crowded."

"You come here a lot?"

"About once a month. And I hardly like to tell you – as

a loyal Englishman – that what I'm doing is getting a ship built. It's a slow business, but not as slow as it would be on the Tyne."

"And cheaper, I suppose."

"A bit. Not all that much. The real trouble with our shipyards is that they never seem able to give you a firm delivery date. My name's Ringland, by the way. You're not in shipping yourself?"

"Hardly," said Hoyland, with a smile at the idea of himself as a shipping magnate. "The only thing I'm interested in shipping is parties of schoolboys."

He explained who he was and what he was doing.

"Not a job I'd care for," said Ringland. "I don't mean your job. That gets you round Europe at the expense of someone else. I'd be all for that. I meant his sort of job. Doesn't look happy, does he?"

This was directed at a serious-looking young man who had come in with twenty rumbustious boys and was spreading them round the empty tables.

Hoyland said, "There's something you can tell me. One of the complaints about the last lot that I'm investigating was that a man going under the name of Hendrik Winkel – some sort of tout I imagine – had tried to get the boys to join him on a trip round the red-light district. Sturmann maintains that this was a normal bit of sight-seeing. Could he be right?"

"Roughly right. Tourists do get taken round the Walletjes in the early part of the evening. The tarts lean out of their windows and shout insults at them and everyone feels they're having a good time. If you're after real business you go along after dark."

"I see," said Hoyland doubtfully. "There was also talk about a strip-tease show."

"Plenty of them. Amsterdam's a pretty tolerant city in some ways. I see that you're a Wellingtonian. Recent vintage?"

"I left three years ago."

"I asked because the son of an old friend of mine has just gone there. He told me he was in the Picton. All the houses are named after Wellington's generals. That's right, isn't it?"

"Correct. But for some odd reason most of them are called dormitories, not houses. I was in the Orange."

"Prince of Orange? The young man who destroyed the King's German Legion at Waterloo by ordering them to charge at the wrong time and in the wrong direction?"

"We skipped that bit of history," said Hoyland, with a smile.

"Hullo! Is that your tout?"

A black-haired, pale-faced man had sidled into the room. He was dressed in a dark three-piece suit, which must have made him quite uncomfortably hot.

"The black crow," said Hoyland. "If his name's Hendrik he's my man. I'll slip out ahead of him and tackle him in the lobby."

The newcomer was not eating. He had pulled up a chair to the end of the table furthest from the master in charge and was chatting up the boys. He seemed to be practising his English on them, whilst they practised their Dutch on him, a proceeding which was giving rise to a lot of giggling.

Hoyland, who found the *smörgåsbord* which was served as a starter more than enough for a whole meal, left the table through a door onto the terrace, circled the hotel and stationed himself in the reception area. The boys, having been served last, came out last. They were followed by Ringland who said, "You've missed your bird. He slipped off the same way that you did."

"Never mind," said Hoyland. "He'll be back."

It was clearly time that he did some serious thinking. He went back to his room in the Reizigerhof, opened the window, pulled up a chair beside it and sat looking down on the traffic which hustled and bustled up Spilbergen Straat.

He had not missed the look of relief on Sturmann's face

when he had told him that he planned to leave on Friday morning. According to the receptionist the present party of boys was leaving on Saturday ('Thank the good Lord.' She had a low opinion of schoolboys). That meant that anything that was going to happen would be timed for Friday night. The idea, quite clearly, was to leave the action until the last moment and then get rid of the boys as quickly as possible.

The more he thought over the problem the more clearly he recognised its difficulties. If the programme was a repeat from last time the boys would leave the hotel by car. No doubt these men had their eyes open. Another car, a taxi or a hire car following them would soon be spotted. His plan, therefore, was to use a bicycle, which he could hire and which was a common enough form of transport in Amsterdam to escape notice. But was it capable of keeping up with an efficiently driven private car, particularly later in the evening when the traffic flow would be reduced? He doubted it.

There was only one answer. He must get some idea of where the studio was, so that he could anticipate the opposition and get into the area ahead of them. Could he do that? A study of the street map had shown him that he might.

The boy in the previous party who had kept his wits about him had noticed that they crossed a stretch of water by one bridge, ran round a bit and came back by another. This stretch of water must be the Amstel, a fact borne out by the reference to hearing the lion roaring. A car crossing the Amstel on Sarphati Straat would run, almost at once, alongside the Artis Park and its zoo. After that it could have fooled round in the Oosterpark area before re-crossing the Amstel. But by which bridge?

There was a choice of two. One was the main Houderskade. The other, just below it, was called the Nieuwamstelbrug. It was on a much smaller road. A car which was not anxious to call attention to itself might well have preferred the quieter route. A further pointer. After crossing, it would have been heading into a maze of small streets, which the map called De Pijp, or the Pipe. Just the sort of area, away from all the main streets, which might have old office properties tucked into it. So far this was surmise, inspired by map-reading. Tomorrow he would take his bicycle and examine the whole area.

Back in his own room after lunch Ringland asked the telephone exchange for an external line and dialled a number in the City of London. This was a direct line at the other end and went straight through to the man he wanted.

He said, "Toby here, Bob. I'm having to take a chance on an open line because this is urgent."

"If it's urgent," said the placid voice at the other end, "fire away. But keep it short."

"Can you locate someone in our circle who's clued up about Wellington? The school in Berkshire, I mean, not the West Country version. Some master or recent old boy. Best would be the man who looks after the OW register."

"Might be able to. What's it all about?"

"There's a character called Hoyland sniffing round the hotel. May be all right. Sturmann says he's got a letter from the East London Education people empowering him to investigate hotels taking youth groups in Amsterdam, Paris and whatever."

"Signed by who?"

"A bod called Wilfred Wetherall. Why? Do you know him?"

The man at the other end chuckled. "Everyone knows old Wetherall. He's about ninety, but an honest old bird. So what's worrying you?"

"It's just a feeling. His coming along so soon after the trouble we had with the other lot. Seemed rather too coincidental. He's been trying to get his hooks into Hendrik. I warned him about this and he slipped out of the dining-room and made off. I've told him to make himself scarce until Friday night."

"Details of Hoyland, please."

"He was in the Orange dormitory. He left about three years ago. And he didn't, I think, go on to the university. What I'd like to know is what he did do. He can't make a living out of occasional jaunts to the Continent. What's his real job?"

"See what I can do. Arthur was at Wellington. Long before your chap, of course. By the way, who's running transport?"

"Jonathan. And that's another worry. If Hoyland got at him he'd blow a gasket."

"Jonathan's a wimp. I'm sorry we ever let him in on this. No use crying over spilt milk. Anything I can find out will have to be with you by the day after tomorrow if it's going to be any use to you. So stay near a telephone."

Hoyland spent the whole of Wednesday exploring the section of Amsterdam that the map called the Old South. He gave most attention to the half of it which lay east of the Ruysdaelkade. West of it the nature of the city changed. It was full of museums and concert halls. The eastern half was much more the sort of area he had in mind, part residential, part business. It had once been prosperous, but had slipped. On some of the blocks of flats 'To Let' notices sprouted as thick as apples in autumn. Other buildings were shuttered and empty. No doubt the renovator would eventually arrive, as he had in the New South. At the moment it was an area that was waiting and hoping.

Starting at the little Sarphati Park in the centre and moving in ever-widening circles, he traversed the whole district, memorising the twists and turns of the streets and picking out landmarks, like the church towers and the pointed roof of the sports hall, which would be useful guides at night. As far as he could judge, the place was poorly lighted. He was glad to see that the bicycle was the almost universal form of transport.

When he had finished he selected a spot from which he could see both of the Amstel bridges. He was fully aware that he was taking a chance. The car might not come that way at all. But it was a better chance than trying to avoid detection when following it from the hotel.

Now one last and very difficult matter had to be attended to. He had somehow to watch the hotel to see when the boys left it and what the car looked like. Useless to think of hanging about in the street. He would be spotted at once.

He took the problem back with him to the hotel and thought about it, lying on his bed. When the solution struck him it was quite simple. The building he was in ran all the way back to the Ortelius Straat and the Witte Raaf hotel was on the opposite side. All he needed was a window in the back of his own hotel. He went out, climbed a further flight of stairs and found himself in an area of small rooms. Some of them had numbers on the doors. He noted particularly three rooms at the back. The doors were locked, but they looked to be what he wanted.

He went downstairs to talk to the proprietress, a motherly woman who clearly had a soft spot for the young man. They talked in French. Hoyland spoke warmly in praise of the bedroom he had been allotted, but regretted that it had one drawback. The traffic in the Spilbergen Straat, which was a main road and a bus route, kept him awake at night. Might it be possible to change it for a smaller room at the back? He explained, with a smile, that he was not seeking to economise. No doubt the room would be smaller, but he was quite prepared to pay the same price for it.

The proprietress smiled too. She said that it would be quite possible. The change-over could be effected that evening. She added that Hoyland reminded her of her own son, who was in the Dutch police.

On Thursday evening Hoyland paid a farewell visit to the Witte Raaf. He explained to Sturmann, with disarming frankness, that the discussions he had held that day with a number of other hotels had not produced a tariff of charges lower than the ones at the Witte Raaf. Indeed, in some cases, they were higher. If Sturmann could assure him that future parties would be more carefully looked after and, in particular, would not be allowed to roam around late at night, then he was prepared to report favourably to the Education Authority.

Sturmann assured him that he was already taking steps in the matter and pointed to an item in the local paper. It invited applications for the post of night porter at the hotel. Hoyland thanked him for this proof of his attention and they parted with expressions of mutual regard.

Satisfied with his day's work, he slept soundly in his garret room.

On Friday morning he set out early, on foot, leaving his bicycle chained up, with others, in the forecourt of the hotel. At a shop in a back street which he had located the day before and which seemed to specialise in sailors' dunnage, he bought an old but respectable-looking suitcase and a seaman's cloak. Once clear of the shop he packed the cloak into the suitcase. He had two hours to kill and spent one hour over a leisurely breakfast and the second on a bench in the Vondelpark, watching the water fowl and reading an English newspaper which he had got from a kiosk. Nothing much seemed to be happening. Most of the cricket matches had petered out in drawn games. For a moment he had an overmastering longing to be back in south London, at the half-empty Oval, watching the leisurely unfolding of County Cricket.

At half past ten he put such thoughts from him, picked up his suitcase and made his way on foot to the Central Station. Eleven o'clock was striking as he arrived. The train for Paris left at noon from platform eight. Platform seven, alongside it, announced a stopping train to Woerden and Rotterdam, leaving ten minutes before the Paris express. He had already noted these timings. He joined the queue at the ticket office and bought a third-class ticket to Abcoude, which was the first station down the line, after which he retired to the station buffet, ordered a cup of coffee and withdrew with it to a table at the back of the room. As he drank it, he kept an eye on the crowd on the concourse. He thought he saw a face that he recognised. Yes. It was Ringland and he was talking to a fair-haired young man. A fellow ship-builder? They strolled up the concourse, turned and came back again and stopped to chat. Blondie had the sort of face that Hoyland particularly disliked. Not much forehead, too much nose and chin; over-poweringly English and upper class. It looked as though they were waiting for someone. But if so, why on that section of the platform which was devoted to departures? He was conscious of a first very faint prickle of uneasiness.

Very well. If they were, for some accountable reason, keeping an eye on him, he would reward them with a full performance.

By the time he reached the barrier Ringland had disappeared. Blondie was pretending, unconvincingly, to read a newspaper. Hoyland presented his ticket and strolled slowly along the platform, examining the Paris train for an empty carriage. He found one at the far end of the platform, dumped his bag in it and then leaned out of the corridor window and shouted to the boy with the trolley for a bottle of beer.

He realised that the next move was going to be tricky, but since the local train was filling up from the rear, there was likely to be a rush of last-minute travellers for the few remaining seats in front. As it came, he slipped across with it, on the leeside of a large Dutch frau who seemed equally afraid of losing her children and the train. With her he landed in a compartment crammed to suffocation.

Ten minutes later he was out on the platform at Abcoude, an uninspiring suburb of Amsterdam, where he had an uninspiring lunch, before catching a bus. After two changes, he found himself in the Duivendrecht district.

This was where the leading diamond merchants had built their houses alongside the golf course. His idea was to keep out of the city until dusk and he could not have chosen a more peaceful place for a siesta. He was too worked up to sleep properly, but managed to doze.

The brightness faded at last from a sky which had turned from dark blue to a threatening bronze. He could feel the thunder in the air and guessed that a storm was brewing up. It took him an hour to walk back to his hotel. There was no one in the lobby. The girl behind the desk was busy on the telephone. He took his key from its hook and padded up the four flights of stairs to his attic room. So far, so good.

He moved a chair across to the window, opened it and sat down. It was an excellent observation post. All he had to do now was to stay awake, not easy after the exertions of the day.

When he found his head nodding he got up and started to walk across the room. Three steps to the door and three back again. As he re-seated himself he heard the distant rumble of thunder. The storm was somewhere over the North Sea. It might not reach the city at all. He rather hoped that it would. Even if it brought rain it would lift some of the heaviness.

He had been on watch for more than two hours when the car arrived. He was certain it was the right one even before he saw Hendrik get out of it and go into the hotel. A long, dark saloon, not unlike the sort of vehicle favoured by undertakers. The back windows were curtained.

Five minutes later the boys appeared, chattering happily. No hurry, said Hoyland to himself. If they follow the same routine there'll be a preliminary session in a Braunen café to loosen the boys up. He watched the car drive off, then walked downstairs and out into the forecourt, unchained his bicycle and pedalled sedately away.

His chosen observation post at the end of Jan Steen Straat was an archway which led to the back of a post office, long closed for the night, its vans parked in a neat row behind a padlocked gate.

No question now of going to sleep. He was wide-awake and worrying. It was perfectly possible that he had made a fool of himself. Even if he had correctly deduced the route of the car on the previous occasion, there was no guarantee that it would follow it a second time.

One crawling hour later he had convinced himself that his plan had failed. A more courageous or a more enterprising operator would have accepted the risk and followed the car. He had just reached this unhappy conclusion when the car appeared, drove over the upper bridge and re-appeared ten minutes later, over the lower one. Precisely according to plan, thought Hoyland. After such a start, all must go well.

The car, which was driving at a reduced speed through these badly lighted and twisting streets, was quite easy to follow. He gave it sufficient law to turn each corner ahead and then pedalled furiously to catch up before it could turn again. The only hitch occurred when it turned down an opening which he knew, from his previous reconnaissance, led to a dead-end, blocked by the sportshall. He guessed that the driver had made a mistake and had turned too soon. This was proved correct when he heard the sudden squeal of brakes and the noise of the car reversing. By the time it emerged, Hoyland had retreated into a handy doorway. He felt certain that the car was very close to its destination.

It turned down the next street and stopped. The night, under its black overcast, was so quiet that he could hear the doors slamming and a crescendo of chattering from the boys. After which all noises were cut off and silence descended.

He left his bicycle in the doorway and went forward on foot. The tail end of the car he had been following showed in the gap between two buildings on the right of the road. The nearer building was boarded up and in darkness. The further one was showing lights.

He eased his way forward.

He could see, now, that ahead of the car and blocking it was a large lorry with a canvas tilt. Both vehicles had been abandoned by their drivers. The lights from the second building came from the upper floors, in one case strong enough to suggest flood lighting. Any doubts Hoyland might have had were set at rest when he lifted the back flap of the lorry and looked inside.

As a keen video amateur he had no difficulty in identifying what he saw. Among a pile of tripods and flex, booms and rifle mikes was at least one Betacam complete with replay adapter and BVF viewfinder. If these were spares, he thought, the studio must be pretty lavishly equipped.

Suddenly a fan of light hit the street. The front door of the building he was watching had been opened. Hoyland was not alarmed. The two vehicles gave him ample cover. If pursued he could move in either direction. However, the man who had come out did not seem to be planning anything hostile. He had lighted a cigarette. Smoking forbidden on the set, thought Hoyland. He's come out for a drag. When the man turned his head he was unsurprised to recognise blondie.

Everything was now in his hands.

He had located the studio, could identify two of the men involved and had noted the numbers of their car and lorry. All he had to do was to get back to base with his treasure.

He decided to abandon the bicycle. His instinct, now, was to keep as low a profile as possible. As blondie went in, slamming the door behind him, he crawled to the far end of the street, got to his feet and started for home.

His quickest route was along the bank of the Amstel Canal for a few hundred yards, then north through the Vondelpark. After that there was a wide choice of ways.

His first idea was to run. He rejected it. Running at night invited suspicion. He would stroll. He had to correct a tendency to keep looking over his shoulder. He told himself that this was nervous reaction, quite unsuitable for an experienced policeman. In any event, the night was so quiet that he would have heard a pursuer long before he caught up with him.

Ahead, at one of the few points where a lamp lit the waters of the canal, a man was coming towards him. He was dressed as a sailor and was singing softly to himself. As Hoyland moved aside to let him pass the man lashed out with the loaded stick he was holding, hitting Hoyland once, on the side of the neck, paralysing him, and a second time on the head as he went down. Then he pivoted, put his foot into the small of Hoyland's back and kicked him into the canal.

He stood for a moment, watching the bubbles coming up, then went on his way, still singing. As he did so a few heavy drops of rain were beginning to fall.

7

Two men, both thick set and distinguishable only because one of them was bald and the other had shoulder-length greasy hair, had been watching Hoyland since he had emerged from Cornelis Straat and crossed the main road. Both were known to the police. Their speciality was robbing any pedestrian who was stupid enough to walk alone on the streets at night. Hoyland, from the moment he appeared, had seemed to them a perfect prospect; unsuspicious in appearance and smartly enough dressed to suggest that his pockets would be well lined.

They had kept level with him by using the street above the canal path, ready to descend at the appropriate moment, and shear this slow-moving young sheep.

What had happened next had outraged their professional feelings. What gross, what unbelievable stupidity to assault this promising subject and kick him into the canal without – for God's sake! – without making the smallest attempt to search him first.

As the sailor disappeared they climbed down the bank, cursing steadily. The rain was belting down now, but this did not worry them. They were going to have to get wet anyway. Both of them slid into the water, feeling with their feet for Hoyland's body. When they located it they heaved it out and laid it on the path.

The inside pocket of the jacket yielded a wallet, promisingly heavy. The other jacket pockets were empty of anything of interest. They found some small change in the trouser pockets and unstrapped and removed Hoyland's wrist-watch. Then, knowing that travellers, particularly Americans, often kept a wad of notes in their back hip pockets, they rolled him over onto his face.

The immediate result of this piece of rough handling was that the pressure as he landed face downwards made Hoyland vomit, bringing up, with the rest of the contents of his stomach, a flood of black liquid mud. Finding nothing in his hip pocket and hearing a car approaching on the road above, they decided to call it a day and left the body lying, in its mess, on the path.

An hour later, when the rain was easing off, the first passer-by on foot, a policeman coming off duty, spotted the body. His natural instinct was to leave it where it was and get home. Then his official feelings prevailed. He plodded off to the nearest police box and summoned the mortuary van. It was when this arrived and the attendants were hoisting up Hoyland's body that one of them noticed his eyelids twitching. The destination of the van was changed from the mortuary to the police infirmary.

When Hoyland finally opened his eyes, the first thing he saw was Petrella's face. The first thing he said was "2A Winder Straat."

"That's all right," said Petrella, who was grinning. "You said it six times before they got you into bed and sedated. As it seemed to be worrying you they sent a police car round to check the place. It was empty. The birds had flown."

Hoyland, whose wits seemed to be coming back to him in instalments, said, "Lot of stuff in that van. Maybe they'd started packing up ready to flit."

"Maybe. Your arrival certainly hastened their departure. And people who leave in a hurry often leave little things behind. Including, in this case, a few small items of equipment and some fingerprints. Which may be useful when they open up their next studio, which, no doubt, they will. However, that'll be a matter for the Dutch police, not for us. And certainly not for you. You'll stay here for a bit."

"For how long?" said Hoyland rebelliously.

"Until the doctor lets you go. You must have an uncommonly hard head. One of those blows might easily have cracked your skull. And, incidentally, you saved your life by being so comprehensively sick. Otherwise, the doctor says you'd probably have choked to death. That's two bits of luck. If I were you, I shouldn't tempt providence again. Not just for a bit, anyway."

But Hoyland wasn't interested in providence. What he wanted to know, very urgently, was where he had gone wrong. How had the opposition got ahead of him? Why, in fact, were they looking for him at all?

"They were meant to think I was on my way to Paris." He explained what he had done. "I certainly thought I'd fooled them."

"You may have fooled one of them. The fair-haired creep you saw sounds like a man called Jonathan Draper. He comes here quite a bit. Alleged to be interested in international re-insurance. Which he may be. Actually he seems to spend most of his time over here at what they call *Blote Boys en Bengels*, meaning Boys' Clubs for Men. You might easily have fooled him. But not, I think, Ringland. He's a very wide-awake character."

"Is he what he said he is?"

"Oh, certainly. He's a shipbuilder, with a lot of money behind him. It seems that what *he* did was he went round to your hotel and chatted up the proprietress. 'Such a nice man,' she said. When she told him that you hadn't given up your room and also mentioned your changing to a room at the back, alarm bells started ringing. No doubt they picked you up when you left the hotel that evening."

"I ought to have thought of that," said Hoyland dismally.

"Don't start blaming yourself. You did all right. You had some good luck and some bad. That's the way things go in our job. Spaan will want to ask you some questions

85

and he'll have some photographs to show you. I'll tell him you're quite fit enough to be grilled."

It was three days before he extracted leave of departure from the doctor, a sour and pessimistic man who only gave it in the end because the bed was needed for someone else. Re-equipped with money, ticket and a temporary passport he made his way to the air terminal building opposite the main line station. Here he had joined a longish line of passengers at the flight reception desk when he saw something that stopped him in his tracks.

Gently, so as not to attract attention to himself, he backed out of the queue and moved away until he was hidden by a newspaper kiosk. A second look confirmed his suspicions. Jonathan Draper was ahead of him in the queue.

His first idea was to telephone Maplin Road, but he rejected it. If Petrella happened to be out, a message from a junior detective, no matter how urgent he labelled it, would go to the bottom of the pile. The number he dialled was the one he had been given for Mr Wetherall. He was relieved to hear the creaking tones of that pedagogue.

He said, "I've got a very urgent message for Superintendent Petrella. I thought you'd be likely to be able to locate him."

"If he's anywhere in East London, I can probably do that."

"I felt sure you could. The message is that Jonathan Draper is on Flight 373 from Amsterdam this morning. It might be a good idea to pick him up on arrival and see where he goes when he gets to London."

"Anything else?"

"No, that's the message. Jonathan – "

"All right. I'm not deaf. Not yet." Clunk.

The receiver at the other end was banged down.

After further reflection Hoyland made his way back to the airline desk and succeeded in changing his ticket for one on the evening flight. Then he retired to the buffet and took as long as he could over two cups of coffee.

Fifty minutes later when the information screen showed that Flight 373 was taking off he started to make some calculations. The flight time was seventy minutes. Adding fifty minutes it totalled just two hours. It was not a lot, but he had great confidence in Mr Wetherall's ability to locate Petrella and Petrella's to organise a suitable reception.

8

"We had quite an elaborate team waiting for Draper," said Petrella. He was sitting in Charlie Kay's office. The superintendent had listened with unconcealed amusement to an account of Hoyland's adventures in Amsterdam. "We had to consider the possibility that he might have left his own car at the airport or perhaps arranged for one of his City friends to pick him up. But in fact he caught a tube train at Heathrow, like a good little boy, got out at Leicester Square and set off on foot, without once looking round."

"Sounds a simple sort of sod," said Kay. "Where was he making for?"

"It turned out to be a second-hand bookshop in Cecil Court – that's one of the passages that join St Martin's Lane and the Lower Charing Cross Road."

"Lot of bookshops there, some clean, some grimy."

"This one called itself the Naughty Nineties."

"Oh, yes. I know that one. When I was with the Porn Squad we gave it the once-over. Classified it as Hemp."

"Come again."

"Harmless – Expensive – Mild – Porn. Semi-respectable stuff. *The Palace of Pleasure*; *The Karma Sutra*; *History of the Rod* by a retired clergyman. You know the sort of stuff."

"It doesn't sound like my favourite reading," said Petrella. "But, yes, I know the sort of books you mean."

"The proprietor's a bod called Maurice Meinhold. Details of his early life a bit vague. No doubt we'd have got some of the facts if we could have thought up grounds for prosecuting him, but no chance of that since Lady Chatterley hit the canvas."

"What sort of customers?"

"The normal ones, I imagine. Overtly respectable middle-class males in search of second-hand material for masturbation."

Petrella said, "My idea was that Draper was acting as postman. I expect they took it in turns to bring a number of videos back. Not really a dangerous job. The cassettes could go in their pockets and the Customs would be unlikely to make a body search of a businessman."

"Highly unlikely. Particularly if they'd seen him before and knew that he'd got some genuine business in Amsterdam. And suppose they did find them. All he'd have to do would be to say, 'I picked them up in a high-street shop and brought them home. I haven't looked at them yet, but I thought they might be amusing.'"

"Breach of Customs' regulations. You have to declare anything you've bought abroad."

"So what? If they pursued the case – which is unlikely – it might result in a small fine."

"Which would be paid by the organisation."

"Organisation?" For the first time Kay looked more than casually interested.

"I think so. Based in London. And with a good deal of money behind it. They're the ones I'm going after."

Many of the details were still unclear, but the outlines of the racket were forming in his mind. The bookshop would be an out-station. The heart of the matter, he was certain, was in the City.

"The best of British," said Kay. "They sound like the sort of shower I spent – or mis-spent – five years of my professional career chasing, but I never seemed to catch up with them. A few tiddlers occasionally, but the big fish had too many emergency exits. I can tell you one thing. If you do catch up with them, watch your step. They've a nasty habit of biting back. Look what they did to poor old Robin."

"Then you think Hood was fixed?"

"Difficult to say. About a month before the *Sentinel* started sniping at him, he told me that he had, at last, got something that looked like hard evidence against a well-known publisher. He wouldn't give me the name, which was odd because, after all, I was his number two. No. He was keeping his cards close to his chest. Next thing was we had all that stuff about him taking all-expenses-paid holidays with one of the porn kings."

"Which he admitted?"

"He couldn't deny the facts. The *Sentinel* had half a dozen affidavits from people who knew about the trip. But Robin maintained it was nothing whatever to do with the investigation he was conducting. Whether or not, it was enough to finish him."

Petrella said, "Yes," and thought for some moments without adding anything, although Kay was clearly expecting something more. In the end Petrella said, "If Hood was conducting an investigation there must be some record of it."

"So you'd have thought. And, of course, we turned out all his working papers and we couldn't find anything about it. There was a chance that he had taken everything home, to work on it there. Towards the end he was getting a bit paranoiac about – well – about treachery in the office. That sort of thing."

"And were there any papers in his house?"

"There may have been. But a few days after his death – his wife was being looked after by her own family and the house was empty – some people broke in. They didn't steal anything, but they rifled his filing cabinets and his desk. So if there were any papers there, they were gone."

Petrella was silent again. What had upset him was Kay's use of the word 'paranoiac'. Did he mean that Hood really was worried that a member of his own team might be playing for the other side, or that he was imagining treachery where no treachery existed?

He was turning it over in his mind as he trudged down Victoria Street and Whitehall and up the Charing Cross Road. The movement of his legs seemed to settle his thoughts into a more logical sequence. Forget Hood. Concentrate on silly Draper, patron of *Blote Boys en Bengels*. Catch hold of *his* coat tails and he might lead them to where they wanted to go.

The Naughty Nineties turned out to be one of three second-hand bookshops in Cecil Court. There was a line of books in a rack outside marked at one pound each, ranging from an old Bradshaw Railway Guide to a *Boys' Book of Cricket*. Dear at half the price, thought Petrella as he pushed on into the shop.

The front room was stacked and packed with books, on stands and shelves, and on the window-ledges and the floor. The only clear space was round an old-fashioned roll-top desk which seemed to be doing duty as a counter. Behind it sat one of the fattest men Petrella had ever seen. Without doubt this was Maurice Meinhold. He had been writing something at a smaller table beside the desk. Now he swivelled round, planted both elbows on the desk and said, "What can we do for you, sir?"

"I was just looking round."

"Is there any subject in which you are particularly interested?"

"Biography," said Petrella firmly. "Military biography."

"I don't think we've much on that. We specialise more in artistic than in military topics. You might be able to find something in the corner over there."

The corner was a dark one. Such light as there was struggled through the diamond panes which fronted the shop. Most of the books seemed to be lives of Victorian and Edwardian painters, sculptors and designers. There were one or two politicians looking a mite uncomfortable in this artistic jamboree. No generals.

He moved along a little to study the books behind the door. Here the emphasis had changed. The shelves were packed with books on Indian personalities and affairs; not only histories and biographies, but Blue Books, Army and Civil Service Lists, records of Vice-Regal and Ministerial Edicts and what looked like a complete set of the *Indian National Gazette* down to 1965. These did not seem to have attracted much attention from the British buyer, and a volume of the letters of Lord Dufferin which he opened emitted an indignant spider and a cloud of dust.

At that moment a shaft of light fell across the shop and he saw that a door at the back had opened. From where he stood he had a clear view into the inner room. It was startlingly different from the front section. He saw a neat, well-ordered office, with a line of filing cabinets on one side and a green and gold safe in the far corner. On a table he could see two telephones and what looked like a word-processor. Petrella was half hidden and the woman who came through the door had clearly no idea that there was a third party in the shop.

She was half Maurice's height, heavily built rather than stout. Her face was not attractive, a lot of pig with a little bit of monkey behind it. She was carrying a number of stout manila envelopes and the way that she handled them when she put them down on the desk suggested that there was an object of some weight in each.

Maurice said, "We have a customer, Mamma."

"I'm sorry. I didn't know you were busy."

As she spoke she was scooping up the envelopes and by the time Petrella had moved back into the shop they had been whisked off the top of the desk and the woman was retreating into the office.

Petrella said, "I couldn't help catching a glimpse of your very businesslike inner room. I hope you'll excuse the comment that it is a surprising contrast to the artistic jumble of your front room."

Maurice did not seem to be upset. He said, "The

difference you have observed, sir, is the difference between my wife and myself. I am an old-fashioned bibliophile. She is a modern business woman."

"Then you make an ideal combination," said Petrella politely. "How much are you asking for this one?"

"The David James biography of Lord Roberts? Only a secondary work, I fear. You may have it for three pounds. But if you are really interested in the life of that great soldier, I have the two-volume edition of his autobiography, *Forty-one Years in India*. A seminal publication."

Petrella said he thought the smaller book would do to start with, paid out the money and escaped. He had already marked down a café at the corner where Cecil Court ran out into St Martin's Lane and here he installed himself to drink coffee and keep an eye on the frontage of the Naughty Nineties. One of its advantages, from his point of view, was that it could hardly have a back door.

He was thinking about those telephones. Normally, if there were two telephones on a desk, one of them would be an outside line and the other an office inter-com. Hardly so in an establishment where the only two rooms were within shouting distance of each other. Could the second one be a private line? Was it possible to have such a thing in London? He would ask his friends in British Telecom, but he thought not. Then a possible explanation occurred to him.

It would be possible to have two telephones with different phone numbers. The first would be the public one that was in the book. Normal customers would use it. The other would be ex-directory and known only to an inner circle of customers or friends.

He looked at his watch. He had been sitting there for nearly an hour. During this period two or three people had stopped to inspect the books in the rack, but after a quick glance at their titles had put them back. No one had entered the shop. Then Mamma Meinhold appeared. She was carrying a bulging brief case which contained, he was sure, those stout manila envelopes. She turned to the left, which meant that she was probably making for the Trafalgar Square post office.

Petrella paid his bill and walked off in the opposite direction. He thought that he had bought a lot of information for three pounds.

His first stop was the library in Charing Cross Road. Here, in the London Telephone Directory, he found the name he needed. Winchip P.L. The address was 6-Z Montague Street, WC1. Montague Street, he remembered, ran along the east side of the British Museum and was thus within easy walking distance. The midday heat made him glad of this.

All the old houses in Montague Street had been pulled down and replaced by six large modern buildings, divided into apartments for the staff and students of London University. Number six was at the far end and T–Y were apartments on the first three floors. Z stood in splendid isolation on the fourth floor. A neat card in the slot said, 'Lt-Colonel Peter Winchip'.

The colonel was a distant relative of his mother, a cousin infinitely removed, who kept in touch with her by means of an annual Christmas card. Petrella knew only two things about him. The first was that he was an acknowledged expert on Indian manuscripts and illustrated missals, on which he was standing adviser to the British Museum. This had, no doubt, secured him his privileged apartment. The second fact was that he was over ninety. Since there was a notice in the hallway announcing that the lift was temporarily out of order, he wondered how he left or returned to his eyrie.

The old man greeted him cheerfully, searching his memory to think who he was. Having finally placed him, he said, "You must be Mirabel Trentham-Foster's son. The one who became a policeman."

"Ten out of ten."

"And you want some help from me? Splendid. It will

give me something to do. I dislike inactivity. Until they mend that lift I'm confined to barracks. Fortunately there's a friendly student – he comes from Nairobi – two floors down. He fetches my provisions. Otherwise I should have been reduced to a diet of Bath Oliver biscuits and sardines. Good for my figure, no doubt."

He was very ready to discuss the subjects which were interesting Petrella.

"Meinhold? Meinhold? Wait a moment. Yes. Sandeman, Meinhold. It was one of the leading Calcutta bookshops. Not perhaps the very biggest, but prosperous enough in the period before the Second World War. I wasn't much in Calcutta myself. Spent most of my time up on the frontier. That was in the twenties, when we were having trouble with the Afridis. But I went down there once or twice on leave. My uncle was stationed there. In the ICS. The boys with brains. Allegedly. Yes. Well, I did get the impression – towards 1939 that would have been – that the shop was finding it difficult to make both ends meet. Usual story. Sandeman was the man with the money. He'd retired and taken his money with him. Am I boring you?"

"Not in the least," said Petrella. "It's just getting interesting."

"Well, if there was a fall-off it must have been partially reversed in 1939 by sales of military handbooks and aircraft manuals. But the end of the war finished all that sort of thing and the downhill run continued. By this time a grandson of the original Meinhold was in charge. Can't remember his name – "

"Maurice?"

"That's right. Maurice Meinhold. The race riots finally finished the shop off and some time in the late sixties poor little Maurice finally had to get out."

"If it's the same Maurice we're thinking about, he's certainly not little now."

"I was speaking figuratively. Anyway, I gather he came back to this country with a packing case full of unsaleable

95

Indian books and a lot of debts. Are you telling me that he's rescued himself and set up here?"

"Either he's rescued himself," said Petrella slowly, "or he's been rescued. Either way it's interesting. And I'm much obliged to you."

"I've enjoyed talking to you, but I'd much rather be doing something. As soon as they get the lift in order. Couldn't I follow someone?"

Petrella reflected that Mr Wetherall, well into his eighties, and Colonel Winchip, in his nineties, were both eager to track down desperadoes. It seemed to him to reflect credit on the older generation.

He said that he'd bear the colonel's offer in mind and departed. He had in his pocket a leaflet which he had picked up at the Naughty Nineties. It contained at least one piece of valuable information: that the shop was owned by a company, Maurice Meinhold Limited. The track he was following now led into the City. He was going to need help and he thought he knew where he could get it.

When he was in Q Division one of his more unusual assistants had been Detective Sergeant Milo Roughead, late of Eton College and the ranks of the Metropolitan Constabulary. His family had tolerated the thought of Milo being a policeman for two or three years, but had then extracted him, almost by force, and installed him in the family stockbroking firm. He had not welcomed the move, maintaining that the East End of London was a more salubrious place than the square mile round the Bank of England. He was now a junior partner in the firm.

When Petrella reached him, through the protective screen of telephonist and secretary, he at once invited him to lunch. Petrella hesitated. He thought of the mound of dockets in his in-tray. Also he knew that he was already spending too much of his time on something which should have been entrusted – if indeed it fell within his manor at all – to a junior officer. He ignored the promptings of his conscience and accepted the invitation.

"Good show," said Milo. "Lovely. One o'clock tomorrow at the Gresham Club. It's a little place in Abchurch Lane, on the left as you come up from Cannon Street. It might help if you could give me a rough idea of what it is you're looking for. Just the general field. Then I could do some preliminary research. Save your time."

"All I can tell you at the moment is that I'm interested in a small outfit called Maurice Meinhold Limited. Anything you can find out about them might be useful."

On the following day the lunch provided by the Gresham Club explained to Petrella why, each time that he met Milo, he looked less like a trim and efficient member of the police force and more like an over-fed business tycoon. It did not worry him. He knew that there was a genuine person underneath the striped suit, starched collar and Old Etonian tie.

When lunch had been disposed of, Milo said, "I got one of our boys to make a search at Companies House. All limited companies have to file their accounts and a certain amount of information about themselves. In this case they seem to have got away with a bare minimum. You know, of course, that they own a bookshop?"

"I've been there. It didn't look very prosperous. Very few customers and an uninteresting stock. Mostly out-of-date books about India. The more modern stuff is mostly very soft porn."

"Well, that's just what the accounts look like. A few books bought, a few sold. Some years a modest profit, other years a small loss. And it seems to have been trundling along in this highly uninteresting way for nearly twenty years."

"Suppose," said Petrella, who was thinking about that back room, "that there was a secondary and highly profitable business carried out under cover of the bookshop, surely there'd have to be some trace of it in the accounts? They'd have to be audited accounts."

"Certainly."

"And the auditors would expect to see bank accounts and records of that sort, wouldn't they?"

"It would be difficult, but not impossible, for a secondary business to be carried on without leaving any trace in the accounts. But only if all the transactions were in cash. Have you any reason to suppose that this secondary business exists?"

"No real proof," said Petrella regretfully. "Mainly instinct. There seemed to me to be a sort of smell about the whole set-up."

"Then I can tell you one curious thing. When the company started, it borrowed twenty thousand pounds from a firm called Mansion House Nominees. It must have been a friendly arrangement, because I can't figure out what security can have been given by the company. Their premises in Cecil Court are leasehold. Not a ground rent, a full rent. That's clear from the profit and loss account. And you say their stock is nothing to write home about. So what equity was there? What did it mortgage?"

"Yes. That certainly sounds odd."

"And here's another thing. Mansion House Nominees seem to have waived interest on the loan. What do you make of that?"

Petrella thought about it while he finished his cup of black coffee. Around him rose the chatter of businessmen talking to businessmen. It sounded like a beehive in June. A contented buzz, as the bees set about manufacturing and storing honey. He said, "You mentioned other information the company had to file. I suppose it tells you about the directors and shareholders and the capital of the company."

"Certainly. The directors are Maurice and Maria Meinhold. Maria is secretary. The registered office is at number 8 Cecil Court. The capital is one hundred shares of one pound each, two of which are held by the Meinholds. The other ninety-eight – surprise, surprise – by Mansion House Nominees."

"So who are they nominees for?"

"You are asking what is sometimes referred to as the sixty-four thousand dollar question."

"Is there any way of finding out?"

Milo did not answer immediately. Then he said, "You've got to remember that you're dealing with the City. I know we've had a bad press lately. The one per cent of villains have grabbed the headlines. But the other ninety-nine per cent are perfectly straightforward businessmen. People who keep their promises, even if it hurts their pockets."

"He that sweareth unto his neighbour and disappointeth him not, though it were to his own hindrance."

"That's the sort of thing. Did you realise that in this electronic age the Stock Exchange still accepts verbal orders – over the telephone – maybe affecting hundreds of thousands of pounds?"

"I didn't, but I'll take your word for it."

"It's the only way business can be done. And it means that people have to trust one another. Not only to do what they promised, but not to talk about it. That's why I was hesitating to take on the job you're suggesting. There are one or two people who owe our firm a favour and might know, or be in a position to find out, who are behind these particular nominees. But if they did tell me, it would be in confidence. I hope you understand what I'm saying, sir."

By adding that 'sir', Milo had reverted, disarmingly, to a junior policeman addressing his boss. Petrella said, "I understand you perfectly. But if you happened, by chance, to be able to ferret out this information *without* involving yourself in a breach of confidence, I take it you'd let me know."

"Of course. Right away."

Milo seemed to have recovered his normal spirits. He ordered two large glasses of the club port.

Since their return from North Africa, Petrella had fallen into the habit of discussing the day's doings each evening

99

with his wife. She was almost as knowledgeable about the by-ways of police politics as he was and her assessments were shrewd and trenchant. When he had finished describing, at some length, his visit to the bookshop and his discussions with Colonel Winchip and Milo, she was silent for so long that he thought that either he had bored her, or that she disapproved of what he was doing. Both guesses were wide of the mark.

In the end her comment surprised him. She said, "So how does Liversedge fit into what you've been doing?"

"Nowhere – as yet."

"That's what I was wondering about. Is he your direct superior, or is he on the sideline? Organisationally, I mean."

"He is unquestionably my superior officer. He's in charge of No. 2 Area and H District is part of his command."

"That's what I thought. So if, for instance, you wanted any help or support you'd have to apply to him."

"Correct."

"Would he give it?"

"He would pass the request up, in triplicate, through the correct channels, to Deputy Commissioner Lovell at the Yard."

"I see."

"You don't seem happy about it."

"I'm not unhappy, but there's a sort of Civil Service feeling about it. Passed to you. That sort of thing."

"I agree. But it happens to be the chain of command. It's the way requests go up and orders come down. However, luckily, it isn't the whole picture. When Robert Mark set up the Serious Crime Squads, he deliberately left them a degree of autonomy. They answer to Morrissey and to him alone. He's now head of the whole bunch – inside London and outside. Twelve squads of twenty picked men. If I needed outside help – particularly if it was help of a somewhat irregular nature – I'd go straight to him."

"Is he a friend of yours?"

"We've met on a number of occasions. On most of them I was being insubordinate and he was being rude, so we got on like a house on fire."

"I'm glad of that," said his wife. "Because I've got a feeling that you're going to need all the help you can get."

9

"The heart of this matter is in the City," said Petrella. "There are big names behind it and a lot of money."

Morrissey said, "But the dirty pictures aren't shot here."

"Until recently they were made in Amsterdam. The arrangement centred on a hotel. Parties of schoolboys went there on what were called educational tours."

"Depends what you mean by education, dunnit? All right. Go on. I don't think it's funny."

"The cassettes come back to England in the pockets of the club members. We managed to have one of them followed." He explained about Draper and the Naughty Nineties. "I think that end of it's quite clear. Meinhold's the middle man. He's the link between the people who take the pictures and the men who use the cassettes."

"Use them? Enjoy them, or sell them?"

"Oh, sell them. The people behind this are businessmen. It cost them twenty thousand pounds to set up that shop. They'd expect a return on their money and they know who's likely to appreciate muck of this sort. So they pass the names to the Meinholds who add them to their mailing list."

"All sales on a cash basis?"

"Certainly. In the first instance the money goes to the Meinholds. In cash. They keep an agreed commission. The balance goes to the big boys in the City. In cash. They'd have plenty of bank accounts in which it could disappear."

Morrissey thought about it.

He said, "It's got a lot going for it. Once someone's bought a cassette he'd be hooked. He'd have to buy others. If he tried to wriggle out he'd be posted round the City as a paedo-porn nut. Right?"

"And might receive a visit from the Farm Boys."

"There's still a lot of guess-work in it. You've no idea who's behind it?"

"Not yet. I may be getting some hard evidence soon."

"So what do you want me to do right now?"

"I'd like to have the Meinholds' telephones tapped and their mail intercepted. It needn't be opened, but I'd like a list of the people it goes to. And if – " this was inserted quickly, to forestall an explosion from Morrissey – "if that's against the idiotic rules we've made, to wrap criminals up in cotton-wool, at least I'd like a watch put on their place and both the Meinholds followed. They live above their shop and there's only one way out, so that shouldn't be too difficult."

"That's three things you want." Morrissey held up his formidably muscled right hand and extended three fingers. "Phone tapped. Mail scanned. Proprietors followed. Sure you wouldn't like anything else? The moon, perhaps. Or one or two stars."

"I want one more thing," said Petrella coldly. "That's for this matter to be taken seriously and for something to be done about it."

"That's not one thing more. It's two things more." Morrissey added his little finger and thumb. "Five, all told." He stared for a moment at his own hand, as if surprised to see it there. Then he cocked his head round and looked at Petrella. He knew that, underneath the reasonable and civilised exterior – a gift from his mother – there lurked a Spanish devil. It was a devil that was almost always kept under strict control, but when it did emerge, wise men took cover.

He said, "Let's look at your last two points. You can

take it from me that all of us here – and that includes the DC – take this business seriously. I've been talking to Charlie Kay about it. No question it's a filthy racket and if it's run the way you think it is, there's a blackmail angle as well. And from what Charlie tells me, it isn't only the videos. He says shots from the film are sold to half a dozen sleazy papers."

"Yes, I've seen one of them."

"It's when we come to your second point that it's not so simple. The main offence is taking the pictures. That's done in Amsterdam and any action there is for the Dutch police. Agreed there's a small matter of bringing the stuff into this country. We might catch one or two carriers. But it wouldn't get us very far. The stuff could come in by post, to an accommodation address. No difficulty."

"Surely the real offence is selling the stuff in this country."

"Maybe. But it's going to take time and a lot of hard work to build up a case against the people we really want to hurt. I mean the slimy sods in the City who are pocketing the cash."

"All right," said Petrella reluctantly. "I do understand that."

"Then let me tell you something that may not have got down to your part of London yet, but is common knowledge up here. That is, that I'm due out at the end of the year. And I'd like to make a good exit. Not to creep out with my bloody tail between my bloody legs."

Petrella looked at him for a long moment. The turn in the discussion had taken him by surprise. Then he said, "Anyone who thinks that the work of the Serious Crime Squads hasn't been successful, can't have read the record."

"That wasn't the way the DC talked when I saw him last Friday. What he said was, couldn't the squads get off their prats and do some fucking work? Well, perhaps those weren't his exact words, but that was the gist of it, and what seemed to be getting up his nose was the doings of two particular lots of villains, both in your manor, incidentally. The Farm Boys and their friends the Torpedoes."

"I know about the Farm Boys. I haven't got round to the Torpedoes yet."

"Then it's time you had a word with young Trench down at CD. He knows all about them. They've nicked so many boats lately you'd think they were aiming to run their own boat show. And things are coming to a head·pretty fast up here, too. Which is why I asked you to be here at half past eleven. Because I've got a man coming round here at twelve that I'd like you to meet."

He lifted the phone and said, "Is Mr Drummond here yet? Ramsbottom too? Good. Sling 'em both up. Does the name Ashley Drummond mean anything to you?"

"Nothing at all."

"He's the boss of the East London Building Organisation – known to one and all as ELBO. Twelve firms under one flag."

"I've seen their placards."

"It's quite an outfit. And Drummond's the man who runs it. Here he is. Introduce Superintendent Petrella. Ramsbottom you've already met."

Petrella, looking at the close-shaven executive face, the firm mouth and the eyes which held a hint of menace, thought that Ashley Drummond might be a good friend, but would certainly be a bad enemy. Ramsbottom looked as though he'd had a taste of his tongue already.

As soon as they were seated Morrissey said, without preamble, "I want to talk about next Friday. That's a week today. And I've got you together because you're the three men likely to be most concerned. Will you kick off, Drummond?"

"Certainly. Easier if we had a map."

Morrissey opened a drawer in his desk and got out a large-scale street map covering the Tower Hamlets district. The three men shifted their chairs until they could see it.

"I'd better explain how we operate. We pay our sub-contractors every other Friday. It's a compromise. I wanted to make it monthly, they wanted it weekly. We settled for fortnightly. It has to be Friday morning, because they pay their own men on Friday afternoon, and it has to be cash, because that's what their men expect."

"To say nothing of their wives," said Morrissey, "who are aiming to do the weekend shopping."

"Right. And that means, like it or not, we're tied to a routine. Our bank is there – " he indicated a point at the bottom of Globe Road. "It's the nearest bank to our headquarters, which are at the top of Globe Road – there. And that means transporting a lot of ready money for half a mile. It never used to worry us. We've got a Securicor-type van – you know the sort of thing – armoured all round and with no external handles. We used it to fetch the cash. No trouble."

Whilst he was talking, Petrella was examining the map. It seemed to him that Globe Road had one disadvantage. There were too many side streets crossing it. And worse, two of the side roads at the north end ran into Limehouse Fields, that centre of West Indian trouble.

"Two or three weeks ago, some of our people picked up a rumour that the cash was going to be hi-jacked. When you remember that we employ over a thousand men, some of them pretty hard cases, it's not surprising that one or two of them should have latched onto it. So last week we tried a diversion. Our van drove into the yard at the back of the bank, waited for ten minutes and then drove out and up Globe Road. The ambush was very skilful. One car came across the road at Chudleigh Street and stalled. The second car came up behind the van from Stepney Way. Two men jumped out and ran up. Upon which our driver activated the switch which opens the door at the back. A development" – Drummond allowed himself a tight smile – "which seems to have surprised them. They could see, quite clearly, that there was nothing in the van at all. The cash

106

had, of course, come by private car, which I drove myself, an hour earlier. The men demonstrated their feelings by kicking the van, but couldn't do much more. The blocking car withdrew and the van proceeded. End of chapter. But not, I fancy, end of story."

"Not end of story," agreed Morrissey. "Because, if there's one thing that really upsets these types it's being made to look stupid. Did your men get a chance to identify them?"

"They were wearing stocking masks and gauntlets. But both of our men were quite sure that they weren't white. West Indians, they thought."

"Which looks like it was the Torpedoes doing the job solo. They won't come alone next week. They'll have a lot of friends and they'll watch your van to make sure it's loaded *and* they'll watch any other cars which might be picking up cash."

"They can watch the front of the bank, but not the courtyard at the back."

"Wrong," said Morrissey. "They can watch that too. The bank only uses the ground floor and basement. There's three sets of offices above and one of them's to let. They'll break into that one and stay in observation as long as necessary."

Petrella said, "I presume the Farm Boys will look after that end."

"That would be the normal division of labour," said Morrissey drily. "They prefer other people to operate at the sharp end."

"So what's your plan?" said Drummond.

Morrissey said, "Globe Road's in your manor, Arthur. It's your plan."

Arthur Ramsbottom looked appealingly at Petrella. It was clear that either he had no plan ready, or was doubtful of any plan of his being accepted by such a critical audience.

Petrella said, "I think, don't you, sir, that this should

be co-ordinated on a district basis? We'll use our men in the first instance, Arthur, but if the opposition puts out any real muscle I could support them with men from other areas. Maybe from you, too, sir?"

"Maybe," said Morrissey, with a grin which exposed two gold-capped teeth. He had been certain that Petrella would take over.

"Right. First we'll need two of your best men, Arthur. They'll be driving this van Mr Drummond mentioned. They'll go into the courtyard behind the bank and be loaded with what looks like cash. Then they drive out, up Globe Road, keeping their eyes open for trouble. Who'll you put in for that job?"

"My first choices would be Sergeant Stark and Sergeant Pearson."

"They should be able to look after themselves. Particularly since they'll both be armed."

This produced a moment of silence. Ramsbottom said, "I don't know that I could accept the responsibility –"

"You don't have to accept any responsibility," said Petrella coldly. "I'll give you instructions about it. In writing, if you wish. They will carry one police-positive .38 revolver each. Six rounds loaded. And no spare ammunition. This is to be checked by you, personally, before they set out."

"I'm longing to hear the end of this exciting story," said Drummond politely.

"I'm afraid it hasn't been written yet," said Petrella. "A lot will depend on the two men in the van. If an attempt is made on the same lines as before they will be heavy enough to break through. No doubt they'll be chased. But since, by that time, the side roads will all be stopped they and their pursuers can only go straight ahead. The idea will be to lead them into Limehouse Fields. Which is, as you can see from the map, a dead-end. Meath Gardens blocks it at the top. It's a private garden and kept locked. The Grand Union Canal shuts off the east side. The only way is back into Globe Road and by that time our reinforcements will be in position."

"And whilst all this is going on, I presume that our cash is coming up by another route altogether."

"Correct."

"Seems all right to me," said Morrissey. "Better if they don't shoot until they're shot at."

Drummond said, "And as long as everyone remembers that the main object is not to stage a Western, but to get our money safely through."

"Agreed," said Morrissey. "All right, Arthur?"

Inspector Ramsbottom said, "Right, sir."

He did not sound happy.

Back in his own office Petrella, too, was wondering why he had shoved his oar in. He could easily have left the whole thing to Ramsbottom. True, the operation fitted in with Morrissey's contention that the people he ought to have his eye on were the Torpedoes and the Farm Boys. He doubted whether it would achieve much against the latter. Morrissey had suggested that they would break into the empty office to be able to observe the loading of the ELBO van and, presumably, to give the signal to the Torpedoes to move in on it. This was pure surmise. There were easier and safer ways of doing it. They could get a legitimate order-to-view the unlet office. Or they could bribe one of the employees in the other firms. Clearly, all the real risks would be taken by the Torpedoes. Which was the way the Farm Boys liked to work.

He wondered, too, why he had stuck his neck out over the carrying of guns. If there was any trouble it was going to bounce back on him. God damn it, he said, if you're not prepared to stake the limit you'll never win the jack-pot. With which dubious piece of self-comfort he turned his attention back to drug-related offences and traffic problems.

Ten minutes later his telephone rang. It was Inspector Trench from the Isle of Dogs, and what he had to say also chimed in neatly with Morrissey's wishes. He said, "I've picked up two pieces of information, sir, which might interest you. One bit's about the lot who call themselves the Torpedoes. The other's about the Farm Boys. I could come up any time you're free – "

"Stay put," said Petrella. "I'll come down to you."

It was a welcome chance to get out of the office. He had not yet succeeded in buying himself a car. What he wanted was a reliable second-hand jalopy at a reasonable price. Unfortunately this was what most of the car buyers in London also seemed to want. He went down to get hold of the station runabout, a seven-year-old Rover, which had had a hard life and was beginning to make noises like a patient with advanced asthma. It was outside its garage, jacked up, with its bonnet open and parts of its interior on a bench beside it. Detective Hoyland emerged from underneath it. He was wearing a pair of overalls, his hands were black and he looked happy.

He said, "I could put everything back, sir, if you wanted to use it."

"Don't bother," said Petrella, "I'll go by train."

This meant risking the Dockland Line, about which he had heard a number of stories. They had not been exaggerated. The train was late, crowded and stopped everywhere.

At the HD station house, in Manchester Road, he found Inspector Trench, who said, "Terrible railway. Can't think why they don't run it properly. You'd have done it just as quickly on foot."

"And more comfortably."

"Much more. Well, I hope you'll think your journey was worthwhile. Here's what I've got. You remember I told you about the motor cruiser that was stolen from Millwall Pier. The man who phoned us about it – a Mr Philips – he sounded quite a respectable type, out to help the police. But I got the impression that he'd been holding something back. So I asked him to come round to see if he could tell us anything more. And this time, out it came. He'd been in the navy himself and he was pretty certain that he knew the man who seemed to be directing operations. It was an ex-petty officer, a sub-mariner, known to one and all as Torpedo Hicks. Seems he'd been made redundant in one of the scaling-down operations in the late seventies and had been unable to land a job and that's why he'd taken to crime. He'd put together a crowd of West Indians – who also thought the world owed them a living – and had been operating with increasing success for some years."

"Interesting," said Petrella. "Pity they didn't keep him in the navy. How definite was the identification?"

"Reasonably definite. He said he knew Hicks from his general appearance and from his voice."

Petrella thought about it. He visualised the evidence being challenged by the defence. It might stand up, but he doubted it. Useful, none the less. It filled in a little corner of the picture. He said, "You mentioned two points."

"I'm afraid the second is even more flimsy than the first. It's a rumour about a boy. This is a great place for rumours. No one knows quite how they start, but when they get under way, they move like a forest fire."

"It's the old dockland sub-world," said Petrella. "It hasn't been driven out by all the modern development. Just driven under."

"Well, this story is firming up. That a boy happened to be in a position to overhear a gang-land trial. You know the sort of thing. What made this one spectacular was that the prisoner – said to have been an informer – was sentenced to death, but beat the sentence by dying first."

"I take it you're talking about the Farm Boys."

"So the rumour has it."

"And the youngster?"

"All I know about him is that his Christian name's said to be Arnold."

"Does the rumour specify the building where this happened?"

"Not in so many words. One or two things seem to be common knowledge. It was a disused ships' chandlery. Of course, we've got dozens of them. In the old days, when the India and Millwall Docks were operating, every other building dealt in ships' stores. But the next point really was interesting. The building is said to be within spitting distance of the river. Almost on the river bank. Now if you look at the map – "

"Yes," said Petrella. "I see what you mean."

"Nearly all the built-up areas are west of the main road. If this particular building was *between* the road and the river, that does narrow it down."

"Only two possibilities, I'd say. The Cold Harbour area, north of the old main-dock entrance, and the Stewart Street area south of it. Both with a lot of old chandlers' stores in them, no doubt."

"Six in one, four in the other. All in the hands of receivers or liquidators. Some of them have been co-operative, sent me a spare key and said I could look over them if I wanted to. Others were sticky. They insisted on a search warrant and one of their representatives accompanying the party, which was the last thing I wanted."

"They were protecting themselves," said Petrella, absently. He was thinking about the two trails which had been opened up. The second was the more promising. Like all gangs, the Farm Boys were traditionalists. If there was occasion for another trial, they would no doubt want to use their old court room. He would have liked to do a little exploring himself. If he had the time –

The telephone answered him. It was Gwilliam. He said, "You're wanted urgently, Skipper. Poston-Pirrie's turned up."

"Where?"

"Right now, he's in the Stepney mortuary. Summerson's

112

doing a preliminary examination. He'd like a word with you."

He had spoken loud enough for Trench to pick up the sense of his message. He said, "I'll run you up in my own car, Skipper."

10

At the Stepney mortuary Petrella found Gwilliam with three other men. Dr Summerson, the Home Office pathologist from Guy's, was deep in discussion with Superintendent Groener of the River Police. Groener had served in the Thames Division, which he now headed, for twenty-five years. He was a standing authority on every aspect of the grey and dangerous stretch of water under his charge. The third man was an ex-policeman called Cracknell, the Stepney coroner's officer. Petrella had met him once before and disliked and distrusted him.

Gwilliam said, "It was one of the superintendent's people who found Poston-Pirrie. He'll tell you about it. It's an odd set-up altogether."

Groener said, "This morning Sergeant Belling – one of my most experienced men – was taking a look at the East Stepney Dock. It's a small dock – it hasn't been used for many years – near the out-flow of the Limehouse Cut. He'd taken his launch into the entrance channel. There's no gate at the river end and it's blocked at the far end by a movable grating. There's a narrow beach of shingle and mud on each side of the channel, just above tide level, and it was on the downstream beach, a few yards in from the river, that he spotted the body. And the real puzzle was how the hell it got there."

"Might it have been dropped from the dock?" said Gwilliam.

"Quite impossible. There was no sign of anyone having broken into the dock, which was strongly barred. And if they had got in, to put the body where it was found would have meant hoisting it over a ten-foot railing of pointed steel spikes."

"And why should anyone have bothered?" said Petrella. "If they wanted to get rid of the body, they'd have weighted it and dropped it into the river, not left it where it was bound to be spotted sooner or later."

"Might it have been brought in from the river?" said Summerson.

"The same objection," said Petrella. "Why do it?"

Having allowed the amateurs to talk nonsense, Groener was now prepared to pronounce a professional judgment. He said, "I don't think anyone brought that body in. Let me explain. On this stretch of the river boats observe a sort of rule of the road. When the tide's ebbing, and they're coming up against it, they're allowed to hug the banks, where there's some slack water. Boats going down use the tidal flow and keep to mid-stream. So what I'm reasonably sure must have happened is that the body was floating down close to the bank and still high in the water."

"Explain that last bit," said Petrella, who was listening intently.

"A body that goes in fully clothed doesn't sink straight away. Which is how quite a few attempted suicides have been saved. Their rescuers have been able to grab them before their clothes get sodden and pull them right down. Now if a barge came past, near the bank and against the stream, its bow wave would be quite strong enough to lift a body that was only just submerged clean out of the water and deposit it on the beach just inside the entrance."

"Which fits in," said Petrella, "with its being found on the down-stream beach. How long would a body float high?"

"That depends on how it was dressed when it went in. I've known a man wearing a heavy overcoat stay up for a quarter of an hour. In this case, in view of the weather, he seems to have been dressed in an open neck shirt and a light jacket."

"So how long? Five minutes – or less?"

"You can't be accurate to a minute. But call it five."

"And at the speed the tide was running, you'd say he went in – how far above the dock – two hundred yards?"

"I wouldn't say anything of the sort," said Groener. He was worried by these attempts at accuracy when none of the factors were certain. "If you insist on a distance, you can call it anything between fifty yards and a quarter of a mile."

They were all looking at the map which Gwilliam had produced.

"Cannon Wharf looks the favourite," said Petrella, unabashed.

Dr Summerson, who knew Petrella well, said, "Might I suggest that you wait for the results of the autopsy before attempting – as policemen so often do – to build a concrete theory on a foundation of uncertainties? However," he added, "in a somewhat cursory preliminary examination I did observe one thing which supports Superintendent Groener's general idea. The body must have left the water soon after it went in, for there are no signs that the fish have been at it. All the damage to it has been done by the wharf rats, who have enjoyed a feast denied to their rivals, the Thames' eels. You can see where the clothing has been torn open and the marks of their teeth in the soft tissues of the body. If you had to rely on the face for identification you'd have been unlucky."

"Too true," said Gwilliam, with a slight shudder. "Luckily we found the wallet in his pocket. There was plenty of identification there. And to make certain, we're sending the dental details direct to the *Sentinel*."

"Then, doctor," said Petrella, "until your autopsy is completed and you are able to give us some estimate of the time of death – surrounded by the normal medical reservations and obfuscations – there is not much more we can do here."

Summerson grinned. He knew that Petrella was getting back at him for his earlier comment.

Cracknell, who had been standing quietly in the background, now said, "I have informed the coroner. He tells me that since identity has been established, the inquest can be opened as soon as Dr Summerson is ready."

"The sooner the better," said Petrella, and Gwilliam nodded agreement. They could visualise the storm that was going to break.

On their way back to Maplin Road Gwilliam said, "I've asked Constable Severn to stand by. He's got some information for you. In view of what's happened, it could be important. He may have been one of the last people to see Poston-Pirrie alive."

Severn was an Essex man, solid, but clearly not unintelligent. He said, "It was on the Friday evening, just two weeks ago, I was passing the end of White Horse Road, when I saw this gentleman coming towards me. He was walking in the middle of the road, sort of tacking from side to side and talking to himself. I did wonder if he might have been drinking at the White Horse."

"Which is where?"

"It's at the top end of the road, where it runs into Stepney Lane."

"Yes. I remember it. Please go on."

"Well, seeing he looked a bit shaken I asked, was there anything I could do for him? He seemed to pull himself together and said, could I direct him to the Athletic Club? Which wasn't difficult as it's a short way up Commercial Road."

"And that's where he went?"

"I imagine so, sir. I didn't see any reason to follow him, but he certainly moved off in that direction."

Petrella thought about it. There were a number of other things he wanted to find out, but he knew the danger of asking Severn leading questions. If he did, Severn might be tempted to tell him what he thought his superior officer wanted to hear rather than the unvarnished truth.

He said, "Did you actually see Poston-Pirrie coming out of the White Horse?"

"No, sir. He was in the middle of the road, like I said."

"Or anyone coming out after him?"

"I got the impression the door was open and someone shutting it. I wasn't paying a lot of attention to it."

"Naturally not. What I was wondering was whether anyone in the pub could have heard Poston-Pirrie telling you that he was looking for the Athletic Club."

Severn smiled slowly. Petrella had no idea of what was coming.

"I can see what you're getting at, sir. It wasn't a question of them over-hearing what was said. Everyone in the White Horse knew where he was going."

"How so?"

"Some of the lads who'd been there were joking about it in the canteen afterwards. It seemed they started pulling his leg. Implied he was chasing small boys."

"You said, 'some of the lads'. Can you give me their names?"

Severn looked unhappy. He said, "Must I do that, sir?"

"Yes," said Petrella gently. "You must."

"Well, two of them were Sergeant Stark and Sergeant Pearson, and there was Ward and Harrington. I can't remember who else."

"Thank you," said Petrella. An unhappy picture was forming in his mind. He could visualise only too clearly how Poston-Pirrie would react to having his leg pulled. He said, "If you didn't follow Poston-Pirrie down Commercial Road, where did you go?"

"My route was along Cable Street, past the church and the rectory. I had a point at Shadwell Station."

"That's quite clear. And very helpful."

When Severn had, thankfully, removed himself Gwilliam said, "I could ask him a few questions if you like. He might speak more freely to me than to you."

"No," said Petrella. "Leave it." Severn was too valuable a witness to be tampered with. "Next stop the Athletic Club. Who's in charge there?"

"The missioner's a man called Branch. Bert Branch. He and the rector do it together. The rector's got the City connections. That's where he gets the money to keep the club going and pay for trips to the Continent."

"And it's Branch who does the day-to-day running?"

"That's right. If you were thinking of going down to have a word with him, I know Bert quite well – "

"Fine," said Petrella. "We'll go together."

As they walked, under the steely blue August sky, down Maplin Street and into Harford Street, each of them was busy with his own thoughts. They passed the HC station house at the foot of Harford Street and crossed over into White Horse Road. The door of the public house on the corner was wide open and one or two customers were drinking in the public bar. No policemen in sight, but they might have been tucked away in the back room. Half-way down the road Gwilliam pointed out an uninspiring block called Grindall Mansions. He said, "Some of the boys have pads there. Stark among others." Petrella nodded, but said nothing. They were approaching the point which, as he was beginning to see, was the centre of one of his problems.

It was a crossroads, Commercial Road ran across it, still busy though evening was closing in.

"Athletic Club down here," said Gwilliam, turning left.

"Hold it," said Petrella. He was looking down the fourth arm of the crossroads. This was Cable Street, which ran towards the river. He remembered going down it when he called on Father Bernard. From where he stood the rectory was hidden, but he could see the squat tower of the church.

119

He said, "As we're here we might as well have a look at Cannon Wharf."

Gwilliam smiled. He was well aware that this was one of the main objects of their excursion.

After fifty yards Cable Street curved to the right. From this point Butcher Row ran straight down to the wharf. It was a stretch of cobbles. Dangerous if wet, Petrella thought. The wharf was a simple affair of planks, unguarded at its entrance and clearly little used.

"Wouldn't care to come down here in the dark," said Gwilliam. Petrella said nothing. He was as certain as he could be that this was the point at which Poston-Pirrie had gone into the river.

Whilst he was watching he saw a barge coming up, against the tide. It was keeping, as Groener had said it would, close to the bank. So close that he wondered, for a moment, if it was going to carry away the pier, but the steersman knew his job and swerved away at the last moment. In the evening light the grey wave he left behind him looked almost solid.

"Seems to bear out Groener's idea," said Gwilliam. Petrella nodded. Accept Groener's hypothesis certainly. But it left the main question unanswered. Had Poston-Pirrie slipped into the water by accident? Or been pushed? Or carried down unconscious and thrown in? Maybe the autopsy would give them an answer. They plodded back, careful not to slip, turned into Commercial Road and made for the club.

Bert Branch was a cheerful tub of a man who looked as though he had come out of the army or the navy. He had, in fact, spent most of his earlier career in the fire brigade. He greeted Gwilliam warmly and didn't seem unduly worried when the object of Petrella's visit was explained to him.

He said, "Yes, I remember that journalist feller. About a fortnight ago, would that be right? Came along around seven o'clock. The club was pretty full."

"As full as it is now?"

"About that."

There were twenty or more boys there, some Brits and others who, he guessed from their colouring and their hair styles, were probably West Indians.

"They get on well enough," said Branch, answering a question that had not been asked.

"They certainly seem to," said Petrella. He moved across to watch a group of three who were playing shove-halfpenny, one white, two West Indians. The white boy was performing as they came up. Petrella noticed his hands. They were like a musician's: long fingers, broad and flat at the end. He seemed to be conjuring the metal discs into the right slots.

"That's Arnold," said Branch. "And Winston and Delroy who are his particular friends. They won't play against him for money."

"Why not?"

"They've got tired of paying out. He always wins."

A darts match was going on at the end of the hall, but the main attraction was a game of table-tennis. A dozen boys were watching what was obviously a needle contest. The two players were both good. They indulged in full-blooded smashes and athletic saving shots.

"If you're talking to them about it," said Branch, "do remember not to call it ping-pong. They take it very seriously. Those two boys both reached the quarter finals of the local league knock-out."

Petrella watched them for some minutes. Then he said, "Is there somewhere we can talk?"

"I've got an office. If you can call it that."

It wasn't large, but the three of them managed to squeeze in and shut the door.

Petrella said, "Tell me, when this journalist turned up – his name was Poston-Pirrie, by the way – what exactly did he do?"

"He talked to the boys."

"About what – do you happen to know?"

"There's precious little goes on here that I *don't* know," said Branch with a smile. "It seems he was fishing. For tit-bits about them and the police. Harassment, bullying, that sort of thing."

"And did he get much out of them?"

"The boys weren't born yesterday. They reckoned that if they were going to rubbish the police they ought to get something in return. When it seemed this chap wasn't going to shell out – he put it to them it was their duty to give him the information – they shut up shop. Gave him a brush-off. They weren't rude about it, just got on with whatever games they were playing. With one exception, that is. Barry Thursday."

As he mentioned the name the missioner's face registered the sort of expression that would have greeted the opening of a tin of over-ripe fish.

"Tell me about Barry."

"He's a bad lot. And I don't mean the sort of harum-scarum kid who gets into trouble. If there's any trouble around Barry, it's the other party who collects it."

"You mean he's a nasty little boy."

"I mean just that. Mind you, some of the blame may go to his mother. He's an only child and she's spoilt him rotten. And she's had plenty of opportunity to do it. Mrs Thursday's the uncrowned queen of Limehouse Fields."

"Then Barry's a West Indian boy."

"He's certainly got a West Indian mother. No one can remember who his father was. I doubt if his mother can."

"And Barry was the only one prepared to talk to Poston-Pirrie."

"Not only prepared. Seemed anxious to. He asked, could he talk to him in private. I let him use this room. They were nearly half an hour together – perhaps not as much, because it was still quite light when he left, though the mist which we get in the evenings was beginning to come up."

"Which makes it, what? About eight o'clock?"

"About that, I should say."

"Can you tell me what they talked about?"

"Seeing I'd been excluded from the discussion, I'm afraid not."

"You didn't ask Barry?"

"I shouldn't have been told the truth if I had. He's a natural liar. And I shouldn't have had much chance anyway. He pushed straight off and hasn't been here since."

"Before this happened, was he a regular attender?"

"Quite regular, yes."

"And for a fortnight he hasn't shown up at all. Did that strike you as odd?"

"When I had time to think about it, I suppose it did."

"I'm sorry," said Petrella, "you're a busy man and I'm taking up a lot of your time. Then one last thing. Can you give me Barry's address?"

"I can look it up for you. Do you think it's important?"

"I think," said Petrella slowly, "that what he said to Poston-Pirrie and what Poston-Pirrie said to him might be very important indeed."

As soon as he got back to Maplin Road he telephoned Ramsbottom. He said, "Could you send a good man to Limehouse Fields? Someone who gets on with the West Indians. His job is to locate a Mrs Thursday – it shouldn't be difficult, apparently she's quite a local character – and find out what's happened to her one and only chick, Barry. When she asks what it's all about he can be a bit cagey and say that the police think he's got some information which might interest them. At which point he can mention that the banks have put out a five-thousand-pound reward in connection with that nasty little wage-snatch at Old Ford last month."

"You mean the one when the girl cashier got her front teeth knocked out?"

"That's the one. It had the hallmarks of a Torpedo–Farm Boys' job."

"And you mean that Barry might be able to pin it to them?"

"To be honest with you, I rather doubt it. But if you dangle that carrot in front of his mum she might persuade Barry to talk to us. I think he knows something which I want to know very badly indeed."

And that, thought Ramsbottom, is all I'm going to get out of him. Close as an oyster. He said, "The best time to find Barry at home will be late afternoon. Wherever he's been he'll turn up for his evening meal."

"All right," said Petrella. "Six o'clock tomorrow. Send your man straight round here with his report – "

"About next Friday," said Ramsbottom. He sounded worried.

Petrella had to think for a moment. Other things had relegated Friday's programme to the back of his mind.

He said, "Yes. I imagine you've made your plans."

"We shan't be short of men. A and B are lending me two crews each. I'm going to block all the side roads at the Globe Road end – "

"Let me have it in writing," said Petrella. "With a sketch plan. And a copy of the instructions you give those cars. Also, of course, for the drivers of the decoy van. Have you picked them yet?"

"Sergeant Stark and Sergeant Pearson."

"That sounds a good choice."

He rang off before Ramsbottom could say anything else. He suspected that he wanted to pass on some of his worries. Petrella had enough of his own without sharing Arthur Ramsbottom's.

It was close to seven o'clock on the following evening when Detective Harrington arrived. Petrella remembered the name. Harrington was one of the men who had been in the back room of the White Horse when Poston-Pirrie had his brush with the police. He was a large, red-faced Father Christmas character; a type calculated to appeal to children and also, hopefully, to West Indians.

He had to report complete failure.

"Really, sir, unless you met her – Mrs Thursday, I mean – you'd hardly credit her. She's huge, heavier than I am, I guess, and I'm no feather-weight. Quite a handsome moustache and her voice! She could sing bass in any choir. I wasn't surprised to hear that she runs Limehouse Fields. Give her half a chance, she'd run the country."

"From which I gather that she wasn't anxious to produce her son."

"That's right, sir. Might as well try to argue with the Rock of Gibraltar. Nor she wasn't interested in money. The way her house was fitted out I'd guess she's got plenty. And she doesn't like the police."

"A pity."

"I did have one idea. *She* mightn't be interested in money, but that's not to say her son wouldn't be."

"Yes," said Petrella. "It's an idea. But if she won't let him loose from her apron strings, how are we going to sell the idea to him?"

"What I thought was, that she couldn't keep him at home for ever. From something she let slip, I gathered that he was keen to get back to that club, where his pals were."

"He hasn't got many friends. All the same, it's an idea. Money jumps all barriers. I'll have a word with the missioner and with Father Freeling. They might be able to work something between them."

When Harrington had rolled away he tried to get on with some of the routine matters which were piling up, but his mind could not focus on them. Traffic control and drug-related offences distanced themselves obstinately from his more immediate problems.

He looked at his watch. It was close to eight o'clock. He had no wish to go home. The flat would be empty. His family had gone for the weekend to stay with one of Jane's many aunts. This one had a house in Broadstairs. In that weather and at that time of the year, the resort would be jam-packed, but better than London, which had baked for so many weeks that its houses, its streets and its inhabitants all seemed to be over-cooked. He was planning to join them on the Sunday, if nothing cropped up to prevent it.

There was still an hour of daylight left and he knew what he wanted to do with it. He had promised himself that, when he had time, he would look at the Cold Harbour area. And he wouldn't repeat that impossible train journey. Quicker on foot, Trench had said. Twenty minutes, if he put his back into it, and a striding walk would help him to sort out the thoughts which were jostling each other in his over-crowded brain.

At the age of nine, during his first Christmas holidays from preparatory school, his mother had taken him to the circus at Olympia. He had an abiding memory of the scenic railway, a towering construction of girders and spars, up which the coaches ground their way towards the summit, pausing there for a moment before the glorious downward swoop. A coach-load on a parallel track would already have begun its descent and young Patrick, even at that age a shrewd observer, had recorded, as in a camera flash, the faces of its occupants; the grown-ups simulating boredom, the children excited, apprehensive or plain scared.

His own coach, he noted, contained a disparate collection. On the back seat, Morrissey and Charlie Kay; in the next one Father Freeling and the sardonic Ashley Drummond; in front of them, youth in the forms of Milo Roughead and Peregrine Hoyland, and indomitable old age in Colonel Winchip and Wilfred Wetherall who shared nearly a hundred and eighty years between them and still wanted to play an active part in the melodrama which, as the coach climbed, was inching towards its climax.

'But something ere the end, some work of noble note may yet be done, not unbecoming men that strove with gods.' Had they striven with gods? Mr Wetherall had certainly striven with a number of education authorities.

Now the opposition coach swung into view. Maurice and Mamma Meinhold smiling smugly in the back seat. Ahead of them a crowd of folk whom he had not yet met in the flesh, some wearing animal masks, others dressed in smart City uniform. In the front seat, leaning dangerously out and waving their hands, were the urchin forms of Arnold, Delroy and Winston.

A policeman, looming ahead of him, brought him down to earth with a bump. He was clearly wondering what this strange man was doing, wandering among these dim deserted buildings. Petrella said, "Could you tell me, is this the area known as Cold Harbour?" The policeman started to say, "Perhaps you could explain why – " Then he recognised Petrella and changed it to, "Yes, sir. That's where you are now. As you see, most of the buildings have been shut down."

"Yes, I can see that," said Petrella. He was peering at a notice pinned to the door of one of them, directing enquirers to Messrs Summerskill and Partners, who were acting for the receiver.

"I know this district pretty well, sir. I wonder if I could help you."

"All I know about the building I'm looking for is that it's an old ships' chandlery and that it's within very easy distance of the river bank. And it probably has some sort of access – a goods shoot or even an air-vent through which an active boy might wriggle."

The constable thought carefully about this. His professional knowledge was being tested. He said, "If I had to guess, I'd have said that the most likely location was the Stewart Street area. That's on the other side of the Blackwall Basin. Packstone Passage is what it sounds like to me. There are one or two buildings there – all shut up now – within what you might call spitting distance of the river. And it's in my mind that the second one along – the Packstone Building – has got some sort of goods hatch in the pavement. I could show you the way if you like."

"I won't take you off your beat," said Petrella. "I'm sure I can find it. And thank you very much."

The evening was closing in now and Packstone Passage, even in broad daylight a gloomy place, was beginning to disappear under the mist which came up from the river at the end of a hot day. The Packstone Building certainly met two of his requirements. There was a goods chute in the pavement, covered by a heavy iron lid over which he had almost tripped as he felt his way along the pavement. And it was certainly very close to the river, separated from it only by a brick wall behind which he could hear the water lipping and splashing as the tide ran out.

As he stood there, in the dusk, he heard something else.

It was the click of metal against metal and it came from almost under his feet.

He withdrew a few yards and wedged himself into a doorway. It was too shallow to hide him properly, but he reckoned that if he rolled his jacket up to hide the white of his shirt, he would pass muster.

Then things started to happen.

First a jet of torchlight came up out of the pavement. Petrella could see, now, that it came from an air-vent which he had overlooked. Then a boy's head appeared. As his body slowly followed, the metallic sound came again. It sounded like the buckle on his belt hitting against some obstruction as he wriggled and heaved.

A voice from below said, "Gerra move on, for Chrissake. We can't hang abaht all night."

The first boy said, "Nearly through." Then a climactic heave brought him, face downward, onto the pavement.

The second boy seemed to have no difficulty in negotiating the narrow exit. He was out before the first boy had got back onto his feet. He said, "And don't flash that fucking torch about."

The light went out, but it had been on long enough for Petrella to recognise Arnold and one of his shove-halfpenny opponents. Delroy or Winston, he couldn't tell which.

Both boys moved away down the passage and were swallowed in the looming dusk.

Petrella had no intention of following them. He had got the information he wanted.

11

Nothing having cropped up to prevent it, Petrella spent Sunday at Broadstairs. It could hardly have been described as a day of rest. Donald was not a restful child. He had a sharp, long-handled spade which he had used to construct a castle on the beach and, later, in an attempt to decapitate a small dog who came sniffing round it. (Settled by apologies.) Afterwards he assaulted a boy who had trespassed in the castle grounds. (Settled by the purchase of ice-cream cornets for both boys.)

Petrella returned to London, perhaps not rested, but certainly refreshed.

Monday was a day of telephone calls. As soon as he got to his office he put through a call to Trench. He described the Packstone Building and said, "You told me that you'd been entrusted with the keys of some of those places. Is Packstone one of them?"

Trench said, "I think so. Hang on a moment." Then came back and said, "Yes, you're in luck."

"Good. Send the key up here. Don't post it. Send it by hand next time you've got someone coming in my direction."

"I'll do that," said Trench. He would bring it up himself. If he did, he might be able to find out what the old man was up to. It was not that he distrusted Petrella, but he liked to have a hand in anything that concerned his own manor.

As soon as he rang off, the telephone went again. Ambrose said, "It's a Mr Callaghan for you."

"Do I know him?"

"Seems he's the editor of the *Sentinel*."

Then Petrella remembered the name. He had seen it in the report of the Robin Hood case. Callaghan had supplied an affidavit. It had not been particularly damning, but it had not helped Hood. "Put him through."

"Superintendent Petrella?" The voice was incisive. "I am telephoning you to let you know that we are offering a reward of twenty thousand pounds for information leading to the identification and conviction of the person responsible for the death of Philip Poston-Pirrie. I have agreed the wording of the announcement with the Assistant Commissioner and it will start appearing tomorrow. I hope this will convince you that we are taking the matter seriously."

Petrella nearly said, 'Oh, we're taking it pretty seriously down here, too,' but realised, in time, that the editor was not the sort of man who would appreciate that sort of comment. So he simply said, "That should be helpful."

"I hope so. And now could you kindly give me an up-date on how your investigations are proceeding?"

"I can only tell you that it looks as though Mr Pirrie went into the river some way above the entrance to the East Stepney Dock, where his body was found."

"Went in? Was pushed in? Thrown in?"

"We shall be better able to judge that when we have the result of the post-mortem. We're expecting this today."

"And who's conducting it? Your police surgeon?"

"No. That would be no part of a police surgeon's job. The autopsy is being carried out by Dr Summerson, at Guy's."

"I see." A measure of grudging respect had come into the editor's voice. Summerson's reputation was international. "In that case we can look for a fair and unbiased report."

"You'd have had that even if we'd been forced to use our own man."

"You'll forgive me, Superintendent, if I say that certain

unhappy episodes in the past have taught me to distrust the police when they make themselves judges in their own affairs."

Petrella said, "Yes." He found this monosyllable useful when his object was to keep his temper.

"The *Sentinel* is instructing one of its foreign correspondents, Murdo Wintringham – I expect the name means something to you?"

"I fancy I have seen him once on television."

"He happens to be in London at the moment. His remit will be to investigate all the circumstances of our man's death. I trust that the police will give him their co-operation. Could you see him tomorrow at three o'clock?"

"Yes."

"He has had a rough passage lately in various parts of Europe and the Far East."

"Then he should be able to survive a few weeks in east London," said Petrella.

This time it was the editor who said, "Yes," and rang off.

Ten minutes later Charlie Kay was on the telephone. He said, "You remember you asked me to see whether our experts here could identify that printer's mark – I.P."

Petrella wrenched his mind back with an effort to that earlier episode. He said, "Any luck?"

"Not at the moment. The mark hasn't been officially registered. Which makes it worth a little more investigation, don't you think?"

"Certainly."

"I remembered that when I was with the porn boys there was a renegade printer – a man called Mal Martiennsen. He knew all the ins and outs of printing dirt and we found him very useful. So I had a word with him. When I mentioned I.P. he turned remarkably coy. But I got a strong impression that he did know something about it."

"Splendid."

"The snag is that he wouldn't open up to me. But he

might talk to you. The one thing that warms his cold and grubby little heart is money. And if you could hint that if he helped he might be qualifying for a share of the *Sentinel* hand-out – "

"Oh, you've heard about that, have you?"

"Nothing shouts louder than money."

"I must admit that I can't, for the moment, see any plausible connection between a sheet of dirty photographs and the death of Poston-Pirrie. But if you think it might give us a line, I'm game to try. Only, things are rather crowding up on me at the moment."

"Could you manage Wednesday evening?"

Petrella looked at his desk diary. If he said yes, it would enable him to side-step a meeting of the Road Safety Committee. He said, "Yes. When and where?"

"Martiennsen suggested six thirty at the Quartermass Club. It's in St Bride's Square. It's a boozing den, much frequented by newspaper men. Fairly disreputable, but not actually criminal. You won't have to sew up your pockets."

"Will you be coming along to introduce me?"

"I think he's more likely to say his piece if I'm not there. You'll have no difficulty in recognising him. He's got a slashing moustache and a terrible squint. And he'll be tucked away in one of the niches at the back of the room."

Petrella said, "All right," and put down the telephone which rang again at once.

Ambrose said, "Dr Summerson. He's been hanging on for you."

Petrella said, "Put him through."

Dr Summerson said, "I thought you'd like to have this at once. Deceased was hit by a powerful swinging blow on the throat. Either from some form of club, or possibly from the fist or the edge of the hand. Maybe a sort of karate chop. It was savage enough to fracture the sound box and severely damage the oesophagus. It would almost certainly have rendered him unconscious."

"But not killed him."

"No. He was alive when he went into the river. There was some water in his lungs. Not much. Enough to suggest that he had gulped once or twice. Then the joint effect of the blow and the shock of the immersion stopped his heart."

"First he was hit," said Petrella slowly. "Then he was thrown into the river."

"It looks like that. I'd guess he'd been dead about twelve days. Difficult to be more accurate. I'll let you have this in writing as soon as I can get it typed out."

After Summerson had rung off, Petrella sat for quite a long time, thinking. Hit by a fist or the side of a hand? Maybe a karate chop. It opened up a train of thought so unpleasant that he hesitated to follow it to its logical conclusion.

He had asked Ambrose to keep callers off his back and was surprised when the telephone rang once again.

Ambrose said, apologetically, "I didn't like to head this one off. It's Sergeant Roughead – ex-sergeant, I should say."

Ambrose and Milo, as he knew, had been close friends in the old days. He sighed and said, "All right. Put him through."

When Milo spoke Petrella realised that the normally imperturbable Etonian was angry. And there was a hint of worry behind the anger. He said, "I've got something for you that I don't really like passing over the telephone. And I know how busy you are – but if I could look in – "

"This afternoon. Any time after four."

"I'll be with you," said Milo.

He was prompt to the minute and looked both excited and worried. Petrella had observed before that when Milo was excited he tended to become incoherent. So he sat him down in a chair and said, "Bear in mind what the King of Hearts said to Alice. Begin at the beginning, go on until you come to the end and then stop."

"All right," said Milo. "The beginning's simple enough. I found out, quite by chance, that the beneficial shareholders in the Mansion House Nominee Company – the crowd that control Meinhold's shop – are another company called Intriguing Publications."

"I.P.," said Petrella softly. "Go on."

"I got the information from someone I'd done a good turn to. It wasn't actually confidential – I mean, it wasn't hedged round with 'Don't tell anyone else' – but in view of the source it came from I was a bit doubtful about passing it on. However, something that happened next changed my mind about that. No, not next, actually. Next but one."

"Chronological order, please."

"Good old chronology. Right. The next thing that happened was that I decided to make a search against I.P. This time I thought I'd do it myself. It looked like another of these tight little, bright little, craft. Directors and secretary imported from a firm of City accountants and shares held by their own service company. But one thing I did find interesting. The memorandum of association."

"Which is, as I understand it, the document that sets out the objects of the company?"

"Correct. And it's usually a rare old hotch-potch, full of things that a small company couldn't possibly do. Like laying railways in Texas and running airlines. All put in to camouflage the real intentions of the promoters. This one was surprisingly definite. I've copied out the interesting bits. Start at sub-clause (J). Then the next two."

Petrella read:

'(J) To pursue all lawful means of reforming the present laws relating to obscenity and obscene publications.

'(K) To publish, distribute and promote magazines, periodicals and pamphlets in furtherance of this object.

'(L) To form and organise institutions and clubs with the like objects.'

"As you say," said Petrella, "all their cards on the table. Nothing illegal about it, of course. Then what?"

"The next thing was, I got a phone call. The man didn't give his name and had the sort of classless accent you find nowadays in four people out of five in our neck of the woods. He said, 'I'm told you have recently been researching our little company, Intriguing Publications –' Pausing there for a moment, I'd heard a rumour that certain crowds in the City did maintain a watch on the Search Room at Companies House. They like to know when stockbrokers or finance houses show an interest in their affairs. I assumed it was one of these people who'd spotted me. I simply said, 'So what?' – or words to that effect. 'Well,' said my caller, 'it did occur to us to wonder whether you'd like to join one of the clubs we promote. The entrance fee is only one thousand pounds and the annual subscription five hundred pounds – at the moment, that is. We've had so many applicants that we may soon be having to put it up, but just now you could get in on the ground floor.'

" 'And what do I find on the ground floor?' I said.

" 'As a member of the club you would be entitled to receive, free of charge, two interesting video cassettes every three months.'

"I said, 'If interesting means what I think it does, then, no, thank you.'

"I was about to ring off when he said, 'I'm sorry you are declining our offer. So be it. But let me give you a word of advice. You will not pass on any part of this conversation to anyone else. If you feel tempted to do so, have a word with one of Bill Thresher's partners first.' Then he rang off."

"And did the name Thresher mean anything to you?"

"Oh, yes. Thresher & Co are well-known metal dealers. And as it happens I knew one of the junior partners personally, so I rang him up and asked if I could have a word with Bill. He said, 'Haven't you heard? It was in the papers only last week. He disturbed some men who were breaking into his flat and got badly beaten up. He's in the London Central now, in their Intensive Care Unit. The latest reports weren't too good.' I said how sorry I was and that my query wasn't important, and rang off."

For a long minute Petrella sat in silence, staring at Milo across the desk. He fully realised the importance of what he had heard.

It had lifted a corner of the curtain which hides the square mile of narrow courts and crooked lanes round Lombard Street and the Minories; an area truly Byzantine in its hierarchic, intricate, tortuous ways; an area peopled by well-dressed, well-groomed men who worship one god only, the Mammon of gain; people who are agreeable to talk to and drink with and are dangerous only if their god is threatened, when they can become very dangerous indeed.

It was Milo who broke the silence. He said, "It occurs to me that it may have been stupid of me to come round here. I could easily have been followed. The last thing I want to do is involve you in what might not be your business."

"It's my business all right," said Petrella. "And I'm involved already. Also I guess I know the people who beat up Thresher. A crowd of bullies calling themselves the Farm Boys. They are the strong-arm side of this particular racket. In fact, I'm beginning to wonder whether they aren't the people who keep the whole thing going. Don't worry about me. I've got plenty of policemen to look after me. It's you who should be careful."

"I shall be all right. My firm's sending me on a six months' attachment to our subsidiary in Japan. I'm flying there next week and until then I assure you I shan't go out alone. And I shan't interfere with anyone who breaks into my flat at night. I shall bolt my bedroom door and scream for the police. I hope what I've told you is going to be useful."

"Extremely useful," said Petrella. "Next stop the London Central Hospital."

Here he had a word with the senior consultant, Dr

137

Burden, who said, "It's not going to be possible for anyone to talk to Thresher, not for some time anyway."

"I don't want to press you," said Petrella. "But it's desperately important to get one fact – possibly a single name – out of him. How long, do you think?"

"Days certainly. Weeks possibly. Maybe never."

"As bad as that, is it?"

"His skull was cracked in two places. A neighbour, coming home late, saw the intruders leaving. He didn't try to stop them, wisely enough – but he managed to get into Thresher's house, through the window they had broken. He found Thresher and rang the hospital before he rang the police. He was a doctor himself and he knew that in a case of cranial injury minutes can be important. If he hadn't done that, Thresher might have died. And if no one had found him until next morning, it's pretty certain he would have been dead."

"Which might have been the object of the exercise," said Petrella thoughtfully. "I'll leave this card with you. It's got my office and my home numbers on it. Would you please ring me as soon as Thresher can say anything at all?"

The doctor, impressed by the urgency in Petrella's voice, promised to do that. Petrella went home.

12

If Petrella had expected that Murdo Wintringham would be a second Poston-Pirrie, he could hardly have been wider of the mark. He remembered seeing him, once before, on television when he was doing a stand-in report for the BBC. On that occasion he had been speaking from somewhere in Manchuria. Since he had been enveloped in a fur hat with side flaps and had spent most of the time with his back to the camera, this was the first chance Petrella had had of getting a clear view of him.

He saw a face that was a map of planes and rugged contours. The left side was seamed and scarred, as though it had been sand-papered by an inefficient carpenter. The result of fire or frost-bite? It was a surprise when he spoke. His voice was soft, even conversational, yet seemed in some way more formidable than the Poston-Pirrie bark.

Petrella said, "Your editor tells me that you've been spending much of your time abroad. Europe, he said, and the Far East."

"Recently Phnom Penh."

"Which is in Cambodia?"

"It is. But out there it's a penal offence to call it that. It is now the Khmer Republic."

"My geography is sadly dated. I still find myself referring to the Persian Gulf."

Wintringham passed that one up. He said, "You know, of course, why I've been called in?"

"I gather that it's to satisfy your editor about the fate of your predecessor."

Wintringham was leaning back in his chair at a dangerous angle. His thoughts seemed to have drifted away. He said, "And here's an odd coincidence for you. Pirrie is said to have been hit and tumbled into the river. Right?"

"Tumbled in, certainly."

"And almost the last thing I saw in Cambodia was a man being knocked on the head and slung into the Mekong River. People were trying to pull him out. I wanted to get close enough to take an action photograph. Unfortunately, the whole thing happened on the far bank and since that was held by the anti-Prince Noradam faction it would have been injudicious to cross over. Their soldiers tended to shoot first and talk about it afterwards. It was soldiers who were doing the pulling out. But he'd been knocked in by a policeman."

As he added the last few words he jerked his chair forward and the comment came across like a sharp smash at the end of a leisurely rally.

Speaking slowly, to recover his balance, Petrella said, "If you weren't close enough to get a picture, how do you know it was a policeman who hit him?"

"Oh, in that part of the world you can always tell. The soldiers slope about in any old outfit. The police are always dressed in neat uniform and move smartly. It's part of their mystique. I think that before we go much further I shall have to ask you to switch off that instrument. Otherwise we shall have to continue our conversation in the back of my car."

Petrella grinned, switched off the box that was standing unobtrusively among a pile of dockets, put it away in the desk cupboard and shut the door.

"All right now?"

"Much better. One likes to keep these things informal as far as possible. I was scouting round at the weekend, getting my bearings. I talked to a number of people. Weekends are useful. You find people at home. One man I talked to – " (a quick glance down at the notebook on his lap) " – was

140

Desmond Cracknell. Previously a policeman, but not now. So, ready to talk."

"As coroner's officer he's in an official position."

"He didn't allow it to inhibit him, not entirely." Wintringham's teeth showed for a moment in the start of a smile, quickly suppressed.

I wonder how much you paid him, thought Petrella.

"He said one thing which interested me a lot. It seems that when you and Dr Summerson were discussing this matter with the top man from the River Police – can't remember his name – "

"Superintendent Groener."

"That's the one. He suggested that Pirrie's body would still have been high in the water when it was caught by the wash of a barge and deposited in the entrance to that dock – "

"As I told your editor when he phoned me."

"The words you used – that conversation incidentally *was* recorded – were, 'It looks as though Mr Pirrie went into the river some way above the dock.' "

"Well?"

" 'Some way'. That was a bit vague, wasn't it? Might have been any old distance. A mile or more. But that wasn't what Groener said. His estimate was anything between fifty yards and a quarter of a mile. And after looking at the map you settled on Cannon Wharf."

"Nothing was settled. It was just one possibility."

"I'm sure it was more than just a possibility, Superintendent. Why, only last Friday you walked down Butcher Row with your number two" – another quick glance at his book – "Inspector Gwilliam. To inspect the wharf, I imagine. I can't think you'd have done that unless you were fairly certain that it was the spot."

And how on earth did you know that? thought Petrella. Surely Gwilliam hasn't been talking.

"And it wasn't Gwilliam who told me that," said Wintringham, answering the unasked question. "The fact

141

is, you're already so well known round here that you can't expect to go anywhere without being spotted."

"All right. Yes. I had a look at Cannon Wharf. And other places as well."

"No doubt. But that's a very important area, isn't it? Pirrie was there on the last night he was known to be alive."

"It was the last night that anyone has admitted seeing him. We've traced him as far as the Athletic Club, in the Commercial Road. He got there around seven o'clock and left some time after eight."

"And walked back, no doubt, the way he had come."

"No evidence of that. Having come so far he might just as well have gone on. He could have picked up a train at Stepney Station."

"But if he did go back, he'd have been walking slap into the middle of the HC area."

Petrella said, speaking slowly to control his anger, "Yes. He'd come back through what you call the HC area."

Wintringham had a street map out now. He seemed to find it intriguing. He said, "The map certainly supports my description. The HC headquarters station is in Harford Street. Grindall Mansions, where a lot of them shack up, and the pub they use are both in White Horse Road."

"Yes. Those facts are correct. What I can't see is what you are trying to make them mean."

"Then let me add one more fact. That Pirrie had been in that pub earlier in the evening and had had some sort of row with a gang of HC detectives."

"And is that something you also picked up from your local informers?"

"It came from the landlord of the White Horse. He might have told me more, but seemed curiously unwilling to open up."

"Perhaps you didn't offer him enough money."

It was now a question of which of two normally self-controlled men was going to lose his temper first. An unbiased observer might have put his money on Petrella, but there was very little in it.

Wintringham drew a deep breath and said, "Money didn't come into it. He was thinking of his own skin. Not only did he deny having heard what was said, but he couldn't, apparently, put names to the men who were there. Which was odd since his back bar was practically a police club room."

"Odd, but possibly true."

"He even denied knowing Sergeant Stark by sight. Really, Superintendent. That was a bit hard to swallow. He's a very well-known local character. As well known as you are."

"It appears to me that you're in for a busy time."

"How so?"

"In as far as I can understand what you're getting at, you seem to be trying to trace anyone who may have spoken to Pirrie on that particular evening, or, of course, for a day or two afterwards."

"Afterwards?"

"Dr Summerson's report, which you'll hear at the inquest – if you're not too busy muck-raking to attend – says that Pirrie had been dead for 'about twelve days'. So there's nothing to show that that *was* the last evening of his life. You'll have to extend your enquiries considerably, both in time and in place, won't you?"

"For the moment I'm concentrating on the most likely area and the most likely time."

"You're not. You're just playing a guessing game."

A flush of annoyance was clear, along the top of Wintringham's prominent cheek bones. He said, "I shouldn't be forced to guess so much if you could see your way to helping me a little more. Do I take it that you have made up your mind to prevent me finding out who was in that back room and what they talked about?"

"You can take it that I'm not going to help you set up some kangaroo court to consider a theory that you've absolutely no evidence to support."

"Then since you're determined to be unhelpful, I shall have to go elsewhere."

"Feel free. Would you like to go up or down? Up to Chief Superintendent Liversedge, at Area, or down to the man who runs HC under me, Chief Inspector Ramsbottom. Some people might object to having their subordinates questioned behind their back, but in this case I've no objection at all."

The thought of what Ramsbottom would say had almost restored his good humour.

"I think I shall have to go a little higher than Area."

"Then the Deputy Commissioner at Central would be the next man for you to see. I'm sure he'd be prepared to talk to you. He was once a barrister himself and is well able to judge the weight of evidence. Or the lack of it."

"There are authorities senior even to a Deputy Commissioner."

"Of course, of course. There's the Home Secretary and the Prime Minister. And even the Queen. Try them all. Why not? And now, if you don't mind – "

He got up. Wintringham rose more slowly. Petrella wondered what his Parthian shot was going to be. When he was at the door he simply said, "I'd rather have you with me than against me." And departed, shutting the door quietly behind him.

At home that evening Petrella recounted as much as he could remember of these exchanges to his wife. She darned and seemed to be listening. He said, "To be honest, I don't think I came out of it as well as he did."

She said, "Isn't that just like a man? To add it all up and see who scored most points. As if it was some sort of game."

"No, I don't think it was a game."

"Surely, all you had to say was, that you couldn't authorise any cross-examination of your men until he produced something that looked like a case."

144

"If he really does go off to our political masters," said Petrella, "and things get tough, I can see I shall have to brief you to represent me. You've got a much more logical mind than I have."

13

Lee Morrissey – her given name, Leah, was used so seldom that she had almost forgotten she owned it – speared a third cream cake and looked thoughtfully across the table at Detective Constable Peregrine Hoyland.

They were in the Cadena Café in Putney High Street. Perry had extracted a grudging afternoon's leave from Inspector Ambrose. ('See that you're back by half past six, sharp.') The tea party was the culmination of a number of earlier and unsuccessful manoeuvres and he had been equally delighted and surprised when a telephone call to her house had found Lee at home and willing to come out and eat cakes at his expense.

Although his kind colleagues would have been the first to suggest it, he was not motivated by the hope of gaining some favour or advantage from Lee's formidable and devious father. It was simpler than that. With her snub nose and urchin face, Lee had reminded him of a boy he had been in love with at school. It was a case of transferred affection.

She said, "I hear that Sergeant Stark has drawn the short straw for Friday."

"That's right. He and Sergeant Pearson – the one they call Lofty – are going to drive the decoy car on Friday. Incidentally, how did you know?"

"Dad told me. He can be quite indiscreet, sometimes."

"That I doubt. My guess would be that he only lets you know things that don't matter, or things he wants you to pass on."

Lee thought about this. She said, "You may be right.

146

He's got a mind like a crossword puzzle. Sometimes he gives you an easy clue and when you fill the answer in it doesn't fit with the words that are there already. But in this case, even if he hadn't said anything, anyone would have guessed that Dod Stark would be number one for this job." She looked at Perry out of the corner of her eye and added, "That's the sort of man I go for."

"Brute force and bloody ignorance."

"That's where you're wrong, bimbo. OK, he clobbers people sometimes, West Indians chiefly, but only to teach them to keep in line."

"He oughtn't to clobber anyone, at any time, for any reason at all."

"You're saying that because you're jealous."

"Certainly not. I try to keep my temper, that's all. If I lost it, and lashed out, I'd be carpeted for sure by the superintendent."

"And we all know that for you the sun shines out of Petrella's bottom."

Hoyland started to be indignant, but found himself guffawing. As soon as he could speak he said, "You really are a vulgar little girl."

"If you'd been brought up by my dad you'd be vulgar." Lee speared a fourth cake. "And I can tell you something else about your sanctified superintendent. He's worrying Dad."

"Worrying him? What about?"

"Seems when they were making arrangements for Friday he was the one who took the responsibility for issuing firearms."

"He isn't afraid of responsibility."

"Didn't say he was. But what Dad said was that if anyone was going to decide about that sort of thing, it should have been his boss at Area."

"Liversedge? He'd have taken a week to make up his mind and then said 'perhaps'."

"You're missing the point. Petrella didn't have to take

it on himself. I'd guess he only did it because he likes to be a big man."

"Unfair."

"OK. But if things go wrong and Stark and Pearson should happen to bump off a couple of black guys, he'll be thrown to the wolves, no question."

"He'll make them a tough meal," said Perry. "Have another cake."

"Why not?" There was an interval of silence as she sank her sharp teeth into a slab of fruit cake. When she had cleared a path for speech, she said, "Your skipper is not the only one with troubles. Dad's got a plateful of his own. First it was Lovell breathing down his neck about the Farm Boys. Now something seems to be blowing up about Lampier."

"Lampier," said Perry. "Yes. Wasn't he going out with you at one time?"

Lee looked at him for a few seconds. Then she said, "How old are you?"

"Twenty-two. Why?"

"When you say things like that, you sound as if you were twelve – maybe fourteen. 'Going out'! For God's sake! Why don't you say what you mean? All right. I was hot for him. And we went the whole way, whenever we got a chance. Which wasn't often. Especially when he took up with those bloody Farm Boys. After that I hardly saw him. Then he got jugged and I had to drop him altogether. If Dad had seen me within a hundred yards of him, he'd have blown his top."

After which unusually lengthy speech she refilled her mouth with cake.

Perry, who had been thinking, said, "Do you remember a bod called Flower? Ernie Flower."

"Yes. Dad told me about Ernie. I had to sit in his office every evening to take calls from him."

Perry said, "And wasn't there a theory that something you let slip – "

He wondered if Lee was going to throw the remaining cakes at him. She managed, with an effort, to control her feelings. She said, "Naturally, all my best friends told me about *that*. It was a filthy rumour and a fucking lie. And anyone who thinks that Dad believes it and that's why he hasn't let me help with whatever he's up to with Lampier, can bloody well stuff it up his arse."

"Sorry I spoke. As a matter of fact I didn't believe it. But tell me this. Have you got any idea what your dad *is* up to? Is Lampier someone he's sold to the Farm Boys to do the job Flower fell down on? Has he allowed him to be jugged and promised him a free pardon, when the curtain comes down and the band is playing 'God Save the Queen'? Or has he really gone over to the opposition? For God's sake, *whose side is he on?*"

Speaking unusually seriously Lee said, "I don't know. Honest I don't. When Dad was running Flower he had quite a team. Lovell and his number two, Chief Superintendent Watterson, and his own number two, Charlie Kay. Now, I really believe he's flying solo. The only hint he's given is that he wants to know whenever Lampier changes his pad. He's got some of his old north London squad looking after that. It's a full-time job. He seems to move almost every week."

"Sounds as though he's running scared."

Lee said, "If you were involved in any sort of play where my father was pulling the strings, you'd be scared."

Perry said, "Have another cake."

He hoped he wouldn't forget what Lee had said, because he intended at the first opportunity to pass on a carefully edited version of it to Petrella. With Ambrose guarding the telephone it wasn't all that easy for a junior detective constable to get alongside the superintendent. He was busy working out a plausible way of doing it, when he reached Maplin Road and the problem was solved for him.

Ambrose said, "The top brass wants you."

"Then I'd better go right up."

"And get your skates on. He's in a hurry."

Hoyland ran up the stairs, knocked on the door and went in without waiting for an answer.

Petrella looked up and grunted when he saw Hoyland. He did not seem to be in an amiable frame of mind. He said, "Were you aware that we possess just one, useful, runabout car?"

"Yes, sir."

"And are you also aware that no car can really be classed as useful when a vital part of its engine has been removed and no one knows where it is?"

"I had the carburettor off to clean it, sir. I can put it back in a couple of minutes."

"I can allow you five. Not a minute more. I take it you can drive?"

Hoyland, who had been messing about with cars since he was twelve and had started driving them at a highly illegal age, said, "Yes, sir."

"Then bring her round to the front. I'll be with you as soon as I've put through one telephone call."

After making the call Petrella pocketed a key from the desk drawer and picked up the heavy lantern torch that lived on his desk. As soon as he was in the car, he started to rap out directions.

"Down to the Mile End Road, along it to the second traffic lights, right into the A1205, down it till you reach the East India Docks Road, left there to the A1206. Turn right and once you're across the Blackwater Basin slow down and wait for instructions."

This was fired at machine-gun speed. And it worried Hoyland. Not because the instructions caused him any sort of difficulty. Before he was transferred to the detective branch he had quartered that area, on foot and in patrol cars, and was exhaustively familiar with every street and turning in it. The directions he had been given were totally unnecessary. All that Petrella had to say was, 'Cubitt

150

Town by the quickest route.' No, what worried him was something different.

He knew that a certain type of senior officer would snap out a string of instructions at top speed in the hope that his subordinate would be forced to ask for a repeat; an opportunity for heavy sarcasm and a rocket for inattention. But he had not thought that Petrella would indulge in such a performance. Which led to a further uncomfortable conclusion.

It was rumoured that the super was running into trouble with his own superiors. Could it be – perish the thought – that he was allowing it to get him down and was losing his cool?

A quick sideways glance went some way to reassuring him. Petrella was smiling. He had noted that his driver, instead of following his careful instructions, had taken an alternative and quicker route. He had snapped out his orders at speed because he was half an hour behind schedule. One of Inspector Trench's men had been keeping an eye on the three boys he was after and his last-minute telephone call had confirmed that they were, very probably, where he wanted them.

The blood-stained history of the Packstone Building had been passed on by Arnold, under excruciating oaths of secrecy, to his two friends, and the place had become a natural meeting place for them, a perfect gang hide-out. But none of them would dare to stop there for one minute after dark, of that he was sure.

"All right," he said. "Hold it. And listen carefully. That turning you can see on the left is Packstone Passage. As soon as you get into it, cut the engine. It's a gentle downhill slope. Half-way along, opposite that big building on the right, there's an old loading bay. You should be able to get into it without having to restart the engine."

Hoyland nodded. He performed the manoeuvre easily and neatly. Petrella, speaking softly now, said, "You've got two jobs. The first is to see that no one steals the car. Something that's very likely to happen in areas like this. The second, and more important, is to keep an eye on that air-shaft in the pavement. I think, and hope, that there are three boys in that building. They go in and out by the air-shaft. If I flush them they may try to get out that way. You won't have much difficulty in stopping their bolt hole."

Hoyland nodded again and Petrella climbed out of the car, being careful to make no noise shutting the door, and crossed the road. He had the key of the front door ready. It was a big key and a heavy lock, but Trench's man had greased it and it opened with no more than a soft click.

The door gave onto three shallow steps leading up to a fair-sized lobby. Double doors on the left led to the main apartment, but the voices, which he could hear quite clearly now, came from somewhere higher up. There were doors in the corner on each side of the hall. Since his first visit he had been careful to keep clear of the building, but the owners had supplied him with a plan and he knew that both of the smaller doors opened onto staircases which led down to the cellars and up to the balcony which circled and overlooked the main apartment. He thought that the voices were slightly closer to the right-hand side, so he opened that door very softly and started upstairs, stepping like an experienced burglar on the edge of the treads to avoid creaking.

The door at the head of the stairs was slightly ajar. He opened it a few inches further and peered through. The boys were there all right, squatting in a semi-circle with their backs to him. They were studying a piece of paper.

"Let's have it again, Arnie," said Winston.

There was more light up here in the balcony than downstairs, but Arnold had no need of it. He had read the document so often that he knew it by heart.

"See, what it says is, the *Sentinel* offers a reward of twenty thousand pounds for information leading to the identification and conviction of the person or persons responsible for the death of Philip Poston-Pirrie."

There was a murmur of gratification. Even if they had to divide it, it would be – what? – near enough seven thousand pounds each.

"Lovely," said Delroy. "So what do we do to get it?"

"What you do," said Arnold, "is you listen to me." The other two were considerably older than him and bigger, but there was no doubt he was the leader. "First thing is this. Last Saturday the coppers were round your place, talking to Barry's mum. Right?"

"That's right. Only it wasn't his mum they wanted to see. It was Barry. Which they couldn't do, because she wouldn't let them."

"Right. Next point. Yesterday was the first time Barry's been to the Athletic for a week – "

"Nearly two," said Winston.

"Hasn't been there," said Delroy, "not since the night that reporter was round wanting us to tell him stories about the police – "

"We might have done," said Winston, "if he'd been going to shell out. What we didn't see was why we should do it for nothing."

Arnold had allowed this brief interruption. Now he brought them back sharply to business. "You haven't forgotten, I suppose, that even if no one else would, Barry *did* talk to him. For half an hour, wasn't it? All alone with him. And when he'd finished, the reporter didn't seem interested any more in the rest of us. He just buggered off. Like as if something Barry had told him had put him in mind of someone he ought to go and see – "

Delroy and Winston nodded their heads. They could follow Arnold's train of thought, and the golden conclusion it led to.

"What you're saying," said Delroy slowly, "is, *if* we knew what Barry told that reporter, we'd know who it was he pushed off to see – "

"And since he disappeared that night," said Winston, "the man he went to see must likely have been the one who pushed him into the river. It's a snip."

"It might be a snip," said Arnold coldly, "*if* we could find out from Barry what he said to the reporter."

"Couldn't we make him tell us?"

Delroy's mind was running on pocket knives and matches. Steel and fire. Arnold, whose mind had been following the same track, said, "Wouldn't work. First, because if you did anything like that you'd have his mum after you."

"Wouldn't want that," agreed Winston hastily.

"Second, because we'd have to catch him alone and take him away somewhere to work him over and that's not on, neither. Didn't you see when he come up yesterday evening one of his crowd – cousin, maybe, something like that – a big buck? He'd been sent with him, I'd guess, to look after him."

"The one who was talking to Bert Branch."

"That's the one. Best part of an hour. While Barry was trying to get someone to take some notice of him. They went away together."

"What we might do," said Winston, "next time he comes. Get him up the other end of the room. Game of shove-halfpenny or dominoes. Something like that. He'd come all right."

"Glad to find he'd got three friends left," agreed Delroy with a smirk.

"OK," said Arnold. "OK. But when we get him there, how do we make him talk if he doesn't want to?"

"Offer to cut him in on the reward," suggested Petrella.

He had never seen three boys move quicker. One moment they were squatting on the floor. The next they had jumped for the far door and hurled themselves down the stairs, Arnold leading. He heard the clatter of their footsteps as they went. They were making for the cellar, he guessed, where they would find the open end of the air-vent, at the top of which they would find Detective Constable Hoyland.

154

So no call for hurry. He followed them at a leisurely pace.

When he reached the cellar Winston was waiting his turn at the air-vent. Delroy was half-way up it and from above him he could hear Arnold, who seemed to have run into trouble.

First, he shut the door at the foot of the stairs, in case the boys tried to double back. Then he grabbed Delroy by the ankles and pulled him back into the cellar, after which Arnold acknowledged defeat and came down.

Petrella unhitched the lantern torch from his belt, switched it on and placed it on an up-ended crate. Then he turned a second crate on its side and used it as a seat for himself. The three boys watched him apprehensively. He let the silence hold. It was a curious little torch-lit tableau.

Stick first, then carrot, thought Petrella.

He said, "I suppose you know that you're trespassing."

This didn't seem to worry them. Trespass was not something that featured high in their list of sins.

"You're infringing the rights of two lots of people. First, there's a firm of accountants who have appointed a receiver."

"Receiver?" said Arnold.

"Not the sort of receiver you're thinking about. It's a legal term."

He noted that the boys were now quite easy. Lawyers and accountants were unfrightening.

"Then there's a second set of people. They haven't exactly got any legal rights, but they probably feel, by now, that they've got some sort of rights." He paused. "I'm talking about the Farm Boys."

This went home, right to the heart.

"I don't think they'd be too pleased if they knew that you'd been making free with this particular building. And I'm certain – " he turned the light of the torch so that it fell directly on Arnold's twitching face – "that they wouldn't

155

be at all pleased if they knew that you had been a witness at one of their so-called trials. Well?"

But Arnold was almost beyond speech. He said what sounded like 'I diddun – ' and then could get no more words out.

"I'll tell you how I stand in the matter. I don't particularly want to see you tied up in a sack, with your hands chopped off, and dropped in the river. Which I imagine is what would happen if I gave them a hint."

He thought for a moment that he had gone too far and that the boy was either going to faint or be sick. He managed with an effort to say something that sounded like, 'You wouldn't do that.'

"I wouldn't. On one condition. That you were prepared to help us."

"Oh, I am. We all are." Three heads jerked up and down. Certainly they would help. No doubt about it at all.

"Then I'll tell you what you can do. It's not difficult. Mention the reward to Barry. He probably knows about it anyway. Then tell him that if he's prepared to let you know just *exactly what he said to that reporter*, you'll be able to fix things so that he's in line – with you – for a share of the twenty thousand pounds."

The boys' faces had cleared as he was speaking.

"We can do that," said Arnold. "We were talking about it when you come in."

"No problem," said Winston. "If we pal up to him and promise him some of the cash, he'll come across, for sure."

"It's got to be done without anyone else knowing."

"What we'll do," said Delroy, "we'll tell him that if anyone else gets to know about it, they'll have to be cut in for a share of the money."

Arnold said, "Can we tell him you've promised us the reward?"

"Certainly not. All I can tell you is that it puts you

in line for it *if* what you tell us leads to the killer being caught. It will be for the *Sentinel* to decide. Perhaps you'd rather forget about it. I could sell the idea to Len Farmer. I expect he and his boys could make Barry talk."

From the energetic shaking of three heads he saw that the point had gone home.

"We'll do it," said Arnold.

"Very well. As soon as you've got the information, let me have it. I've written down two telephone numbers. One's my office. The other's my flat. And there's one thing more. If you really mean to help us, that is. You know this area pretty well, I guess." Three nods. "Then keep your eyes open. If our farming friends come back, I'd like to hear about that, too. Money for telephones." Some coins changed hands. "And now push off before I change my mind. You can make a proper exit. By the front door."

Once out in the street the boys lost no time, slipping away like small animals let loose. Petrella said, "Home to base." And when the car had been backed out and turned, "Do you want me to give you directions?"

"No, sir," said Hoyland gravely. "I think I can manage."

He had no idea what the superintendent had been up to, but since he was grinning it seemed that it must have gone well. In view of the change in climate he was encouraged, on the way back, to pass on some of the things Lee had said, particularly about Lampier. Petrella listened in silence.

14

"Members of the jury," said the coroner, "we are here as the result of the discovery of a body inside the entrance channel of the East Stepney Dock. You have all been provided with plans to enable you to follow the evidence, which I hope you will do very carefully. The body was on the mud and shingle beach, a short distance in from the river. A cross on the plan indicates the spot."

The coroner had examined the jury as they were being sworn. He could see at least one who would need careful handling; a grey-haired woman with a powerful nose, who was known to him as a member of a number of east London committees dedicated to improving the welfare of their fellows.

Petrella was more interested in the onlookers than in the jury. He hated inquests. In a court of law you knew where you were. It was a straight fight, with the prosecution and the police on one side, the accused and his legal champions on the other. An inquest was without form and void. He had to be present because, as senior police officer in the district where the body was found, he had been charged with collecting the necessary witnesses and taking statements from them; statements to which they would, hopefully, adhere when giving evidence.

In the middle of the front row of spectators was a man he identified as Frank Callaghan, editor of the *Sentinel*; flanked by Murdo Wintringham and a foxy-faced man, probably the *Sentinel*'s legal eagle. Seats had been kept in this row for three or four well-dressed City types, none of whom he knew, but he had made arrangements to find out about them.

The coroner said, "The body was discovered last Friday, so you will appreciate that the police have had only five days, so far, to prosecute their enquiries. However, at the request of the *Sentinel* newspaper – a request which the police have not resisted – it was decided to hold this preliminary hearing forthwith, in order to dispose of two important matters. The first, as always, is the identity of the deceased. Fortunately, as you will hear, that presents no real difficulty. The second is the cause and likely date and place of death. When these points have been disposed of – " the coroner glanced sharply at the *Sentinel* block – "I shall adjourn the hearing in order to allow the police to continue their investigations. It may then be necessary to recall you."

Interesting, thought Petrella. It looked as though the coroner had been pressed by the newspaper to go further than he wanted. However, Dr Guy was a stubborn Welshman, about as susceptible to pressure as the Rock of Gibraltar. He looked at the list in front of him and said, "Sergeant Belling, if you please."

The sergeant explained that it was one of the duties of the Thames Division to make periodical inspections of the many derelict docks in the area. It was during one of these inspections that he had found the body.

"Can you tell us," said the coroner, "how the body can have lain there so long – nearly a fortnight, it seems from evidence we shall be hearing – without being seen by anyone else?"

"There are only two points, sir, from which it could have been seen. From the dock itself, which is very tightly locked and barred, or by taking a boat, as I did, up the entrance channel. It's marked as 'Private' and none of the boats which normally use the river have any reason to go up it."

"When you found the body, Sergeant, just exactly how was it lying?"

"On its side, sir. A yard clear of the water."

"Did you have any idea how it got there?"

"Well, sir, that was a bit of a puzzler – "

The coroner, who had been examining his list, said, "I see that Superintendent Groener is to give evidence. He is, as I know, greatly experienced in everything connected with the river. Probably he will be able to give us his ideas on that point."

Sergeant Belling agreed and was about to leave the box when the coroner noticed that one of the jury had a hand raised.

"Yes, Mrs Winlaw."

The grey-haired lady said, "We are frequently told that our police force is under-manned and over-worked. Why should it have to spend its time inspecting this dock?"

"We inspect all the docks, madam."

"Yes, but why?"

"To see that no one has been tampering with the gates or the dock fixtures." Here he shot a quick look at the coroner before adding, "Also to take samples of the water."

The coroner picked up his cue. He said, with well-simulated surprise, "Now why would you do that?"

"When a dock is closed, sir, local factories sometimes see it as an opportunity to discharge illegal waste into it."

"Thank you, Sergeant." The coroner noted with pleasure that this answer had been recorded by the reporters, who were present in force.

Mrs Winlaw had resumed her seat.

"Normally," said the coroner, "identity is established by a member of the family. In this case, no family witnesses being available, we are relying on the employer – I should say the presumed employer – of the deceased. If you please, Mr Callaghan."

Mr Callaghan observed the formalities calmly and stated that a wallet discovered in the deceased's pocket had contained a letter on *Sentinel* notepaper and signed by the news editor. This, coupled with the clothing and general appearance of the deceased, had raised a strong presumption that he was the man whom the letter was addressed to – a Mr Poston-Pirrie who had been pursuing enquiries in that area on behalf of the paper. The matter had then been conclusively settled by dental evidence. If any doubt of any sort arose the dentist could give evidence in person.

"At the moment," said the coroner, "I am content to rely on the evidence we have and we will proceed on the assumption that the deceased was, in fact, Philip Poston-Pirrie. Yes, Mrs Winlaw?"

"I was only wondering, sir, why the more normal method was not adopted. I mean, identification by the features of the deceased."

"I understand," said the coroner, "that the deceased had no face. All the softer portions, including the eyes and tongue, had been eaten by the rats which infest – oh, dear – better take her out."

A lady in the second row was hustled out of the room, but the door was not closed in time to shut out the sound of her distress.

"While my court is open to the public," said the coroner testily, "people should surely realise that some of the details they hear will be unpleasant. Thank you, Mr Callaghan. Superintendent Groener, please."

The superintendent explained his idea of how the body had got into the dock entrance, but speaking, Petrella noticed, with increased conviction. He had evidently thought the matter through and could see no alternative solution. His conclusions were listened to respectfully.

The coroner said, "Enlighten us on one point, Superintendent. When you speak of barge traffic one visualises a string of barges towed by a tug. But that is not what you had in mind on this occasion?"

"I'm sorry I wasn't clearer, sir. The sort of vessel I was talking about would be a self-propelled load carrier. It would probably be proceeding by itself. They come in all shapes and sizes and in most cases are directed by a man standing on some sort of raised platform at the back. They sometimes have a second man as look-out in the bow."

"Thank you, Superintendent."

The foxy-faced gentleman stood up. He said, "Andrew Batson of counsel, representing the *Sentinel* newspaper."

"Yes, Mr Batson?"

"I wasn't clear if the superintendent had finished. But since he had reached a point on which I have instructions, I should like to put one or two questions to him."

The coroner thought about it. He had heard of Andrew Batson, QC, as an expert in running-down cases. He was quite capable of saying 'No' even to leading counsel. He thought he would let him have a little rope.

"If your questions bear directly on the matters we have to decide today, you may put them to the witness."

"I am obliged. They concern two matters which you yourself indicated were in front of us. The time and the place of death."

"Very well."

"Let me preface my questions, Superintendent, by saying that no one here – I include myself – knows as much about the river Thames as you do."

Groener smiled, but said nothing. He had met Andrew Batson before.

"Then tell me, is not the method by which barges are steered open to some criticism?"

"It has been criticised, yes."

"In a recent case of collision with a pleasure steamer?"

"In that case the other vessel was a dredger."

"Agreed. But was not the method of steering the same? A man at the back, with rather limited powers of observation, and a second one in the bows."

"Yes."

"We are, of course, dealing here with a theoretical barge. But supposing it to be of that type and suppose that a half-submerged body floats past, quite close to the barge, might I put it to you that the only circumstance in which it could have been overlooked would be if the incident happened in the dusk."

"Or at first light."

Since this did not fit in with the theory that counsel was trying to build, he ignored it. He said, "On the last day that Mr Pirrie is known to have been alive, sunset in London was at five minutes past eight. Allow half an hour of twilight after the sun had gone and that brings us to around eight thirty. I am suggesting that this was the probable time that the deceased went into the river."

"Possible. Not probable."

"I'll compromise on possible, if you insist. So much for time. Now, as to place. I believe that, when the point was first put to you, you said, 'Between fifty yards and a quarter of a mile.'"

"If I said anything of the kind, and I can't pretend to remember my exact words, it would have been when I was discussing the matter with Superintendent Petrella and Dr Summerson. Mr Cracknell, I remember, was also present." He swung round as he said this and Cracknell was seen to shift uncomfortably in his seat. "If this snap judgment seems important to you, sir, they could be asked about it."

The coroner said, "I don't think that your snap judgment is of any importance. What we want is your present considered opinion."

Batson said, "I agree, of course. But snap shots sometimes hit the target. And if we take the distances which you mentioned – fifty yards and a quarter of a mile – and look at the map" – he had one open in front of him – "does it not stand out that Cannon Wharf is the most likely place?"

"One of several possible places."

"Such as?"

"Shadwell Pier or Hermitage Wharf, to name two."

Counsel was busy with a ruler. He said, "One of these

is four hundred yards up river. The other eight hundred and twenty yards."

Groener said, with a smile, "I haven't measured the distance myself, but I'm quite prepared to accept your *snap* measurements."

"Then surely you must agree that Cannon Wharf is the most likely candidate?"

"No, I don't agree."

"Why not?"

"Because you are asking me to arrive at a specific answer to a sum where both the relevant factors are unknown. One of them is the speed of the river, at the moment when Mr Pirrie went into it. A speed which can vary widely, from day to day and hour to hour, depending on such matters as the state of the tide, the direction of the wind, the management of the up-river weirs and regulation at the Thames Barrier. Again, the state of the deceased's clothing is equally full of imponderables, which are so obvious that I needn't elaborate on it."

"Even agreeing with those points, Superintendent, I must return to my original suggestion, that Cannon Wharf is the most likely place."

"I can't prevent you returning to it," said Groener politely, "but by doing so you don't make it any more – or any less – probable."

"Really, Superintendent, aren't you being a little unreasonable – "

"I think we've had enough," said the coroner. "You started by complimenting the witness on his knowledge of the river. Now you're suggesting that you know more about it than he does."

"I only wanted – "

"I said, enough. Has anyone else any questions? Thank you, Superintendent. Dr Summerson, please."

Dr Summerson, with one eye on his notes, repeated what he had told Petrella. He added that a further examination was proceeding, but had, as yet, taken him no further.

The coroner said, "This blow that knocked out the deceased: if he had been standing near the river, it could, I presume, have knocked him into it?"

"It's possible. Though there's nothing to show whether a period of time might have elapsed between the time when the blow was given and the deceased was thrown into the river."

"And in either event, if he went into the water unconscious, and in that damaged state, he would have died almost at once?"

"Certainly. A supposition borne out by the very small amount of water in his lungs."

"That seems quite clear. You spoke of continuing your examination. What would be the object of that?"

"Simply to negative any suggested alternative causes of death – by poison, for instance. Also to show whether he might have been under the influence of alcohol when he went into the river."

"He was practically a teetotaller," said Callaghan loudly.

The coroner looked at him over his spectacles for a long moment. Then he said, "If you have further evidence to give it should be given formally. Not by interrupting the proceedings. Particularly with irrelevant statements. Dr Summerson was *not* suggesting that the deceased was intoxicated. He was saying that it was part of his duty to *show* that he was not."

The editor, who was unused to having his face slapped in public, looked as though he would have liked to have said something, but evidently thought better of it.

"Thank you, doctor. If that is all – yes, Mr Batson?"

"A couple of questions, if I might."

The coroner had had almost enough of Mr Batson. However, having snubbed his employer he thought he ought to allow him one more short innings. He nodded to the barrister.

"When you were describing the fatal blow you gave us

165

a number of alternatives. Club. Fist. Open hand. Is it not possible to be more precise?"

"The difficulty about being precise about that point is that the blow appears to have landed on the throat. Normally there would have been imprints or bruises or other marks which would have suggested the source of the blow. In this case the outer portion of the skin and flesh of the throat had been destroyed by the rats. My deductions about the point of impact and the force of the blow had to be made by following its effect. As, for instance, the destruction of the sound box, the fracture of the hyoid bone and the damage to the oesophagus."

"But you think it was the only blow?"

"If there had been blows on other parts of the body, they would have left signs which we would have seen."

"So if the damage was done by one hard and skilful blow, does this suggest to you that it might have been delivered by someone expert in karate or unarmed combat?"

"The most I can say is that it is possible."

Mr Batson, who could see that official patience was wearing thin, subsided. Dr Guy said to the jury, "There is no reason, at this point, to ask you for a formal verdict. Thank you, Dr Summerson. I understand, Superintendent, that police enquiries are proceeding."

"That is so, sir."

"Then I will adjourn the hearing for fourteen days. If that is not sufficient, I could adjourn it further."

Petrella said, "Thank you." Since the coroner was addressing him he had stood up.

Mr Batson, also rising, said, "May I take it, sir, that the superintendent will himself be giving evidence at the adjourned hearing?"

"If he has anything of importance to tell us, yes."

Mr Callaghan and Mr Batson were looking at him. Like two hungry tigers, he thought.

15

After a snatched lunch at the police canteen, Petrella returned to his desk. There were a number of things to be attended to. The first was a call to Milo Roughead's office. He was told that Milo was out at lunch, but would be back soon and would ring as soon as he returned. Idle financiers obviously took longer over their lunches than hard-working police officers. The matter he had to put to him was not urgent, but it could lead to important developments.

As the police officer in charge of the inquest proceedings he had been able to take certain precautions. He had put two men on the door and had instructed them that all comers were to be asked to identify themselves. With members of the public something informal would do: bank card, driving licence, even a recently delivered letter. Where people were attending as representatives, they were to be asked to demonstrate their connection with the body sending them.

Petrella had had no particular motive for insisting on this, beyond a desire for good order, but it had paid an unexpected dividend.

The three City types in the front row when challenged had simply produced their business cards. It appeared that they were Derek Chambers, from Franz Mittelbach, insurance brokers, J.C. Adamson from the Anglo-Netherland Shipbuilding Company, and T.H. Milford from Angus, Hardy and Glenister, merchant bankers. Petrella was not interested in Chambers, Adamson and Milford. They were clearly junior types, sent along to report, but there was food for thought in the outfits they represented.

The Ringland whom Hoyland had encountered in Amsterdam had mentioned that he was a shipbuilder and 'Anglo-Netherland' suggested a connection with Amsterdam. The name Glenister also rang a bell. There was a folder of documents locked in one of the drawers of his desk. From it he extracted the brochure which Father Freeling had given him. He was right. One of the supporters of the Athletic Club holiday fund was Ray Glenister.

He was starting to think about this when Milo came through. Petrella explained what he wanted. He said, "I expect I could get it out of directories and books of reference, but you'll be able to do it much quicker and better."

"You want the names of all the directors or senior types in those three outfits?"

"Particularly the top man."

"Easy enough with the company. I'm not sure about the other two. Merchant bankers and insurance brokers are a secretive bunch."

"I'm sure you'll be able to get it. And as quickly as you can."

"The noise you heard," said Milo, "was the clatter of my feet, sprinting to do your bidding."

Some time later, happening to look at his desk diary, Petrella had a shock. He had forgotten all about his promised visit to the Quartermass Club. When Charlie Kay had first mentioned the name to him it had rung a faint bell. It was only much later and when he was thinking of something different that the circumstances in which he had heard it before had recurred to him. If he was going to visit it, there were things to be done first. But did he really want to go? He reflected that Kay must have gone to some trouble to fix the meeting and that it might produce some interesting information.

He grabbed the telephone.

* * *

In his busy life Petrella had had little time for clubs. The word suggested to him, at one end of the scale, an austere building full of bishops and senior members of the Bench and Bar; at the other end night clubs, which he had occasionally entered in pursuit of undesirable characters. When he got there he found that the Quartermass Club fitted into neither of these slots.

It seemed to cater for a wide range of age and class. The noisier element was young office workers filling in as much time as possible between leaving their desks and returning to their lonely bed-sits. The next age group, a little more serious and drinking more selectively, consisted, he judged, of in-work and out-of-work journalists. They were all equally sloppily dressed, but the in-work ones looked a little happier. At the top end of the age scale there was a sprinkling of elderly men.

Petrella, who had the policeman's habit of trying to identify and categorise people he met, found himself handicapped by the odd lighting arrangements. These centred on a battery of bulbs over the bar which occasionally and disconcertingly changed strength and colour. At one moment the room would be flooded by a wash of clear light, the next moment plunged into near-darkness lit by flashes of red and blue.

None of this seemed to worry the members, or the two waiters who circulated busily between the tables.

Following the directions he had been given he made his way towards a number of recesses at the far end of the room. From Charlie Kay's description he had no difficulty in recognising Mal Martiennsen.

He was sitting on a padded bench behind a table which nearly filled the niche. There were two glasses on the table, one full, the other half-empty. Petrella squeezed his way in beside him, apologising to two elderly men who were playing draughts. He was not surprised that, when Mal opened his mouth, the words which came out were accompanied by a smell of past drinks and careless tooth-cleaning. What did surprise him was the voice, which was educated.

"Lovely to see you, Super. I've taken the liberty of ordering you a glass of vino. In this hell-hole it's better to keep clear of spirits. I suspect the proprietor of boiling up the gin in his bath and the whisky tastes as though he strained it through his socks. But he can't muck about with the wine. This is a Sancerre. Quite drinkable." He pushed the full glass towards Petrella, who restored it to its original position. He said, "I make it a rule not to drink on business. And business is something I've come to discuss with you. I was told by Charlie – "

A look at his companion's face showed him that he had nearly been guilty of an indiscretion. He amended it. "I was told by a police officer known to both of us that you might be in a position to help me with an enquiry."

"Always pleased to be helpful."

"What I have to discover is the origin – or perhaps I should say the true originator of these photographs."

He laid the crumpled sheet on the table. Mal looked at it impassively, then produced a lens from his pocket, turned the sheet over and examined the back.

"Easier if they weren't playing silly buggers with the lights," he said.

As though in answer to this the lights suddenly blazed out. Mal said, "Thank you. That's a lot better. Yes, I think I can help you. This comes from one of the papers put out by a company called Intriguing Publications. More honest if they called themselves obscene publications."

"Thank you," said Petrella politely. "We'd got as far as that. What we want to know is who actually owns the company. And I don't mean the names in the register. They're dummies. I want the real owners."

"The beneficial owners," said Mal thoughtfully. "Well, that's different. Now you really have asked me a question." He looked at Petrella out of the corner of his eye. "I don't actually know the answer. Not definitively. But I'm not saying I couldn't obtain it."

"Then please do so."

"The thing is I'd have to offer some money – quite a lot of money – in the right quarters." His red-rimmed eyes blinked hopefully.

"You seem to be under a misapprehension," said Petrella. He was getting tired of Mal and was beginning to be sorry that he had risked the visit. "The police have not got unlimited sums of money at their disposal to hand out to people in return for their help. Help which any right-thinking citizen should be glad to give. If you do get this information, then get in touch with me and I'll consider how much it's worth. But be clear about this: I'm not promising you anything."

As he spoke he was extracting himself with some difficulty from behind the table. Mal put out a hand as though to stop him, but seeing that his mind was made up said, "Then all I can do is apologise for wasting your time."

"On reflection, I'm not sure that you have wasted it," said Petrella agreeably. "That we shall see."

The genius behind the bar selected this moment for plunging the room into semi-darkness, causing him to knock over the draughtboard. He apologised to the players, picked up the pieces and fought his way through the crowd and out into the street. The young man on the other side of the road observed his exit and made a note.

On the face of it an inconclusive meeting, but the more he thought about it the clearer did certain aspects of it appear. Some helpful, one particularly unhelpful and unpleasant.

Whilst he had been in the club there had been a change in the weather. He had noticed that the clouds were closing up. They had hidden the moon and were now shutting down the whole sky. It seemed that the long drought was coming to an end.

He managed to reach home before the heavens opened and poured down their benison onto the parched and thirsty earth. He stood with Jane at the open window and watched the rain beating onto the roofs and rebounding in spray. Presently they were joined by their pyjama-clad son.

"This is something like it, isn't it just?" said Donald.

"What it's something like," said his mother, "is time you got back into bed."

"Couldn't I stop and watch, just for a few minutes?"

"Certainly not. Trotting about in pyjamas. You're asking for a cold."

Donald moved very slowly towards the door, stopping there to say, "If I got back into bed just now I expect I should get a cold."

"What are you talking about?"

"The rain's been coming straight down onto it, through the window. It's pretty damp – "

"You evil child," said his mother. "Why didn't you say so at once?"

Petrella, left behind at the window, found himself laughing and was grateful. There hadn't been a lot to laugh about lately.

The rain hardly stopped during the night and was still coming down steadily as he made his way to his office next morning. The change in the weather seemed to have had one good effect. It had damped down the number of people who wanted to distract him. Ramsbottom rang him twice with queries about the arrangements for the ELBO cash run next day. He began to wonder whether he ought not to go across to Harford Street and pick up the reins, but decided that any interference at this point could only be counter-productive.

He managed to focus his mind on a number of routine matters. Went up West that evening for a game of squash with a friend at the RAC and came home feeling better.

During Thursday night the rain eased off and London next day was alternately dripping and drying under intervals of hot sun interrupted by sudden fierce downpours.

The break in the weather seemed to have improved everyone's temper. He hoped that this was a favourable omen for what was going to be a difficult day.

The decoy car was timed to leave the bank at eleven o'clock. He was aware that a good deal of his own future hung on what happened in the next few minutes. He had an illogical faith in the ability in action of Sergeant Stark and very little in the organising power of the sergeant's superior officer. Maybe the two things would balance out. Unable to sit still he opened the window and leaned out, ignoring a steady drip of water from the blocked gutter above him.

His office was no more than 400 yards in a direct line from the bottom of Globe Road and perhaps half a mile from the top. Whilst the rain was beating down he could hear nothing, but when it stopped there was an interval of silence. It was during this that he heard what he had been listening for, and hoping not to hear. Two shots. Then, a full minute later, two more. After that the rain belted down again. Petrella shut the window and mopped his head. Ten minutes later his telephone sounded. As expected, it was Ramsbottom. He sounded as though he had lost a dear relative. Petrella cut him short. He said, "Don't explain anything. Just send Stark and Pearson straight round here," and replaced the receiver gently, but firmly.

When the two sergeants appeared they were wet, but looked cheerful. Petrella said, "Well?"

"Didn't go too badly," said Stark. "Not a hundred per cent success."

"Goalless draw," said Pearson.

"Let's have it all – sit down – from the start."

"The start was when this big estate car pulled out across our bows. The idea was that we would force our way past, let them chase us and lead them into Limehouse Fields, which being a dead-end they couldn't get out of. By that time the supports would be coming up behind us and we'd have them bottled."

"And it didn't work like that?"

"It worked all right. But the wrong way round. To start with, the spot they'd chosen to stop us had been chosen – well – pretty craftily."

"You mean bloody craftily. That's what you were going to say, wasn't it?"

"Right. But seeing as how this is an official report – "

"Your official report can come later. In writing. For now let's have it in your own words."

"Right, sir. Bloody crafty is what it was. A lamp-post on one pavement and a direction post on the other. No chance of squeezing past. So we started to extract ourselves from the van and sort them out."

"Them?"

"The two bastards who'd jumped out of the car – they must have spotted me and Lofty." Stark grinned. "We're pretty well known in that part. Whilst we were climbing out, they got the car turned and pissed off up Globe Road with us on their tails. If I'd had a little more speed I'd have rammed them, but they kept ahead until they tried a skid turn into the road that leads to Limehouse Fields. Whilst they were doing that they ran up onto the pavement and hit a gate post. No real damage. They started backing, but I was out by this time and put two bullets into the car engine."

Whilst he paused for breath, Petrella said, "Let me be clear about one thing. They were deliberately heading for Limehouse Fields?"

"No doubt about it. And now they were on foot and we were back in the van. With the upper hand, you'd have thought. Then, when we turned the corner, we saw the crowd waiting for us. West Indian hunkies. Fifteen or twenty of them. The two men dived in among them. We couldn't drive after them, not without starting a massacre, so we jumped out. The crowd was deliberately blocking us – "

"Laid on for the purpose," agreed Pearson. "All part of the organisation."

" – so I fired two more shots over their heads. This scattered them all right and we got through. A bit too late. By that time their reserve car was on the spot. It must have been hidden in that private garden."

"Meath Gardens?"

"That's the one. Easy enough to get a key, I suppose. The men jumped on board and set off down the track beside the canal. By that time we had got back in the van and started after them, pushing past a few stupid buggers who were trying to commit suicide. Faint, but pursuing, you might say. The canal track wasn't no sort of motorway and the rain had made it so slippery that I thought once or twice we were going into the drink. The other car was doing better. Maybe it had chains on. I don't know. They seem to have thought of most things."

"But," said Petrella, who had been following all this on the map, "they couldn't get away. The path runs up to the Jewish cemetery and stops there."

"So you might think," said Stark with a grin. "I don't know whether that part was good luck or good staff work, but a funeral happened to be going on and both gates were open. They ran straight through and out into the Mile End Road. When we arrived, the gates were shut. Seems they didn't approve of people barging through their sacred ceremonies. Can't blame them, really. By the time we'd explained who we were and they'd let us through there wasn't any point in going on, so we came home."

Petrella thought about it. He supposed that a very careful man would have blocked the cemetery exit gate, but since it was normally kept locked it was hard to blame Ramsbottom for this. And there were more important things to attend to. He said, "When you fired the second time, you said you fired high."

"That's right. I put the shots into the trunk of one of the trees in Meath Gardens, about twelve foot up."

"Both shots?"

"Hit it both times. Not a difficult target."

"Good. I saw from your record that you did the three-month explosive recognition course at Woolwich."

"Most of us did that before we went to Ireland."

"Have you kept in touch with any of the instructors?"

Stark pondered. Pearson said, "Hector's still there. I saw him the other day."

"Sergeant Instructor Hector Lambie. Yes, a good bloke."

"See if you can get hold of him."

"Now?"

"Right away. Tell him that what's wanted urgently is a piece of aid by the military to the civil arm. If there's any trouble I'll square it with his CO."

Whilst Stark was looking up the number and dialling, Petrella went down to talk to Ambrose. He said, "Can you lay on a truck for me with a ladder at least twelve-foot high and have it standing by with a full crew?"

Ambrose said, "Sure." One of his many virtues was that he never asked unnecessary questions.

When Petrella got back to his office he found Stark looking ruffled. He said, "Crowd of box-wallahs. Professional obstructors. What was my name? What did I want? Where was I speaking from? However, I got through in the end. He's coming."

"Excellent."

"One thing I forgot to tell you. I thought I recognised the driver of the get-away car. Not well enough to swear to it in court. Boy I was at the Matthew Holder School with. Len Lampier. Younger than I was, of course. I thought he was a decent sort of kid. Don't know what he's been playing at lately."

"That's something I'd give a lot to know myself," said Petrella. He was thinking about what Lee Morrissey had said; duly reported to him by Hoyland.

They sat in silence for some minutes. Then Stark said, "I hope you won't think it out of order, but there's something I've been meaning to ask you and now seems a chance to mention it." Petrella wondered what was coming. All his guesses were wide of the mark.

"People were saying that when you were on leave you got into a bit of trouble in the desert."

"That's a friendly way of putting it. The truth is, I made a stupid mess of my direction-finding and nearly wrote myself off. That was when I was coming back. Going out I'd noted down directions and distances for each leg. That should have meant that if I followed the reverse directions for the same distances I'd get back to the place I'd started from. It didn't work out. I can only suppose there was something wrong with my compass."

"In some parts of the desert they say there's a lot of ironstone under the sand. Enough to throw an ordinary compass off a point or two. That's why the SAS and the Long Range Desert Group used the sun compass."

Petrella did some hasty arithmetic. He said, "You couldn't have been old enough to take any part in the desert war."

"Old enough? I wasn't even a gleam in my old man's eye. But he used to talk to us about it. He'd enjoyed it, you see. It was clean fighting. Same thing in the SAS when I joined. Operation Jaguar and the action round Mirbat. We were soldiers then, not policemen. The change came when we were sent to Northern Ireland. Not a job for a soldier. Should have been left to armed policemen. That was where I blotted my copybook. I expect you heard about it?"

"I heard about it and I couldn't see that you were to blame."

"I guess that's what the court of enquiry thought. When you've got a situation where one side tries to keep the rules and the other side breaks them all the time, accidents are bound to happen."

He didn't sound bitter about it. A man hardened by hard experiences. He would not allow his feelings to interfere with the notion he had of his duty. If an IRA supporter went into action against you, with one hand under his jacket, that hand might hold a loaded pistol or it might not. Don't chance it. Shoot first. Aim at the arm or leg if possible, but don't hesitate. If a West Indian became aggressive hit him hard, once, where it would hurt. If a reporter was looking for trouble –

At this point the arrival of Sergeant Instructor Hector Lambie interrupted a train of thought that had become uncomfortable.

Lambie was a formidable hunk of regular soldier, not a man to take liberties with, but friendly for the moment because he knew and clearly approved of Stark. Petrella explained briefly what was wanted.

He said, "Meath Gardens is private property and kept locked. The opposition must have picked the lock or broken it. Anyway, I imagine the gate will still be open. We go in there with a ladder and I want you to see if you can locate the tree and the two bullets Sergeant Stark fired into it. About twelve foot up, he says. Then see if you can dig them out. And if you can calculate the angle they went in at, well, that'd be a bonus."

"Doesn't sound too difficult."

"The West Indians who hang out round there may spot us and be hostile. However, we'll have a crew with us who'll be able to keep them quiet while you're doing your stuff."

There was no opposition. Half an hour later they were back in Petrella's office examining the two pieces of lead that Lambie had extracted from the tree. One was twisted out of shape, but the other, which must have gone into a softer part of the tree, was practically intact.

"Police Positive thirty-eight," said Lambie. "No doubt about that."

"Assume," said Petrella, "that the crowd was pretty well filling up that end of the square and the sergeant was standing – how far from the nearest man?"

"About a yard." He looked at Pearson, who nodded and said, "About that."

"And that he fired those two shots which hit the tree twelve foot up."

"Thirteen," said Lambie. "I measured it." As he spoke he was drawing a plan showing the relevant heights and distances.

"Could he have hit anyone in the crowd?"

"Well, now," said Lambie, "by my calculations if one of the men in the crowd was ten feet high, he might have parted his hair for him."

Everyone laughed. Petrella said, "Could you let me have a short report in writing? No need to mention names. Set it out as a problem in geometry. X standing there. Y there. The bullet hitting the tree at point Z."

"I could do that all right," said Lambie. "But if I'm going to have to swear to it in court, I'd need to go higher up to get permission. They're a bit shy about getting mixed up in legal matters."

"We'll cross that bridge when we come to it. I think it's most unlikely that we're heading for court. None the less, I'll feel happier with that report in my pocket."

"Are you expecting trouble, then?"

"All I can say at the moment is that I've a feeling there's a storm coming. The barometer's going down and there are some nasty looking black clouds on the horizon. When a prudent mariner feels like that he shortens sail and makes all as safe as he can."

16

Her Majesty's Secretary of State for Home Affairs, the Honourable Geoffrey Tredinnick, was certainly no fool. The worst the Opposition could find to say about him was that his early training in the City would have fitted him better to be Chancellor of the Exchequer. And he knew and respected Frank Lovell. As Deputy Commissioner, Lovell headed all CID operations and was a very hot tip to be the next Commissioner. If the central pivot of police power was to mesh smoothly, they would have to work hand in glove.

He had summoned Lovell to his room and got straight down to business.

"I don't need to remind you," he said, "that in the late seventies and early eighties the relationship between the police and the press was at a very low ebb. No doubt there were faults on both sides. When Robert Mark became Commissioner one of his greatest achievements was to rebuild confidence. He did it by insisting that the papers should be given the facts, in every case, no matter how damaging they might be to individuals. If you don't give them the facts, he used to say, they'll invent them. There was considerable opposition in police circles, but it proved to be the right answer. You agree?"

"I think there are still a few cases," said Lovell, "where, as far as the great British public are concerned, ignorance is bliss. But in general, yes, I agree with you. What particular case had you in mind?"

"No secret about that. I had half an hour yesterday

evening with Callaghan, the editor of the *Sentinel*. Not a bad chap, as editors go. Ruthless as all come, but not unwilling to co-operate. I didn't care much for the lawyer he brought with him. A barrister called Andrew Batson. We had him in a case when I was in the City. He won it, by bullying the witnesses on the other side."

Lovell said, "He was on his feet a good deal during the inquest on Poston-Pirrie. I wasn't there, but I've read the report. The coroner kept a firm hand on him, I was glad to see."

"If you've read the report you'll appreciate the case he was trying to set up."

"Surely. He was fixing the locus of the crime as Cannon Wharf – or maybe a short distance above it at a place where Cable Street crosses the Commercial Road. In his scenario that is the place where Sergeant Stark – who knew that Poston-Pirrie was visiting the Athletic Club – was waiting to continue an argument which had started in the bar of the White Horse. All that his script lacked was an account of what had actually happened in that bar."

"Which, I gather, he hasn't been able to find out."

"His man, Wintringham, had another session with the landlord. Reading between the lines I guess he must have tried to frighten him, by waving subpoenas at him, and only succeeded in gumming him up entirely. In fact, he not only went dumb, but took back anything he had said before."

"The whole thing sounded a bit thin to me," said Tredinnick. "Whatever was said, could it have been so offensive that Stark was prepared to wait, for an hour or more, and then to hit Pirrie so hard that – whether he meant it to or not – it finished him?"

"Their whole case rests on their estimate of Stark's character. Based on his record in Ireland and the things he has done since he came here."

"The things he has done here?"

"Hitting any West Indian who talked out of turn.

And firing into a crowd of them to clear them out of his way."

Both men thought about it for an appreciable time.

Then Lovell said, "If the case had been put to me when I was at the Bar I'd have said that it had a fatal hole in it. And until that hole was filled, my clients would be ill-advised to take it to court."

"And how would you have suggested that they set about filling it? If they don't know who was in the bar and no one's prepared to tell them, they're stuck."

"Only one thing to do. They'd have to persuade the men's superintendent to co-operate."

"Petrella?"

"Right. I'm sure he knows exactly who was there. And if he passed the names to Batson and allowed him to cross-examine them, he'd soon have the whole story."

"Do you think he'd be likely to agree?"

"Difficult to say. In theory, I'm sure he'd support the Robert Mark thesis. Let the truth be told whoever it hurts. But it's difficult to be certain. He's got a mind of his own. In fact, a remarkable man all round. If he doesn't blot his copybook now, he could go right to the top."

"Then let's hope he will co-operate. Because, from something Callaghan let drop, I gather they're busy constructing a bomb to blow him up. With enthusiastic help from some City types. He wasn't very forthcoming about that part of it, but I gathered that the superintendent had been after one of their pet rackets and was beginning to tread on their heels. If that's true it's a formidable combination. Press and City."

"However formidable, they can only smear someone if they've got dirt to do it with."

"Don't you believe it," said Tredinnick. "If they gave their horrible minds to it they could smear the Archangel Gabriel."

Lovell thought about it. Then he said, "Best will be to

get Morrissey to talk to him. He mightn't listen to me, but he'll listen to him."

At the same time an equally important, if slightly lower-level, conference was taking place. Arnold, Delroy and Winston were deep in discussion. They no longer dared to use the Packstone Building. Their new meeting place was a very large packing-case which had once contained the works of a diesel engine and had been dumped at the back of Murgatroyd's Shipyard. Since the shipyard had been closed months before and was unlikely to re-open, they felt reasonably secure from outside interference.

Which was as well, in view of the matters they had to discuss.

"How much did we get last night?" said Winston.

"All he had," said Arnold. "Every last penny. We cleaned him right out." Any other boy would have laughed. Arnold only smiled; the tight smile of a professional gambler.

"All *and* a bit more," said Delroy. "He had to borrow from the gr'iller who comes to look after him. Nor he wasn't keen to let him have the money neither. I heard him say, 'You pay me back tomorrow or I'll tell your ma.' "

Winston said, "She'd belt him good if she found out he'd been playing cards for money."

"And he knows it," said Delroy.

The skinning of Barry had gone according to plan. In three evening sessions they had scooped up all of his generous pocket money and now he was in debt.

"What's the next move?" said Winston.

"When he turns up this evening – "

"If he turns up."

"He'll come all right. He's got to try and win back some of what he's lost, hasn't he?"

Losers always did that.

"Like I was saying, we offer him cash for his information."

"How much?" said Winston and Delroy in unison.

"How much have we got?"

Pockets were turned out and a count was taken.

"Eleven pounds eighty. Right. We offer Barry ten quid."

The other two boys normally followed Arnold without demur. On this occasion there were rumblings of dissent.

From Winston, "Suppose we give him the money and he hasn't really got anything to tell us." And from Delroy, "Or if he hangs onto the money we give him and asks for more."

"If he did anything like that, he knows what'd happen to him. He's yellow, see. He doesn't like the idea of being hurt. If he takes our money he's *got* to come across with something good, or he'll be half-killed. He knows that. And anyway, what have we got to lose? It's his money."

His allies considered the point. It was perfectly true. Any money that was paid him would have come out of his own pocket.

"OK," said Winston. "But where's *our* pay-off?"

"Our pay-off comes when I see that superintendent and pass on what Barry has told us. And I tell him it cost us ten quid to get it. He'll fork up."

"Tell him twenty quid," said Delroy.

"All right. Twenty quid." He'd been going to ask for that anyway and pocket the difference. Now he'd have to make it twenty-five. The trouble with having greedy allies.

Morrissey had been a sergeant in the uniform branch when Lovell was a recruit, and though Lovell had climbed further and faster, a little of the old relationship still remained. In all matters affecting the conduct and well-being of their service they looked with a single eye. The police were a band of brothers. There were two enemies: the criminal whom it was their job to pursue and the public who got under their feet when they were chasing him.

Later that morning Lovell passed on, with minimal omissions, what the Home Secretary had said to him. It appeared that he had been talked into accepting Stark in the Metropolitan Police by the head of the Anti-Terrorist Branch. It had been put to him that this was necessary protection of the sergeant and an acknowledgment of his services in Northern Ireland. The *Sentinel*, which had been critical of his conduct at the time of the incident in Northern Ireland and had denounced his acquittal as a political job, now had all its guns pointed at him. They were convinced that he was responsible for the death of their man Poston-Pirrie.

"Do you believe that?" said Morrissey.

"Speaking as a lawyer, I'd say they haven't got a legal case, but quite enough to make a newspaper case."

"Based on the fact that killing Poston-Pirrie was an act of violence and Stark is a violent man?"

"If you like to put it that way, yes. They've got a long list of individual acts of violence. And now this business of firing into a crowd to disperse it. I gather that one of the West Indians was lucky to escape with a bullet hole in the sleeve of his jacket. He's given them an affidavit."

"And has produced the jacket as evidence?" said Morrissey repressing a grin.

"I imagine so. What's the joke?"

Morrissey laid in front of him a copy which Petrella had sent him of Lambie's statement, with a plan attached to it. Lovell read it through twice. At the second reading he, too, was smiling.

Morrissey said, "He's had the other two bullets dug out of the car engine as well. Stark's gun and ammunition were checked when he got back to the station. Four shots fired, four bullets used. He's got that in writing from Ramsbottom."

"He *is* being careful, isn't he?" said Lovell.

Morrissey said, "He's an odd mixture. Part of the time he plays the police game straight down the middle like a real professional – like he's done over these bullets. Other times he behaves like a reckless amateur. I've got two whole squads deployed in this area. They aren't there to spy on Petrella, but somehow they always seem to be running up against him. He's been seen more than once in the Isle of Dogs with three street urchins of murky character. And one of my men who was watching the Quartermass Club – incidentally, both Farmer and Hicks are known to use it – noted him making at least one visit there, when it seems he was drinking with a notorious pornographer."

"Are you telling me that this is another Hood case?"

"No. I think he's too crafty and too experienced to let himself be led by the nose down that track. The real trouble is that the wild side of his character makes him like and approve of Stark."

Lovell was looking at the diagram on the paper in front of him, with its careful annotation by Sergeant Instructor Lambie. He said, "OK, I agree. He's got a complete answer to the charge of shooting into the crowd. But what about all the other charges? The *Sentinel* has got a long list, ranging from casual brutality to actual assault. What I was wondering was, is Ramsbottom the right man to control Stark? And if he's allowed to carry on unchecked, may we be provoking a West Indian riot?"

Morrissey took his time over answering this. The possibility was one which hung over them all the time. In the end he said, "No, I don't think so. I'd have said that, for the most part, our second generation West Indians are settling down. A lot of them are making money. They don't want trouble. Only one lot – the Limehouse Fields crowd – are really dangerous. And that's because they're organised by some remarkable men. The character known as Torpedo Hicks and the Farm Boys. Leonard Farmer is the boss. He actually is a farmer, of sorts. He's got a few acres out at Hagley, mostly pasture which he leases to people with horses. His wife, who's as bad as he is, looks after it. The others are professional thugs. Buller is a part-time butcher. Henty, who they call Dog, is a bookmaker's runner in his spare time. Goat Glibbery looks after a second-hand clothes shop, and Soltau, known as Piggy – in my view the nastiest of a nasty bunch – he used to be a doctor, but got struck off and jugged after a messy abortion which killed the girl. When he came out he got a job at a garage, which will do surprising things to your car."

"If you managed to get them on the run, which of them do you think would be most likely to crack and come across?"

"My money would be on Soltau. But he'll only talk if the others are safely locked up."

"So what comes next?"

"Friday week could be D-Day – if we chose to play it that way. They've now failed, twice, to get their hands on the ELBO pay packet and everyone knows it. This time they'll put out their full strength. Hicks can call out a couple of dozen West Indians, or more."

"And if we field enough men to hold them, that'll mean open war. Which will give the papers a field day."

"Right. And that's why I'd like to wrap up the top men *before* war breaks out."

"Do you think you can do it?"

"With an average amount of luck," said Morrissey, placing one thumb firmly on the wooden desk in front of him, "I think I can."

"We didn't have much luck with Flower."

"Not a lot. But it taught me a lesson. One or two lessons in fact."

"The main one," said Lovell, with the hint of a smile lifting his tight lawyer's mouth, "was to keep your plans to yourself."

"Right. And I'm aiming for them to stay that way, for the moment. If you're agreeable, that is."

"Provided you tell me, personally, what you're planning to do, before you do it, not after."

"I read that as a vote of confidence," said Morrissey smiling in his turn. "And now, since we don't want two wars on our hands at once, I'd better try and get Petrella to pacify the *Sentinel*. I'll talk to him on Monday. I find people tend to be a bit more receptive after a quiet weekend with their families."

"I don't think I've met his wife."

"She's a grand girl. Used to be in the Probation Service. And I guess she's about the only person in the world that would get him to change his mind once he's made it up."

The weekend was quiet, but Monday was another busy day. A hotch-potch of things Petrella wanted to do and things he had to do. Just before lunch Milo telephoned. He said, "Those three outfits you asked me to look up. Have you got your pencil poised? Right. The directors of the Anglo-Netherland Shipbuilding Company are James Hardaker, William Piper, Colin Mayle -- spelt with a 'y' – Toby Ringland and Graham Mayle. None of the names meant anything to me, though they may do to you."

"One of them does," said Petrella. "On you go."

"The merchant bankers, Angus, Hardy and Glenister, are just that. Donald Angus, David Hardy and Ray Glenister. They're a newish outfit. Been going for less than ten years. The insurance brokers were a bit of a problem. They don't print the names of their partners on their note paper. It used to be obligatory, but now they can get away with a statement that 'A list of the names of partners is maintained at their head office and can be inspected by appointment during business hours.' In the light of what you told me I didn't think you'd want me ferreting round at their office, but one of our boys has had dealings with them lately and he said that the man who made all the decisions was a chap called Bob Seamark. Does that give you what you want?"

"It gives me exactly what I want," said Petrella. Or almost exactly, as he told himself after Milo had rung off. Glenister was mentioned in Father Freeling's brochure. Ringland had featured in Hoyland's adventures and misadventures in Amsterdam. The brochure listed Franz Mittelbach and Partners as one of the corporate contributors and if Bob Seamark was the man who pulled the strings, it was reasonable to suppose that it was he who had decided that the partnership should contribute to this excellent charity.

Toby Ringland, Bob Seamark.

The odds were shortening.

Coming back from lunch in the nearest sandwich bar, he found Morrissey occupying the visitor's chair. He was smoking a filthy black pipe and looked relaxed and comfortable. He said, "I've been talking to the DC." Pause for a puff of smoke. "And he's been talking to the Home Secretary." Puff. "They're both singing the same song. They don't want trouble with the West Indian community."

"You can add my voice to that chorus," said Petrella.

"Or with the press."

He cocked a weather eye at Petrella as he said this and noted the slight stiffening in his attitude.

He said, "It depends what you mean. If it's simply that we shouldn't go out of our way to antagonise the press, then I'd go along with that. But if you mean that we should do exactly what they want us to, I'm afraid I should have to reserve judgment."

"Really, it's half-way between the two." It was clear to Petrella that Morrissey was picking his words with great care. "Seems we might be on collision course with both of 'em. Equally, it seems we could avoid any sort of confrontation easily enough. The key figure in both spots of trouble is your Sergeant Stark. The *Sentinel* are sure that he either killed Poston-Pirrie or had a hand in his death. And they think that you're keeping the truth from them."

"Indeed. Just how am I supposed to be doing that?"

"You're doing it by not letting them have the facts they want. You could cut both knots by allowing Batson to

189

question the men who were at the White Horse that evening."

"I have no control over Batson. If he wants to question them, it's up to him to try. I don't think he'll get much joy out of it."

"What's preventing him from trying it," said Morrissey, with another gentle puff from his pipe, "is that he doesn't know who was there. But you do know."

"Yes. I know who was there. Or most of them."

"So you give the names to the *Sentinel*. And tell the men that if they're questioned it's with your consent. Nothing more. You don't press them to talk to Batson. You just don't stand in his way."

"In fact," said Petrella, "they want my help in setting up one of my own men for trial by the press."

"Put it that way, it sounds dirty," agreed Morrissey. "Put it another way, all they're asking for is the facts."

"Which they'll twist to suit their own brief." When Morrissey said nothing he added, "What happens if I tell them to take a running jump at themselves?"

"If you won't co-operate, likely you'll find yourself in trouble."

"The same sort of trouble that Hood found himself in?"

He said this so coldly that Morrissey, who was not the most sensitive of men, felt the ice and the steel in his voice and was, for a moment, shaken.

He had spent a lot of time recently looking up Petrella's record. He was fully aware of his good points, which were many, and his bad points, which were few, but he had never before seen his feelings stripped bare. To gain time he said, "The answer is yes and no. No, because Hood was a fool and you're not. The DC enjoyed the ten-foot West Indian who got his hair parted by a shot that went through his sleeve. But yes, because it seems the *Sentinel* has been doing a strip search of your past, present and future. Particularly your activities in the City. And they've been getting enthusiastic help from certain high-ups there. Have you been buying any shares lately?"

"Yes. As a matter of fact, I have. I was given full pay whilst I was away and as I was living with, and on, my father, my expenses were trivial. So I found I'd got a bit of capital. I asked an old friend of mine, Milo Roughead – he used to be one of my sergeants – to invest it for me."

"Do you know what he put it into?"

"No. I left that to him."

"I see," said Morrissey thoughtfully. "It's never easy to sort out this sort of thing at second-hand. Why don't you have a word with Lovell?"

"I don't imagine that the Deputy Commissioner really wants to waste time gossiping with a junior superintendent."

"It was his suggestion. I was to tell you that he'd be available at ten o'clock on Wednesday – if that fitted in with your commitments."

Petrella looked at his desk diary, but it was only a gesture. He knew very well that a suggestion from the Deputy Commissioner was tantamount to an order. He said, "I've got nothing I can't put off."

Noting the mule-like expression on his face Morrissey said, "One thing you've got to remember, Lovell's a lot more important in your young life than I am. Come the end of the year I go out. He goes up."

"I'll bear it in mind," said Petrella.

The telephone call from the hospital came at half past four on Tuesday afternoon. Petrella had just concluded two long and tiresome conversations, the first with Ramsbottom at HC, the second, as long, but less tiresome, with Trench at HD. Dr Burden sounded upset. He said, "I've been trying to get through to you for nearly an hour. Now, it may be too late."

"Damn, damn and damn," said Petrella. "When you

told them who you were, why the hell didn't someone have the sense to put you through?"

"Can't be helped. If you come round quickly you may still – "

Without giving him time to finish the sentence, Petrella slammed down the receiver, and sprinted for the basement garage. Fortunately both Hoyland and the runabout were there. He gave his instructions as he was getting into the car, adding, "As quick as you like."

For the next few minutes he wondered whether he had been rash, but providence turned all the red lights green.

When, still breathless, he was shown up to the small room in the Intensive Care Unit where the hospital had been fighting for Thresher's life, he met the doctor and the nurse coming out and knew that he was too late.

"I've noticed before," said Dr Burden, "that when a patient has been in a coma for a long period, there is often a short moment of lucidity when he comes out of it. In fact, that's usually a signal that the end is near."

"And that's what happened?"

"Yes. Very briefly. It was clear that he wanted, desperately, to say something. I was sitting on one side of the bed and the nurse was on the other side and he was turning his head, first to one of us, then the other, and I could see his lips moving. Then he said something. A few words and something that could have been a name. But too softly for me to make any sense of it."

"And then?"

"That was all."

"I'm truly sorry," said Petrella.

"No need to be. If you'd been here in time it wouldn't have made any difference."

As they were speaking they were walking down a long corridor, with doors on either side of it. The doctor paused outside one of the wards, offered his hand to Petrella in a gesture of sympathy, and disappeared into it.

The nurse had gone through a door on the other

side of the corridor into a room which contained two benches, a row of shining brass taps and a number of empty bedpans. Looking at her for the first time he noticed two things. First, that though no longer young she was an attractive-looking woman, with a face which carried lines of experience and determination. Clearly one of the senior nurses. The second thing, which was equally clear, was that she had something to say to him.

He followed her into the room and, obeying a small gesture of her hand, shut the door. When she spoke, her voice placed her, as her face had done, in the upper reaches of the middle class.

She said, "I'm afraid Dr Burden was not being entirely frank with you."

"No?"

"As he told you, we were sitting on either side of the patient when he died."

She did not say 'went' or 'passed on'. She had seen death too many times to be mealy-mouthed about it.

"We could both hear anything that Mr Thresher said. In fact, when he did speak he was facing the doctor, but although his head was turned away from me I could hear him perfectly clearly. He said, 'The man who let me in for this was called Seamark.' Then, again, 'Tell the police, Bob Seamark.' "

The silence which followed seemed to last a long time. Then Petrella gave a little sigh, as though he was emptying his lungs of their last fraction of breath, and said, "You're quite sure about the name?"

"Oh, quite sure."

"If you had to stand up in court and swear to it, do you think you could do that?"

"I could swear that that's what Thresher said. Dr Burden would swear that he said nothing. When a doctor and a nurse disagree, it's the doctor's version that's accepted. That's a matter of protocol, you understand."

"Then you think Dr Burden would be prepared to lie, on oath."

"In this case, I think he might do so."

"Why in this case?"

"Sir Robert Seamark is chairman of the Hospital Finance Committee. And they say he's made very generous contributions to our funds out of his own pocket."

"I see," said Petrella. A number of things were becoming plainer. "You realise that if you give evidence it will almost certainly get you into trouble?"

"Trouble?" said the nurse. "There's so much of it around these days that everyone's bound to run into it sooner or later, don't you think?"

Looking at her face, composed, but resolute, Petrella thought what an excellent witness she would make.

"Poor old boy," she said. "It was his last wish and it cost him all the life that was left in him to get it out. How could I stand by and let it be brushed aside and buried? As for the money Sir Robert handed over, that didn't weigh with me. Why should it? He's probably got plenty." With the beginning of a smile she added, "I might have been more sympathetic if it hadn't all been spent on fancy equipment and a little of it had gone to improving our pay."

17

At nine o'clock on Wednesday morning, Petrella warned
Ambrose that he would be away and unavailable for two
hours, and told him where he was going. Ambrose said,
with a smile, "If you're taking the station runabout you'd
better let Hoyland drive it. He seems to have adopted that
machine and constituted himself your chauffeur."

"Thank you," said Petrella. "I've only just recovered
from my last experience of being driven by Hoyland in
a hurry. This time I've got plenty of time and I'm going
on foot."

It was a perfect morning. A succession of showers had
washed away the dirt and depression of the long summer
drought and the sun was shining once more, but without
its previous ferocity. August had turned the corner into
September and there was already a faint foretaste of
autumn in the air.

He set out, following the Commercial Road until it
became Fenchurch Street, thrust through the confusion
round the Bank and made his way up Cheapside where
the dome of St Paul's rode above the City. Here he had
a choice of ways and decided to strike south, onto the
Embankment, which he could follow as far as the other
great London church, at Westminster. Here he was within
easy distance of his destination.

How many days ago was it that he had taken that
other walk down to the Isle of Dogs, visualising, as he
went along, the roller-coaster on which he was a captive
passenger? Only now the other car had a different crew.

The Farm Boys and Hicks were still there, but relegated to the second seat. The front row was full of well-dressed City types, arm-in-arm in token of friendship and community of purpose. Men who would give money to hospitals and subscribe to sending poor boys abroad. Yes, and would recoup their outlay by making obscene video films and selling them to their acquaintances, and using the muscle of the thugs sitting behind them to keep those acquaintances in line.

There was one odd thing about the set-up. Surely a properly thought out roller-coaster was designed so that the cars followed each other. Here it seemed that when his car started on its downward sweep it must run head first into the other car grinding its way up.

"Odd sort of construction," he said.

"I beg your pardon," said a young man who had come up close behind him.

"Talking to myself," said Petrella. "Bad habit." He turned into the steel and glass battleship which was New Scotland Yard. He was shown straight up to the Deputy Commissioner's office. Lovell, who seemed also to have been influenced by the weather, was at his most charming and persuasive. He wasted no time on preliminaries. In exactly the way that he would, at the Bar, have opened a case to the jury, he subjected Petrella to a closely reasoned, quietly convincing pattern of argument. As the interlocking sentences followed each other, Petrella was guiltily aware that he was paying them less attention than he should have done.

His mind was running on different rails.

He was aware that Lovell held most of the cards. Whilst he could not sack him – at least, not without some definite and demonstrable grounds – there was nothing to prevent him taking him away from his present job and shunting him into some administrative siding where he would be harmless. He realised, too, that if Lovell really was in line for the top job, the one thing that might stop him being promoted to such a politically sensitive post was bad trouble with the West Indians.

Having sorted this out in his mind he was able to ignore the special pleading and concentrate on the single point that mattered to him personally.

Accordingly, when the time came for him to speak, he said, "It's true that I know the names of most of the men who were present in the back room of the White Horse at the time you mentioned. And I know, in outline, what was said. The information was entrusted to me by one of the men who was there, in the confidence, I'm sure, that I should not repeat it. You're therefore asking me to do something which is totally repugnant to me. If the *Sentinel* raise the matter again, you'll have to tell them that I won't help them to set up a newspaper tribunal to try Sergeant Stark. Either for general brutality, or on the specific charge, which I personally don't believe, of having been responsible for the death of their man Poston-Pirrie."

When saying this he managed to keep his voice and delivery as matter-of-fact and unemphatic as possible. He did not wish to sound as though he was making a speech from the scaffold.

Lovell accepted the rebuff calmly. He said, "As long as you realise that you're charging headlong at one of the most powerful and unscrupulous outfits in London."

Petrella said, with a smile, "Have you ever seen a bull fight, sir?"

"Never. And never wanted to."

"If you had, you'd realise that the matador doesn't charge headlong at the bull. He waits for the bull to charge at him."

Lovell said, "Yes, I suppose that's right."

After Petrella had left he sat for several minutes, looking down at his desk. Oddly enough, he was not thinking about Petrella at all. He was thinking about his father, Colonel of Police Gregorio Petrella, whom he had met once, at a conference in Paris, and who had impressed him greatly.

He knew that he had spent most of his career as a young man protecting Franco from assassination. Now retired from active policing, he was an accepted authority on the combating of terrorism. There had been a suggestion that he was planning to come to England. If he did, Lovell wondered whether he might be able to divert his son from the dangerous course he seemed set on.

When he left the DC's room Petrella made his way down to the basement. In one of the cell-like rooms at the back he found the man he was looking for, an old friend from Highside days, Detective Sergeant Golightly, who said, "Wotcher, Patrick. I mean, hullo, sir."

"Stick to Patrick."

Golightly grinned and said, "What can the scientific boys do for you?"

"I just wanted to know something." He extracted from his pocket the much creased page of pictures which had caused so much trouble to a harmless newsagent. He pointed to the faint mark on the back. "Assume, as I think you can, that that's I.P. Would it be difficult for you to identify the publication?"

"With a little bit of luck," said Golightly, "it would take me all of sixty seconds."

He went across to a filing cabinet in the corner. The files seemed to be arranged alphabetically. He extracted one of them, flipped through it and said, "It looks like an outfit called Intriguing Publications. They publish quite a few magazines. This would be one of them." He examined the page of pictures. "Looks like something that wouldn't be a great loss. Are you planning to shut them up?"

"Ultimately, possibly. For the moment, all I wanted to know was whether it was difficult to identify the mark."

"By my watch, forty-five seconds," said Golightly smugly.

That evening after both the children were in bed, Jane suspended her evening sewing marathon to say, "You're worried about something. If it's confidential don't tell me, but if it isn't, it might help you to get it off your chest."

"It isn't confidential. In fact, it's no more than a rather uncomfortable idea I got after I'd been to that club."

"The one you told me about. The Quartermass?"

"That's the one. It looked such an obvious set-up. It was the place where photographs had been taken of Hood drinking with known pornographers. And there was one of them, with drinks on the table, one of them all ready to be pushed across in my direction."

"But you didn't pick it up."

"Actually, I pushed it back again. But in a photograph taken from one side, it wouldn't be possible to say that it wasn't my drink. And I don't doubt there were other known porno characters, ready to surge up. Maybe a group picture was planned. That's why I got out so fast. But I couldn't help reflecting that *if* it was a trap, it was Charlie Kay who got me into it."

"I follow that," said Jane. "But it's not conclusive. This porno character could have suggested to Kay that he had a hot tip for you and Kay could have passed the news to you without realising what he might be letting you in for."

"That's what I told myself. I didn't want to think that Kay was bent. I've known him, on and off, for years and always liked him. I was glad to give him the fullest benefit of any doubt there was. Then this afternoon something else happened. I'd asked him to locate a printer's mark for me. A day or two later he told me that he couldn't do it. It wasn't registered. Golightly, who works in that department, found it at once."

"Might that simply have been slackness on Kay's part? He didn't want to bother about it, so he simply told you it wasn't on."

"Yes, I thought of that, too. And what's more, all things being equal, it was no part of my job to suggest that one of the bods in Central was playing for both sides. But all things weren't equal, or not quite. The trouble is I know

199

that Morrissey's plans to deal with the Farm Boys are coming to the boil."

"How do you know that?"

"His daughter, Lee, guessed he was up to something. She told Hoyland and he told me."

"Third hand."

"It may be third hand, but I've worked with the old boy before and I'm as sure as I can be that he's got something devious in the offing. So far he's been keeping his cards close to his chest, but when the moment comes, he may need help. Suppose he plans to bring Kay in on it. He did last time."

"And last time," said Jane thoughtfully, "his plans were blown."

"Yes. I thought about that, too."

"But if you do say anything to Morrissey, and Kay's innocent, you could be doing him irreparable harm."

"All right. Those are the facts. Let's have the judgment of the court."

Jane thought about it whilst she concluded a line of stitching and snapped the cotton. Then, once more, she succeeded in surprising him.

She said, "It seems to me more an ethical problem than a practical one. Do you accept the responsibility of keeping your mouth shut, or do you risk hurting Kay? I had a phone call from Father Freeling this morning. He told me he has a short service every Thursday morning at eight. If we went along we could be back by nine. Mrs Gamage would keep an eye on the kids." Mrs Gamage was the widow of a police sergeant who lived in the flat below.

"You're not suggesting that I should put the problem to Freeling?"

"Certainly not. What I thought was that the excursion might clear your mind."

"Well, so it might," said Petrella. "I'm willing to try."

When they reached the church next morning and slipped into a seat at the back, the nave was nearly half-full; an astonishing congregation for a London church on a week-day. The congregation consisted mostly of middle-aged and elderly women with a scattering of men and a few children. The service was a shortened form of morning prayer.

When Father Freeling preached, Petrella decided that he was communing with himself rather than with the congregation. For most of the time he was looking down at the book-rest on the pulpit, as though he was reading his sermon, although clearly he was doing no such thing. On one occasion, when he lifted his eyes to the back of the church, he seemed to be speaking directly to Petrella and his wife.

"All of us, at one time or another," he said, "are faced with a problem to which there seems to be no rational solution. In such cases it is best to take the course which may hurt you, but will do as little harm as possible to anyone else."

When the service was over he moved to the door, not to speak to people as they went out, but to smile at them and shake an occasional hand. He smiled with particular kindness at the Petrellas.

As they were walking home Petrella said, "Well, I asked for guidance and I certainly got it. I'm to say nothing about Kay and hope for the best."

Jane said, "I wonder. Were you so engrossed with your own problem that you didn't think about his?"

"Father Freeling. Has he got a problem?"

"He's a deeply troubled man," said Jane. But said no more until they got home and encountered an apologetic Mrs Gamage on the stairs.

"I hope I did right to let him in," she said. "Seeing he was only a boy I diddun think he could do any harm."

"That's all right," said Jane. "I expect it's some school friend of Donald's."

"Diddun look like a school friend," said Mrs Gamage doubtfully.

They found Donald sitting at one side of the dining-room

table. Arnold was on the other side. Donald's money-box had been up-ended and there was one pile of coins beside him and a smaller one beside Arnold, who was shuffling a greasy pack of cards.

"I've been gammelling," said Donald.

"Born lucky, that boy," said Arnold. "He's got more of my money than I done of his."

"It was a very intresting game," said Donald. "Lucy squawked once, but I put a pillow over her face to stop her."

"You did *what*?" said his mother, racing from the room.

Donald winked at his father. "Of course I didn't do that. I just told her to pipe down. She always does what I say."

Lucinda, back with her mother and freed from the iron control of her brother, had started to give tongue. Petrella said, coldly, "I imagine that you've come here because you've got something important to tell me."

"That's right," said Arnold. He was pocketing his pile of coins and seemed unperturbed. "Better if I told you private, really."

"We can talk in the kitchen."

When Jane came back with a pacified Lucinda she set about clearing the table of cards and money and laying breakfast. The conversation continued in the kitchen. Most of it was in Arnold's voice. When it finished and Petrella led the way out, he was feeling for his note-case. After a moment of thought he extracted one ten-pound and two five-pound notes and handed them to Arnold.

"For the moment," he said, "that's all you can have. If what you've told me leads to a definite conclusion, then there'll be more. Another twenty at least."

Arnold pocketed the notes. He seemed neither pleased nor sorry. As he went he was followed by a thoughtful look from Donald who seemed to be thinking that, given half a chance, he could win back some of the money his father was dishing out so freely.

"Now if I might be allowed back into the kitchen," said

Jane, "I could carry on cooking breakfast." Then she saw the look on Petrella's face and said, "Was it bad?"

"If it was true, it could be very bad. I shall have to telephone. I'll use the one in the bedroom." First he tried the rectory and got no answer. Even if Martha was in, he supposed that she was too deaf to hear the bell. The church had a number in the book. Presumably a telephone in the vestry. He tried this and after a few rings a woman's voice said, "Yes?"

"I was wondering whether I could speak to Father Freeling."

"He's been gone some time. I'm not sure where he'd be. This is Mrs Parks. I'm the vicar's warden. Can I help?"

"If you could get a message to him. It's Superintendent Petrella speaking. I'd like a word with him. Could you suggest tomorrow at nine o'clock, at the rectory?"

"He's a very busy man these days. I'm not sure whether – "

"If you tell him that it's about Barry, I'm sure he'll make himself available."

"Barry?"

"That's right. It's a boy's name. He'll understand."

"Do what I can," said Mrs Parks.

Petrella did not sleep well that night, but he got more sleep than many of the staff of the *Sentinel*. The result of their night's work appeared next morning in the form of a leading article.

It had been closely scrutinised by the paper's legal advisers, who had expressed misgivings. A lengthy debate had been closed by the editor who had said, "It's my responsibility. If it raises a storm, we can weather it. And if the winds blow hard enough they may blow away that bully, Stark, and his bloody superintendent."

The article was headed by the single word, 'Obstruction'.

From time to time this paper has been critical of the

actions of the SAS Regiment in Northern Ireland. It was appreciated that they were faced with a difficult problem. In many ways they were on active service, fighting an enemy as well armed as they were and a lot freer to use those arms. Our comments, therefore, were made, we hope, in a constructive way. On the other hand we did criticise, very strongly, the action of the authorities in electing to bring back a particular member of the SAS, removing him from the restraints and discipline of his regiment and enrolling him as a member of the Metropolitan Police Force. Since his arrival in east London this paper has received a string of complaints of the brutal treatment of West Indians in this area. Many of them may have been exaggerated and it was certainly not our intention to mount a campaign against one man when the complaints were of a type which has, unfortunately, become very general.

Now our hand has been forced. A representative of the paper was pursuing enquiries in this district. Some days ago his body was recovered from the entrance channel of one of the disused docks. The pathologist, Dr Summerson, whose opinion is widely and rightly respected, reported that he could have been killed or rendered unconscious by a single blow, from a fist or hand, before being tumbled into the river.

If only in support and protection of its own staff, the *Sentinel* felt bound to investigate the matter as thoroughly as possible and to offer a substantial reward for information. A curious story came to light. It seems – and for reasons which will become clear we can go no further at the moment than to say it seems – that on the evening of what proved to be the last day of his life, our man was involved in an argument, in a public house in White Horse Road, with the ex-member of the SAS and a number of his colleagues. We fully realised that this did not, of itself, amount to any sort of proof that the SAS man might have continued the argument later that evening, and that it might have been his hand, trained as it was to violence, that had struck the fatal blow. Almost everything depended on what had, in fact, taken place in that public house.

We wanted only to arrive at the truth. If the argument had been a friendly one, then it was highly unlikely that a member of the Metropolitan Police would have tried to take the law into his own hands. On the other hand, if the argument was violent and acrimonious, the possibility did exist and needed investigation.

Unfortunately the well-known tactic of the police, to close ranks if one of their members might be in trouble, has hampered our investigation. Is it too much to ask the authorities to order a full disclosure of the facts and to remind the superintendent concerned that he owes a duty to the public, as well as to his own force?

Since the *Sentinel* was not his normal morning paper, Petrella had not read this thundering effusion when setting out for the rectory. On his previous visit the front door had stood hospitably open. Now it was shut, and ringing and knocking produced no answer. When he suspended his assault and listened he thought he heard the sound of someone moving about. This worried him enough to send him round to the back of the house, where he found the kitchen door not only unlocked, but half open. He knocked again and now heard, quite clearly, the sound of shuffling footsteps, but no one appeared.

He went in, and crossed the kitchen. There was a breakfast tray of congealed and uneaten food on the table. The omens were unpleasantly clear.

Standing in the hall he listened again. The shuffling footsteps on the floor above had now stopped and the only sound he could hear was the ticking of the grandfather clock, keeping time with the beating of his own heart, as he climbed the stairs.

Martha was crouched outside one of the bedroom doors.

She hardly looked up as Petrella approached, but continued muttering and mumbling without producing any words that made sense. Petrella opened the door and went in. He had known for some minutes what he would find.

The rector was lying on his bed, on his side, covered by a single blanket. His knees were drawn half-way up to his chest as though by some sharp agony which, at the last moment, he had tried to control. He had clearly been dead for some hours. On the table, by the bed, was an envelope which Petrella noted, without surprise, was addressed to him. He opened it. The writing which covered two folded sheets of paper was firm and well spaced.

I got your message and knew what it meant and what I had to do. There have been boys in the past with whom I have had silly little affairs. None of them went very far. This boy was different. I am not writing his name and hope it may not be necessary to publish it. He was more than willing for me to take such liberties with him as I wished. Also I knew that in this case, unlike the others, he would demand money to keep quiet and if I did not pay him – or did not pay enough – he would talk. I was proved right about this almost at once. He told his story to the reporter, Pirrie, no doubt with every detail, and if he enjoyed doing it I'm sure Pirrie enjoyed it too. Pirrie came straight down from the club to see me. Martha told him I was taking my usual evening stroll down by the river. No time to waste. He came straight down to tell me, with a horrible feigned regret, that reluctantly he felt it to be his duty – I could see him mouthing the words and savouring them – to report the facts to the police. I hit him, once. The blow was meant for his chin and landed on his throat. I was certain I had killed him and can only say I felt no remorse. I carried him to the end of the jetty and lowered him into the river. As I was doing it a boat was coming up. It was dusk, not dark, and I wondered if they had seen me. Apparently not, since the boat went straight on. That's all.

Good night.

There was much to do.

The original document, carefully handled, had to be tested for finger prints. If any were found they could be compared with the rector's prints, of which there would be plenty in the house. This was a routine precaution in case anyone sought to question the authenticity of the document; unlikely, seeing that it was written throughout in Father Freeling's distinctive hand. Then several photocopies had to be made, one of which must go, by hand, to the coroner's officer for transmission to the coroner.

Petrella accompanied it with a short note, explaining where it had been found. Cracknell would arrange for the moving of the body to the mortuary. Next, to alert Dr Summerson and to preserve, for his examination, the bottle of tablets and the nearly empty half-bottle of whisky which he had found by the bed.

There being nothing more to be done for the moment, he decided that he would go home for lunch. He could take the opportunity of telling his wife what had happened.

Jane said, "I knew something was wrong. The advice he gave wasn't for you. It was for himself. To take things on his own shoulders and try to avoid hurting anyone else. I didn't know what was behind it, but I could see that much."

"Whether it was meant for him or me," said Petrella, "it was good advice."

Jane said, "I nearly forgot. I've had three people round this morning and the telephone's been going non-stop. It's an article in the *Sentinel*. One of them left his copy with me."

Petrella read the leading article in silence. Then he said, "Looks as though someone's going to have to apologise to Sergeant Stark, doesn't it?"

More than a simple apology was going to be needed. This was due to the activity of ex-Detective Constable Cracknell. From time to time all coroner's officers got early news of sensational happenings. Most of them were discreet. Cracknell was an exception. He had a standing arrangement with the news editor of the *Messenger*. This paper had already been critical of the *Sentinel*'s anti-SAS stance. Now their leading hatchet man got to work. He avoided any high-flown rhetoric and headed his article 'Egg on Face'.

The 184,499 registered readers of the *Sentinel* (figures confirmed by the Press Bureau) must have been thrilled to the marrow by yesterday's leading article. Enveloped, like a coy Victorian maiden, in swathes of 'maybes' and careful qualifications, the story it told was brutally clear. There was, in east London, a villainous police sergeant. The proof of his villainy? That was simple. Before becoming a policeman he had been a member of the SAS. His latest victim, it seemed, was an employee of the *Sentinel*, a Mr Pirrie, who had been ferreting round in the sergeant's manor and was said, on one occasion, to have got into an argument with him. Mr Pirrie's body was recovered from the Thames. He had been killed (wait for it!) by a karate chop as taught to all members of the SAS. Moreover, and clinching evidence, it seems that he may have gone into the river in the very area in which the sergeant lived (some 5,000 other Londoners lived there too, but don't let that bother you). The killer of Mr Pirrie has now taken his own life, leaving behind him an unquestionable confession. All details will no doubt be made public when the inquest on Mr Pirrie is re-opened. So what happens next? Does the maligned policeman look to the courts for redress? Even more intriguingly, does the *Sentinel* publish a most abject apology?

This journalistic cross-fire was studied by other interested parties.

Lovell was summoned once more to the Home Secretary's office. Copies of the two articles were on his desk. He said, "I take it you've read these effusions."

"I certainly have," said Lovell. "The first one made me angry. The second one made me laugh."

"It's not your reactions that interest me. It's your considered opinion on what is going to happen next."

"I'm afraid there's no doubt about that, sir. The *Sentinel* has loaded what you might call a double-barrelled gun. One barrel was pointed at Sergeant Stark. That having missed – or rather, having blown up in their face – they'll be particularly anxious to see that the second barrel is effective."

"Meaning?"

"That they'll make sure it hits the target."

"The target being Superintendent Petrella."

"I'm afraid so. Our Complaints Department is already studying a sheaf of documentary evidence brought over by hand this morning. I could have copies made for you – "

"Let me have it in your own words."

"The documents – copies of letters, statements, board minutes and things like that – seem to show that Petrella consorts with pornographers and is helpful to them. In consideration for his services he has received 2,000 shares in a company which promotes pornographic magazines."

"He got them free?"

"Yes. A gratuitous allotment."

"And you consider the evidence conclusive?"

"For the most part, no. It is largely composed of statements by people who are evidently hangers-on of the pornographers, ready to give evidence at the drop of a hat – "

"Or the drop of a ten-pound note."

"A suitable number of ten-pound notes would certainly unlock their tongues. On the other hand, there are two

209

items which do require explanation. Some photographs and the share transaction, which is fully documented."

The Home Secretary rolled it round in his mind. He had witnessed many assaults on people's reputations. Had been the subject of more than one himself.

Lovell said, "It seems to me to be an ideal case for a PDE."

"Yes. That would be appropriate. One thing puzzles me. I find it hard to believe that an experienced man like Petrella – incidentally I've read his record. A remarkable man in many ways – should have allowed himself to be framed without fighting back."

"When I was discussing it with him he said that in a bull fight the matador didn't attack the bull. He waited for it to attack him."

"And then?"

"I've never actually seen a bull fight, but I imagine that he whisks aside the cloak the bull has been charging and sticks his sword into the animal as it goes past."

The Home Secretary thought about certain members of the Opposition who had been plaguing him lately.

"How gratifying it would be," he said, "if life was as simple as bull fighting."

Piggy Soltau was sitting, with his feet up on the table, in the room he occupied above Goat Glibbery's second-hand clothes and general junk shop. He was smoking his tenth cigarette of the day, and he was thinking.

He was the best educated and the least pleasant of the Farm Boys. Starting his career as an RAMC orderly he had been discharged for stealing and selling drugs from the medical kits. After which, using some of the morphia syrettes he had brought away with him, he had set up as an abortionist. His last effort, which had resulted in the death of the girl concerned, had landed him in gaol. On getting out he had found work at a garage, where he had performed on the engines of cars the sort of forceful and unskilled surgery he had used on girls. It was here that he had made the acquaintance of Goat Glibbery.

Soltau was, and he knew it, the only one of the Farm Boys capable, in intellect and character, of standing up to Len Farmer. Buller and Dog Henty were muscle-bound oafs. His present landlord, Glibbery, was a nonentity, used by the others as an odd-job man and errand boy.

He stubbed out his cigarette, lit the last one in the packet and thought about the situation. If something had to be done, if some definite action was called for, then he would have to initiate it. And it might be called for, sooner rather than later.

Farmer was becoming dangerously over-confident. If he had not been, he would not have agreed to play a part – even a minor part – in the ELBO cash job next Friday. Apparently he was not worried by Morrissey. Morrissey, said Farmer, was an empty old wind-bag, a bluffer. He said this more than once. He said it so often that Soltau had begun to wonder. For his part, instead of shooting his mouth off, he had kept his eyes open and his ear to the ground. He had noted a number of arrivals in the district, men who seemed to have little to do except hang about on the corners of streets and in the saloon bars of the public houses he used. He had sniffed them with his piggy little snout and they smelled like policemen.

There might be nothing in it. It was easy to imagine things like that. East London had a shifting population. One had to balance between scaring oneself by shadows and taking sensible precautions.

When he opened a drawer in the table to get out a fresh packet of cigarettes his eye lighted on something else that was there. It was a plastic bag. Well, that might serve as a precaution of sorts. If the worst came to the worst.

Keep your wits about you, boyo, and play both sides of the table. That's the game.

18

Since no legal proceedings seemed to be involved the weekend papers were able to express themselves about the Freeling case with unusual freedom. They stirred up the bubbling cauldron enthusiastically. The *Sentinel* did not seem to have many friends in Fleet Street.

At midday on Saturday, Petrella received the summons from Chief Superintendent Liversedge which he had been expecting. He was driven to Shepherdess Walk by Hoyland, who seemed to have appointed himself his private chauffeur.

Liversedge said, "You've been causing some excitement, young fellow."

He said it disapprovingly. Excitement was not catered for in his book of rules.

Petrella said, "Several people have told me that I should be in for a PDE. It's a new procedure, isn't it? Could you explain about it?"

"It's a Preliminary Disciplinary Enquiry. It was introduced into Police Orders, by a directive of the Home Secretary, in February of this year. Where there has been what seems to be a serious complaint against a police officer – I said, 'seems' – "

"Yes," said Petrella. "You said 'seems'."

"I didn't want it to be supposed that I had prejudged the matter. Particularly since I may be concerned in it myself."

Petrella waited patiently. He knew better than to try to hurry Liversedge.

"The procedure is that a panel of three senior officers is convened to consider the evidence and to see whether it warrants any further action."

"Like the old Grand Jury."

"I had not considered the point, but yes. It is similar in function to the old Grand Jury. The panel comprises one officer from the area to which the man complained of is attached, one from the Complaints Section and a chairman from Central."

"A balanced body."

"Certainly. Great care is taken that there shall be no prejudice against the man complained of. The man from the Complaints Section will have the assistance of their legal staff."

"A barrister or solicitor?"

"Something of that sort," said Liversedge, compressing his lips. He had the serving policeman's inherent dislike of lawyers whatever shape they came in.

"And the accused?"

"He is invited, if he wishes, to bring a best friend with him to speak for him."

"Then, if a balance is to be maintained, his best friend should be a barrister or solicitor."

"There is nothing in the rules to forbid it."

"Do we know who will sit on this particular tribunal?"

"Chief Superintendent Roper from the Complaints Department. Myself, as your local member. Chief Superintendent Watterson as chairman. I see that you have the right – " Liversedge had the book of rules open in front of him, " – which must be exercised, in writing, within seven days, to object to any one or more of the selected persons."

"I have no objection to any of them."

"Then all that remains is to agree a date. The official view is that the sooner the matter is dealt with, the better."

"My view, too," said Petrella. "Today is Saturday. I

should like to have Monday free to – er – consult my best friend. Also to hunt out a few relevant papers."

"Then let us say the afternoon of Tuesday. I will give you the exact time and place later. Meanwhile, here are copies of the documents it is intended to rely on." He pushed a heavy folder of papers across the desk. "If it is sought to introduce any extraneous matters you have the right to object."

Petrella weighed the folder thoughtfully in his hand. He said, "It certainly seems enough to be going on with."

That afternoon Morrissey spoke to John Anderson. When Morrissey had run the No. 1 Regional Crime Squad, John had been his second in command. Now that he headed the squads nationally, John had moved up with him and combined running the four Metropolitan squads with acting as his unofficial number two.

Morrissey said, "I take it you're all lined up for the ELBO cash delivery on Friday."

"I'm looking after it myself this time," said Anderson.

"It'll be adequately guarded, I hope."

"It could hardly have more protection if it was the Royal Family."

Morrissey didn't sound worried. He knew that if Anderson was in charge it would be done properly. He said, "Now tell me about Lampier."

"He could give points to the wandering Jew, that boy. Do you know he's changed his pad three times in the last fortnight? He arranges the moves by telephone and carries them out after dark."

"But he hasn't slipped you?"

"No chance. I've got eight men on the job. His last move ended in a bed-sit in Earlham Street, behind the West India Dock Road, which was a bit of luck for us, because one of my men happened to know the owner of that house. He's got some form and is suspected of being a fence. Which gave us an opportunity to twist his arm. He'll let us know when Lampier plans to move again."

"Excellent," said Morrissey. He said it absent-mindedly. The map he was examining was not a street map of London. It was a large-scale map of the Essex bank of the Thames between Creekmouth and Cyprus point, an area of marsh and meadowland, with a few scattered buildings. He had circled one of these buildings in red pencil. It seemed to be a farmhouse. Anderson looked at it curiously. He thought that if it was connected with any criminal activity it must surely be smuggling.

"What I want from you," said Morrissey, "is a man with some experience of signalling. Someone who had a Post Office job, or maybe someone who spent a few years in the Royal Corps of Signals."

Anderson conducted a mental roll-call of his men and said, "I should be able to find one or two men like that."

"There's another even more important qualification. He's got to be a man who's capable of keeping his trap shut. Because I can tell you frankly, Johnnie, that what I'm planning to do is some way outside the book of the rules."

Anderson felt a surge of excitement. Morrissey only called him 'Johnnie' when he was feeling pleased with himself; when he had everything lined up and was ready to blow the whistle. He said, "How soon do you want this man?"

"I want him in place by Tuesday evening."

On the following day, as Sunday lunch was drawing to its sticky close, Petrella had a telephone call which surprised and pleased him. It was from his father, ex-Colonel of Police Gregorio Petrella. He was speaking from Boulogne.

He said, "I've just missed one boat. If the next one runs to time I should be in Dover by six o'clock. Six o'clock your

215

time, that is. Would it be possible for you to meet me and give me a bed for a few days?"

"An enthusiastic 'yes' to both of those. And I've got someone here who's just as keen to see you again as I am."

Donald, who had been listening, grabbed the telephone and shouted down it, "Wait for me. Wait for me. I'm coming to fetch you."

"We shall have to ask your mother about that," said Petrella. "It may mean keeping you up rather late."

This seemed to Donald to be a curious objection; an advantage rather than a drawback. In the end Jane said 'yes' and after a scrambled tea the two of them set out in the car that Petrella had, at last, managed to buy; an aged, but reliable, Volkswagen.

Left to herself Jane put Lucy in her day cot by the open window and settled down to her tapestry work. It was the time of day which she liked best, when Grove Road was quiet with occasional interruptions from the traffic in Maplin Road. She knew that her husband was involved in some difficult business, but had not grasped the extent to which his doings were becoming a matter of public interest.

The immediate effect of a long and imperious ringing on the doorbell was to wake up Lucy, who protested. Jane picked her up, went to the door and opened it. Bearing in mind her husband's instructions she left it on the chain.

There was a young man outside, with a camera slung from one shoulder. He said, "Might I come in?"

"That depends," said Jane, "on who you are and what you want."

"I'm from the *Messenger*. You'll have noticed that we are strongly on your husband's side in his dispute with the *Sentinel*. I expect you read our article on Saturday. I wondered if you might have some comment for our readers. And perhaps a photograph."

Jane was relieved to see that the prolonged ringing of

the doorbell and the sound of voices had brought Mrs Gamage out onto the landing below and that she was listening unashamedly.

Jane said, "My message for you is that you should go away and stop pestering me."

"Surely you can do better than that," said the young man with a smile. "At least let me take a photograph – "

Jane said, "Mrs Gamage."

"Yes, ducky."

"Would you be so good as to nip round to Maplin Road and fetch a policeman? Tell him that this man has been making improper suggestions."

"I'll go right round," said Mrs Gamage, much gratified. The young man, having concluded that discretion was the better part of valour, followed her down. Lucy saluted his departure with a scream which was a mixture of dislike and triumph.

The only other interruption was the return of Mrs Gamage with a constable – luckily one that Jane knew. He said, "Don't you worry, Mrs Petrella. We'll keep our eyes open. The super wouldn't want you to be upset, that's for sure."

Mrs Gamage said, "If one of them nasty creatures comes round again just give us a shout. I'll hear you."

Thus doubly guarded Jane returned to her embroidery.

It was after ten o'clock when the boat party got back. Donald did most of the talking. He said, "And do you know what? We stopped at a place on the way back and had sausages to eat. I had four."

"Off to bed," said Jane.

"I'm not a bit tired."

"We're not all as tough as you," said his grandfather. "I've driven four hundred miles today and I'm so tired I could sleep on a rockery. I think I'll take those papers to bed with me."

"They'll lull you to sleep," said Petrella.

On the following morning, in the intervals of putting

away a large breakfast, his father said, "I leafed through that dossier before I got up. When I was working for General Franco I was threatened no less than three times with fabricated accusations. They were a good deal more carefully rigged than this one. This is a house of cards, resting on two premisses. One of them questionable, the other simply wrong." He explained what he meant and added, "One or two facts are still not quite plain. If I'm to give you the whole picture I shall have to do some telephoning. It'll be a question of locating one man and seeing if he can put me on to another man."

"Do all the telephoning you want," said Petrella. "I shan't be here. I've got a date with my best friend."

Geoff Tasker was a full-jowled, black-haired character who conducted a one-man solicitor's practice near the Oval cricket ground. He worked a twelve-hour day for most of the year and closed his office for the complete period of the London Test Matches. He did a lot of police-court work, appearing indiscriminately for and against the police. Petrella knew him well.

He spent ten minutes looking at the papers and photographs Petrella had produced and at the end of it said, "Your father's right. Most of this is piss and wind. The only points of substance are the photographs and the share transaction. We shall have to decide what line we're going to take about those."

"I think," said Petrella carefully, "that the line has been indicated to us by the opposition. Let me explain."

He spoke for ten minutes and produced two further documents. Mr Tasker rarely smiled, but at one point he actually laughed out loud. When Petrella had finished he said, "One thing puzzles me. Instead of all this share pushing why didn't they just pay money into your bank?"

"It wouldn't work. Nothing can be paid into my account until I've signed the paying-in slip. I imagine that's why they rigged this share business. It might have come off too, if they hadn't run up against my father."

"Yes," said Mr Tasker thoughtfully, "I suppose it might."

Lovell, although he approved in principle of Morrissey's reticence, felt that, on this occasion, he was carrying it too far. He summoned him to his office and put the matter to him squarely.

Morrissey said, "Of course you're right, sir. The difficulty is that my tactics hinge on one fact that I'm not, even now, quite certain about. Though I'm taking steps to remedy this."

As he spoke Lovell's face grew grimmer and grimmer. He said, "When are you going to know the truth?"

"If all goes as I expect, I'll know by tomorrow evening."

"What really worries me," said Lovell, "is the fact that you're doing all this yourself. I appreciate your reasons. We don't want a repeat of the Ernie Flower balls-up. And the less people who know a secret the likelier it is to stay secret. But suppose something had happened to you. Suppose you were run over by a bus."

"I look both ways before I cross any road."

"Maybe. But all the same I'd like you to bring Frank Watterson in on it."

"No objection," said Morrissey. "In fact, while I'm at it, I'll brief both him and Kay."

Lovell thought about this for quite a long time before he said, "Yes. That might be the best way."

19

On the Tuesday afternoon, when Petrella and Mr Tasker
were shown into Chief Superintendent Watterson's office,
they found four men there. In addition to Watterson they
were Liversedge, Chief Superintendent Roper, head of MS
15, the Police Disciplinary and Complaints Section, and,
to Petrella's surprise, Mr Batson, QC. As soon as they
were seated he scribbled a note for Mr Tasker, who read
it impassively and added it to his other papers.

Watterson opened the batting.

He said, "This is a new procedure. You might call it
an experiment. It is designed to sort out those cases –
we've had far too many of them – where some member of
the public blows off steam against a police officer, maybe
justified and something in it; but maybe out of spite and
nothing in it, resulting in a smeared policeman and a waste
of everyone's time. However, since we have stated, more
than once, that *all* complaints against the police would
be looked into, we have designed the PDE as a sieve,
through which complaints can be passed. A quick and
simple hearing, in private, to arrive at a speedy conclusion.
The proceedings are recorded on tape."

Petrella had already noticed the squat boxes, one on
each side of the table, and had guessed their purpose.

"If we conclude that there is substance in the allegations,
then the recording goes forward to the disciplinary hearing
which will follow. If we conclude that there is no real
substance, then the complainer is so informed, the tape is
destroyed and the matter is concluded. All clear so far?"

Petrella and Mr Tasker nodded.

"The other point which I have to make is that this is not a court of law. We keep it simple. No speeches, no examination and cross-examination of witnesses. The procedure we have developed is that the complaint, and all evidence in support of it, is supplied to the person complained of, in writing. He is invited to give such explanation as he thinks necessary and we, or any one of us, can question that explanation or ask for further details. Whilst no witnesses are called, it is open to the accused to put forward what his witness would have said in the form of a written statement signed by that witness. If the matter does go further, then that witness can be called and examined and cross-examined in the usual way. Over to you, Mr Tasker."

Mr Tasker swivelled round, looking at all four men in turn, focusing finally on the lawyer. He said, "Before I start I'd like to clear up one point. Who does Mr Batson represent?"

Batson said, "I represent the police and am instructed by MS 15."

"And were you instructed by them also at the inquest on Poston-Pirrie?"

A flush of annoyance appeared on Mr Batson's face and he said, "Certainly not."

"Then might I ask who instructed you on that occasion?"

"The question is irrelevant and I decline to answer it."

Mr Tasker raised one of his heavy eyebrows and looked at Watterson, who said, "Really, Mr Batson. Even if the question is irrelevant I see no reason why you shouldn't answer it."

Mr Batson was clearly tempted to ignore this suggestion, but he may have reflected that it was bad tactics to start by upsetting the chairman. Also he suspected that Geoff Tasker had raised the matter simply to needle him, a tactic for which he was notorious.

He said, "If you so rule, sir. I have no objection to stating that on that occasion I was instructed by the *Sentinel* newspaper. I still fail to see the relevance of this line of enquiry."

"Surely it is relevant," said Mr Tasker. "We are dealing here with complaints that originated from the *Sentinel*. If you were instructed by them so recently, would it not have been preferable for the police to instruct some other barrister to take part in this enquiry?"

Mr Batson looked at Watterson, who said, with a smile, "You yourself, Mr Tasker, appear one day for the police and the next day against them. I think we must allow Mr Batson to be similarly dispassionate."

Mr Tasker said, "Very well, sir. I'm sure he'll do his best to be dispassionate. Now, I do not propose to trouble the tribunal about the first part of this case. I refer to the vague and unauthenticated items" – he examined the document in his hand with evident distaste – "which, we are told, one Ted Lewis passed to one Roy Saunders, or which one Arthur Basset heard from one Frank Cole and passed on to one Sam Levy. If these gentlemen ultimately appear to enlarge on these tit-bits of gossip we may find out who they are, where they come from and what weight is to be attached to their table talk – or should I say their public-bar talk? If, and when, they are called I shall be delighted to cross-examine them on these matters. Until then I submit that their evidence is worth less than the paper it is written on." He then placed the document at the bottom of the pile of papers he had in front of him.

Mr Batson said, "If I might, sir. I would agree with my friend that if the two main charges fail, then these preliminary matters, which he is lightly dismissing, cannot stand by themselves. I would submit, however, that if the main charges *are* substantiated these auxiliary matters lend a certain weight and colour to the allegations affecting, as they do, the general repute of the officer in question."

"When you say colour," said Mr Tasker, "I imagine

you refer to the redness of our old friend the red herring. However, since I am confident that what you call the two main charges will both be dismissed, I am more than happy to go forward on that basis. These two photographs show Superintendent Petrella, in a club of dubious repute, in the company of a man identified as Mal Martiennsen, a printer and distributor of pornography. They show other things which I shall come to in a moment. However, I will now ask the superintendent to tell us how he came to be there."

Petrella explained the message he had had from Superintendent Kay. Mr Batson said, "I should like to be clear about this. Did Kay suggest the meeting, or did Martiennsen suggest it?"

"The suggestion came from Martiennsen. Kay passed it on."

"And when you decided to act on this suggestion," said Mr Tasker, "what did you do?"

"I made an entry in the station Occurrences Book."

This reply was so unexpected that it produced a moment of silence.

"I have here a photo-copy of the relevant page," said Mr Tasker. "As you will see, it records that the superintendent would be away from the station for about an hour to meet a Mr Martiennsen who might have some information for him. This does not tell us anything we didn't know already, but it does at least demonstrate that there was no secrecy about the meeting. Please note that the entry is timed six thirty. So, what happened next?"

"The suggested time of the meeting was six thirty and I was already late. So I grabbed a taxi and went right along. Arriving, I suppose, around seven o'clock. Perhaps a little earlier."

"And then?"

"The meeting was brief and I suppose I was back in my office not much later than half past seven."

"Again by taxi?"

"Yes. This one was a bit faster as the rush hour was easing up."

Mr Tasker said, "Since these timings are important, I shall be confirming them from a number of different sources later. For the moment I suggest that you examine the photographs. You all have copies? Good. The first point, again, is one of timing. If you look closely you will see that there is a man in the background lighting a cigarette. In photograph number one he is clicking on his lighter. In number two he is applying it to his cigarette. Suggested interval, not more than five seconds. I make the point since otherwise it might be supposed that there was a considerable interval between the photographs and that they record a conversation of some length. They do no such thing. They record the opening moment of an extremely brief conversation."

"Where are these photographs taken from?" said Watterson.

"It seems, sir, that the whole business is controlled from behind the bar. At intervals brighter lighting is switched on and the cameras, which are in a gallery beside the lights, come into action."

Watterson made a note on the pad in front of him. The silence whilst he did so had a hint of storm weather behind it. When he had finished he said, "Please continue, Mr Tasker."

"You said, Superintendent, that the interview was brief."

"Brief and unsatisfactory. I wanted to know who was behind a company called 'Intriguing Publications'. After fluffing around he said that he might be able to find out, but it would cost me money. Upon which I gave him up and departed."

"Leaving your drink behind you?" said Watterson. "Do you know what it was?"

"Allegedly white wine, sir. He pushed it at me. I pushed it back and it finished up in no-man's-land."

There was a further brief silence, broken by Roper, who said, "The story from the *Sentinel* which accompanied these pictures is, as you will have seen from the documents supplied to you, radically different. It is based on the testimony of Martiennsen. In his version you had a friendly talk, which lasted for more than an hour, accompanied by a number of drinks, of which the one on the table was only the first. And that, at the conclusion of it, he promised you a substantial sum of money if you would drop your enquiries into this company, 'Intriguing Publications'."

"And what did I do?" said Petrella, who seemed to be more amused than alarmed.

"You promised to consider the matter." Turning to Watterson, Roper added, "So far, this seems to me to be one man's word against another's."

"Fortunately," said Mr Tasker, "that is not so. Other men were involved. In one case, quite closely involved. Two of them were playing a game of draughts at a table not more than a yard away. Statements which have been taken from them are practically identical, so I will only trouble you for the moment with one of them." He read from a sheet of notepaper which was scrawled across with crabbed writing. " 'I observed the curious conduct of the two men at the table behind us. On account of the general din, which seemed to be a permanent feature of that place, I was unable to hear much of their conversation, but the black-haired man seemed to be making the running. He pushed a drink towards Superintendent Petrella, who pushed it back again. Their subsequent exchanges were brief and, I thought, rather bad tempered. After about five minutes the superintendent got up and left. Our table was so close to his that he accidentally knocked it over when squeezing his way out.' "

"Who are these men?" said Watterson.

"One of them, sir, was Lieutenant-Colonel Peter Winchip, late of the Indian Army, now standing adviser to the British

Museum on Indian manuscripts and illustrated missals. The other was a Mr Wilfred Wetherall – "

"Good heavens!" said Watterson. "Is he still alive?"

"You knew him?"

"If you mean the man who was once head of the South Borough Secondary School, certainly I knew him. Both my sons were there. The boys used to call him Wellington Wetherall, on account of the shape of his nose and a certain rigidity of character."

Mr Tasker said, "I hope I am right in assuming that you would place more reliance on the evidence of two men like that than on the unsupported testimony of a self-confessed pornographer."

"Certainly," said Watterson, turning to Roper. "Quite apart from the character of the witnesses, I make the odds three to one."

"You will find," said Mr Tasker smoothly, "that the odds are even longer than that." He picked up another piece of paper. "For some time Superintendent Morrissey has been suspicious of the Quartermass Club. Some of the villains he was particularly interested in – among others Leonard Farmer and Andy Hicks – were known to frequent it and he had put the club under surveillance. Two of his men were on duty that evening. They both knew Superintendent Petrella by sight. In their report there is a note of his time of arrival – six fifty-five – and his departure – seven fifteen."

"Five to one. Game, set and match," said Watterson. Liversedge nodded. Roper said, "Then this means that Martiennsen was lying."

"It means," said Watterson coldly, "that if he dares to repeat his statement on oath he will be in very bad trouble indeed."

Speaking for the first time Liversedge said to Petrella, "I assume that you knew Winchip and Wetherall and that they knew you. Was it a coincidence that they should happen to have been there?"

"Certainly not. In the ordinary way neither of them would have been seen dead in a place like that. They went there to oblige me."

"Fortunately, as it turned out. But why did you ask them?"

"When I heard the name of the club, I remembered that it was the place where those photographs were taken that weighed so heavily against Superintendent Hood."

No one seemed anxious to break the silence which followed. Eventually, speaking slowly, as if he was dictating an official report, Roper said, "Superintendent Hood was investigated by my office. It is true that the evidence against him did contain photographs taken at that club. But they were only a small part of the total evidence."

"Just so," said Watterson hastily. "I think we are being led off the track. Please proceed, Mr Tasker."

"About what has been referred to as the second main charge, I have very little to say. It seems to have been totally misconceived. The principal document in support of it is, as you have seen, a photocopy of a board minute of Intriguing Publications. It runs: 'The directors considered an application for shares from Pedro Casimir Petrella of Flat B, 27 Grove Road, E14. Resolved: In view of the services the applicant had rendered to the company that 2,000 ordinary shares be allotted to him gratuitously. The secretary to be instructed to forward the relevant share certificate in due course.' And there is a note dated August 30th that the certificate was duly despatched."

"I was given to understand," said Roper, "that Pedro Casimir was the correct form in Spanish of your given name and that this is your address."

"Half right," said Petrella. "This is my address, but not my name. I am, and always have been, Patrick. Pedro Casimir is my cousin, the son of my father's younger brother. A letter which arrived recently and which I forwarded to him contained, I understand, the share certificate referred to."

Mr Batson, who had been silent for some time, looked up from leafing through a sheaf of memoranda. He said, "I find this puzzling. I know, of course, that the superintendent is commonly referred to as Patrick, but in the light of this document I, too, supposed that it was the English form of his name."

"Not so," said Petrella. "If Pedro had to be reproduced in English it would surely be Peter, not Patrick. In any event, it does not arise. Mr Tasker has all the relevant documents."

"Dealing first with the cousin," said Mr Tasker. "His birth was registered, in the normal way, in Spain. I have here a faxed copy of the original certificate showing the names, as you can see, Pedro Casimir. With regard to the superintendent, the situation is rather more complicated. He was born when his parents were, temporarily, in Beirut. In accordance with local regulations, his birth was registered at the Spanish Consulate. Unfortunately, this building, like so many others in Beirut, was totally destroyed in the subsequent fighting and its records perished with it. However, when the family, which seems to have been continually on the move, arrived in England, the superintendent's mother, an Englishwoman, insisted that the child should be baptised and this was carried out at St Michael's Church, Portsmouth. I have the baptismal certificate here, signed by the rector. It shows the child's name as Patrick. No other names."

Silence fell as this information was digested. Mr Tasker added helpfully, "Mrs Petrella senior is still alive and if any doubt is felt about these facts, a statement can easily be obtained from her."

"For myself, I can see not the slightest reason for doubt," said Watterson.

Liversedge once again nodded. Roper said, "If this Pedro Petrella is your cousin and not you, can you explain why his address is given as 27 Grove Road?"

Petrella explained about his cousin's use of the flat and

added, "When he left there he was on the move and he kept it as his permanent address. Letters for him came there, including the one with the share certificate in it. When we spoke about it on the telephone he could only say that he never looked a gift horse in the mouth."

But the heat had gone out of the enquiry.

Summing up, Watterson turned to Roper and said, "Since the complaint came to you, Jim, at MS 15, it will be for you to communicate with the *Sentinel*. I suggest that you send them two letters. A formal one, saying that we have examined the evidence and that it does not reflect in any way on the officer concerned, and a personal and confidential one to the editor indicating just where he has gone off the track. That should prevent him from pursuing the matter any further."

Roper said, "Very well." Petrella thought that he did not sound happy.

20

On Wednesday morning Petrella had a telephone call from Morrissey. The old man sounded uncommonly cheerful. He said, "You really had them by the short and curlies yesterday, didn't you?"

"At the PDE, you mean? Yes, it went very well. I'd always thought that if we could persuade the bull to charge we'd get a chance to stick him as he went past."

"Stick him? You cut his balls off! And I can tell you, it caused a lot of pleasure, not to say hilarity, at this end."

"Then the news has got round?"

"You can't keep a good story down. And have you seen the *Sentinel* this morning?"

"I don't get time to read the papers until I get home in the evening. What surprise has it cooked up for us now?"

"The surprise is that for the first time in six months there's nothing in it about the police. Not a word. Now they're getting worried about Iraq."

"Plenty of room for worry there."

"And you remember that chap Wintringham? He's gone back to Baghdad."

"He'll be happier there, I expect, than he was in London."

Morrissey said, "Tell me how you rigged it. That business of the names."

"That was my father, not me. It's an odd story and we haven't got to the bottom of it yet. A few weeks ago – just after young Hoyland had muddied the water in Amsterdam – a man calling himself Harrington turned up in Casablanca. Seems he wanted to set up there the sort of outfit he'd had in Amsterdam. Plenty of young talent available. Nothing to do with my father, of course. But Harrington called on him, made some polite conversation, said he had met me in London. When he was going – very casual this – said he'd heard me called Patrick. Was this my real name, or was there some Spanish equivalent? Well, my parent, who was already deeply distrustful of the smooth Mr Harrington, didn't see why he shouldn't pull his leg, so he gave him my cousin's names and thought no more about it – until they turned up on that absurd charge sheet. Then he got busy."

"Doing what?"

"Finding out Harrington's real name. He'll do it, too. He's got a lot of contacts."

Morrissey said, "Interesting. Very interesting. Got to ring off now. I've got a high-powered conference coming up about the ELBO cash run on Friday."

As Petrella put down the telephone one thing was puzzling him. However high-powered the conference, should he not have been summoned to it? Did that indicate dissatisfaction of his handling of the arrangements on the previous occasion? He put the thought aside and turned to half a dozen other matters that were clamouring for his attention. He noted that the unhappy Sergeant Kortwright had put in an application for transfer to another area. Could it really have been only a month ago that he had formed up to discuss his difficulties with Sergeant Stark?

So much had happened in the interval that it might have been six months ago.

"Well, gentlemen," said Morrissey, "you all know what we're here for."

Realising that the numbers present would have over-filled his own office he had secured the use of one of the small conference rooms for his meeting. Like many such rooms in the building it was wired for sound.

Present, in support of him, was John Anderson his number two, Chief Superintendent Watterson and Superintendent Kay representing Central. Chief Superintendent Liversedge was there from No. 2 Area with a nervous Superintendent Ramsbottom hiding behind him. Ashley Drummond had brought along his chief cashier, thus marginally restoring the balance between policemen and civilians.

"This Friday we have another cash run from the bank to the head office of ELBO. And this time we're not only going to see that the cash goes through, but we're going to gather in anyone who makes the slightest effort to stop it. Now I've had a certain amount of information lately, from a man we've very carefully planted, about the opposition plan. Their scheme is to leave the cash carrier alone until he gets nearly to the top of Globe Road – to be precise, until he reaches the last right-hand turning, the one that goes past Meath Gardens into Limehouse Fields. Here they are going to mass every West Indian they can recruit. There'll be no shortage of volunteers and no doubt additional help can be bribed or bullied. They count on having at least sixty – possibly seventy or eighty – men in Limehouse Fields. These erupt into Globe Road, block it, force the driver to open up by threatening to set the van on fire, collar the cash and disperse. Everyone with me?"

The seven men who had been following this on their maps indicated that they were with him.

"Now you'll remember that last time the opposition got hold of duplicate keys of Meath Gardens and hid the get-away car there. This time the lock's been changed and we've got the only keys. Our plan is to feed fifty men into Meath Gardens by the north-west gate in Roman Road. They'll go in on Thursday night and lie low. A second lot of fifty men will come up into Limehouse Fields from the south, using the track beside the canal. Additional reserves will be on the west side of Globe Road, ready to come out from Chudleigh Street or Stepney Way."

Drummond said, "Will they be armed?"

"With motor-cycle crash-helmets, to protect their heads, and with truncheons."

"To use on the heads of the sambos," said Kay happily.

"Should be worth watching," said Drummond.

"We might be able to fix you up with an observation post."

Everyone seemed satisfied with these arrangements, except for Watterson. But he refrained from criticism.

That evening Len Farmer left his house on the Essex marshes and drove north by a private road until he reached Newham Way. Here he turned left and left again down to the Blackwall Tunnel, emerging, as the last of the light died over the Kentish hills, into that desolate area of half-built and half-destroyed houses which surrounds the tunnel entrance. He drove with confidence, as one who knew the area well. His objective was a small river-side public house. Considered as a building it had much in common with the prostitutes who frequented it, being both flashy and dirty. Here he was evidently well known and the lady who doubled as bartender and madame showed him straight into her private parlour.

Torpedo Hicks was waiting for him.

When the ritual drinks had been consumed, Farmer leaned forward with both elbows on the table and said, "I've got some news for you. Hot from the press." Whereupon he repeated, almost word for word, what Morrissey had told the meeting that morning.

"I suppose this is straight goods," said Hicks, scratching his chin with one great thumb. "You're not being sold a load of old cobblers by any chance?"

"My informant has been perfectly reliable in the past."

Hicks grunted, took a long pull at his drink and said, "OK. So what do we do?"

The fact that he was being deferred to by Hicks, coupled

with the manner of his speech, would have made it clear to a listener that Farmer was the leader. He said, "Someone once remarked that the best general was the man who had his troops on the field fifteen minutes before his opponent. I propose to turn that upside down."

"Meaning what?"

"Meaning that we do nothing – for the moment. Let them mobilise a hundred and fifty men – two hundred if they like – this Friday, next Friday and the Friday after. They'll soon get tired of it. They can't keep it up for long. And as soon as we hear that they're letting up, we go in. Right?"

"All right," said Hicks. "I'll pass the message on. To tell you the truth, some of them won't be sorry. They wouldn't have enjoyed a stand-up fight on level terms. Six to one is their idea of good odds. One thing worries me. And when I explain the scenario to them it'll worry them too. It seems that Morrissey knew a bloody sight too much about *our* plans."

"The fact had not escaped me. When he was talking to the others, he didn't actually name his informant, but he gave a pretty broad hint. He said, 'a man we've very carefully planted'. Can only be one person."

"That ex-cop Lampier."

"Must be."

"And now that you know – "

"Now that I know," said Farmer, with a butcher's smile on his broad red face, "I propose to abate the nuisance."

"How are you going to find him?"

"No problem. My informant has supplied me with his current address. We'll pick him up tomorrow and put him on trial for his crimes. If we're not going for the ELBO cash, it'll be a useful diversion. Give them something to do. The boys always enjoy it. Piggy suggested that you might like to watch."

"Look forward to it," said Hicks.

* * *

At around midday on the following day Lampier was sitting in the front room on the second floor of a house in Earlham Street. Among a number of things that he wanted, the most urgent was a cigarette.

He had suggested to his landlord that perhaps he would oblige by nipping round to the corner shop and buying him a couple of packets. His landlord, who had one eye and a number of convictions for minor offences, had said that it was no part of his fucking job to run errands for his fucking tenants. If his tenant wanted cigarettes, why didn't he fucking go out and buy them?

Lampier, unwilling to give him the real reason, which was that recently he had felt increasingly nervous about being seen on the street before dark, had withdrawn the suggestion and was suffering in silence.

The half-hour striking from the church up the road seemed to make up his mind for him. It was the lunch-hour and the street which he could see from his window was practically empty. Chance it.

He crept down the front stairs and out into the hall. The house was as quiet as the street outside. He opened the front door, thumbing down the catch so that he could get in again. Then he was out in the street, sliding along the south side of the road in the shadow cast by the midday sun.

Through the open door of his ground-floor sitting-room his landlord watched him go. He suspected that he might never see him again, but since he had taken a week's rent in advance the thought did not trouble him unduly.

When Lampier came out of the tobacconist there were two men on the pavement and a car drawn up at the kerb with a driver behind the wheel and its rear door open. Each of the two men grabbed one of Lampier's arms, lugged him, struggling and kicking, across the pavement, pitched him head first into the car and climbed in after him.

The car drove off.

Two ladies with shopping baskets saw this happening and decided it was nothing to do with them. A man watching from a window opposite picked up a telephone and started to dial. A car, parked further up the street, edged out and started to move.

In the confined space at the back of the car Lampier had very little room for manoeuvre. Henty and Buller were both stronger than he was. They twisted his arms behind his back and slipped handcuffs over his wrists. Lampier had by this time recovered his wits sufficiently to say, "What the bloody hell – " when a broad strip of sticking plaster was slapped over his mouth.

Henty said, "Shackle his feet?"

"Would mean carrying the bastard," said Buller. He put his mouth down close to Lampier's ear and said, "Listen, boyo. If you try to run away you'll lose both knee caps. Understood?"

Lampier nodded. It was the only movement left to him.

When they reached Glibbery's shop the car drove into the back yard. Lampier was pushed out and punted towards the back door which Glibbery was holding open. When he stumbled, Buller helped him on his way with a swinging kick which landed an inch below the bottom of his spine.

Once they were all inside and the door was shut, Glibbery showed them a cupboard. It was full of musty clothing, in bundles and boxes, but there was just room for Lampier.

"Keep an eye on him," said Henty, showing his dog's teeth. "We want him in one piece. He's our main course for this evening."

"Well, gentlemen," said Farmer, "the court's open."

"Before we get down to business," said Piggy, "I wonder if I might make a suggestion."

"Provided it is made respectfully and in accordance with our customs and usages, you may do so."

"Just to say that the quicker we get rid of this bastard" – he indicated Lampier, even more securely roped – "the happier I should be. Speaking personally, that is."

"Have you any reason for suggesting this change in our procedure?"

"The reason is, I don't trust that shower Morrissey. He's brought in a lot of men round here lately. He's up to something, no question."

Whilst Piggy had been talking, Farmer had been thinking. Lately, he had noticed, Soltau had taken to making suggestions. Some of them quite sensible. It had been his idea to invite Hicks to that evening's proceedings. But he didn't really approve of his subordinates making suggestions. Could Piggy be angling for the leadership? And was Morrissey really moving in on them? If Lampier was on his payroll they would, no doubt, have been keeping an eye on him. So they could have seen him being picked up. It was possible. But one thing he was sure of. No one could have followed them to the Packstone Building. Their approach to it was very carefully organised. They came by separate routes, which were designed to make undetected following impossible. Having thought this through, he decided to compromise.

"What I'll do," he said, "is to present the case for the prosecution. If you find it convincing, OK. We can skip any further talk and decide how the prisoner is to depart this life. Right? Then let me tell you that a very reliable contact in the ranks of our enemies gave me, yesterday, three pieces of information. The first was that Morrissey knew exactly what our plans were for tomorrow. Plans, incidentally, which we've now changed. The second was a broad hint that the information had come from this piece of filth you see on the floor. The third, which was obliging, was the address where we could find him. I don't think – "

he looked round his audience – "that there's much room for doubt."

There was a murmur of agreement.

"Then, if the prisoner has nothing to say – "

Here it became apparent that the prisoner did want to say something.

"A speech from the scaffold," said Farmer genially. "Let's have it."

Buller grinned and ripped the plaster from Lampier's mouth.

Lampier said, in the high, squeaky voice of a frightened child, "That's a lot of balls. How could I tell Morrissey what your plans were? How was I supposed to know them? No one ever told me anything."

This produced a moment of thoughtful silence.

Before Farmer could speak, Soltau said, "I think I can deal with that." He turned to Hicks. "I assume that you've had to explain tomorrow's plans to some of your boys."

"To the leading ones. Yes."

"Well, two evenings ago I saw some of them in the bar of the Deptford Giant and the prisoner was chatting them up. No doubt he'd have picked up enough to guess the outline of the plan."

Farmer said, "How he found out isn't important. The fact that he did find out is proved by the fact that he passed on the information."

The faulty logic in this escaped his audience. They didn't want talk. They wanted action. "Now, any suggestions?"

Dog said, "String the bugger up and dump him in the river. If the body turns up, so what! It's just another nasty little grass has got his come-uppance."

There was a murmur of agreement.

"Then if that's a unanimous decision – you've got the rope, Bull. Sling it over the beam, would you? And lock the door, Goat."

"There ain't no key."

238

"Then bolt both doors, stupid. Top and bottom. We don't want any visitors, do we? Not now that we've reached the most important part of our proceedings. Right. All ready. Then haul away."

"On the whole," said Petrella, "I shouldn't do it. Or rather, all I can really say is that if I was in your shoes I'd let it go."

"The paper wasn't all that kind to *you*," said Stark. "Though we've all noticed that they seem to have turned the tap off a bit sudden. What happened? Did they run into a brick wall?"

"You might put it that way."

"And you really think I'd have no chance, if I started an action?"

"I think you'd have a fifty-fifty chance. Which is the most fatal thing in the world. Because you dive in without really knowing if the water's deep enough. And if it isn't, you get the hell of a crack on the head. Another thing. If you did start an action it'd be for libel and you'd have to find the money out of your own pocket. You can't get legal aid in a libel action."

"That's a clincher," said Stark with a grin. "All the same, I'd have liked to have a smack at them. Not because of suggesting I bumped off that journalist. I'd have given them a kick on the bottom for that. No. It's what they said about me in Ireland – "

At that point the telephone rang. When Petrella picked up the receiver he heard the voice of Arnold, high with pleasure, excitement and incipient hysteria.

"They're at it again. You told us to watch. We saw them drag him in – "

Petrella put down the receiver and said, "You wanted action. Come on." He raced downstairs. It seemed that the meaning of Arnold's message had been appreciated by Inspector Ambrose, who said, "Hoyland's here with your car, sir."

"How many of our patrol cars are on the streets?"

"Two, at the moment."

"Tell them to rendezvous at the corner of Manchester Road and Sterndale Street." And to Hoyland, who was waiting by the car with the door open, "The Packstone Building. As fast as you can, but don't break our necks."

His impression of the next five minutes was a succession of hair-raising twists and turns as Hoyland, avoiding traffic lights, manoeuvred the car out of the main streets and through uncrowded by-ways. Stark spoke only once. He said, "The boy's wasted here. He ought to be on a race track."

Petrella said, "Slow down before you turn into Packstone Passage." As he said it the car jerked to a halt. A metal barrier, with a red light winking in the middle of it, blocked the mouth of the passage. As Petrella jumped out he saw John Anderson, leaning against one corner of the barrier, grinning.

He said, "I've got orders to stop everyone, but I expect the old man wouldn't say no to you. Or the sergeant. A bit of extra muscle."

Petrella said to Hoyland, "Bring the other two cars up here, but tell them to wait." Then he set off down the pavement with Stark padding like a silent shadow behind him.

The front door of the Packstone Building was ajar. He pushed it open and they went up into the foyer. This was full of men. Ten at least, he thought. But he had eyes only for Morrissey who was crouching in front of the inner door, his eye to the keyhole. As Petrella moved forward he straightened up and said, "Now."

This seemed to be an agreed signal. Petrella saw that an eight-foot length of telegraph pole lay on the floor. Four men picked it up, swung it a couple of times, then smashed it against the double doors where they joined, carrying both away, bolts and all. The men dropped the pole and surged through.

Petrella, coming behind them, got a photo flash of the scene in the room before it dissolved in movement. Six men staring, in different states of shock and unbelief, and Lampier strung to a beam in the ceiling, eyes staring and face empurpled, swinging in a slow arc in front of them.

The only man to show fight was Buller. He charged forward with a bellow of rage, straight at Stark. The sergeant moved aside, buried his left fist in Buller's stomach and, as he keeled over, hit him in the face with the full swing of his right arm.

21

The cars were stationary. Petrella wondered what had happened. Perhaps the power had failed. He hoped not. Peering over the side he saw that it would be a long climb down. One advantage of not moving was that he could examine the car opposite more closely. There were significant differences from last time. No more Farm Boys. All the seats were filled by well-dressed, smiling, City types, chatting amiably to each other. So crowded were they that the only intruders, Maurice and Mamma Meinhold, had given up their seats and were clinging to the outside of the car.

"When the car starts they'll be in danger of falling off," said Petrella.

His wife said, "I don't know what you're talking about, but it's high time you snapped out of it."

Petrella rolled over in bed. "Sorry," he said. "A dream. Or was it the end of a nightmare?" He looked at his watch. "Christ! We'll have to hurry breakfast. I'm seeing Morrissey at ten. He wants to have a general discussion before we see the Crown Prosecution bods at eleven."

"So that you both tell the same story," said his wife drily.

"That's the idea, I imagine."

Two weeks had passed. The equinoctial gales had blown away the last remnants of that long, hot summer. The Farm Boys and Hicks had come up twice at Bow Street and twice had been remanded in custody. The five were charged with the murder of Flower; the five, with Hicks, with the attempted murder of Lampier.

Morrissey was in excellent spirits and had good reason to be.

He had done the job his superiors had wanted and was being rewarded for it.

"You'll see it in Orders, when the idle slobs get round to publishing it. I'm being put up to commander."

"That's splendid," said Petrella. "Too late, but splendid."

"It's good for me. Means that when I go out in December my pension will be based on a commander's pay. And good for Johnnie when he takes over from me, as he will. Incidentally – " he looked out of the corner of his eye at Petrella – "that means finding someone to take over the four London squads. I suppose you wouldn't be interested?"

"Do you mean that I'm to be offered the job?"

"When I spoke to Lovell, he seemed to have it in mind."

"Before I decided on anything, I'd have to have his reactions to a memorandum I sent him a week ago."

"Yes," said Morrissey thoughtfully. "I read it. Interesting stuff. A real-life who-dunnit. Trouble is that one of your suspects was at school with Lovell. Makes it difficult for him to be dispassionate."

"But not impossible," said Petrella coldly.

"Let's hope not. However, that's not what you came to talk about."

"What I want to understand is exactly how you pulled off that pantomime at the Packstone Building."

"Pantomime?" said Morrissey thoughtfully. "Is that what it looked like to you?"

"A mixture between a pantomime and the last act in *Hamlet* – with you as producer and stage manager."

There was a moment of silence before Morrissey said, "If we're going to bring down the curtain without any last-minute hitches, maybe you ought to know what was going on behind the scenes. But anything I tell you, stops with you."

"I'm not likely to pass it on to the *Sentinel*."

"Can't stop you discussing it with your wife. But it goes no further. Right? Well, then, you knew that Kay was in Farmer's pocket?"

"I suspected it, but I wasn't sure."

"Same with me. So I bloody well made sure. I let him in on my plans at the very last moment. The only way he could get it across in time to Farmer was on the blower. From a public box, of course. So I tapped Farmer's own phone and I had Kay followed. Result, we know that he made a call at five that evening from a box, duly received by Farmer *and* recorded by our man. So I knew where I stood. Next step was to get my hooks on one of the Farm Boys. Soltau seemed the most likely and I'd been treading on his heels for some days. My men were told to haunt him – quietly. Shop at the same shops, drink at the same pubs. I calculated that his nerve would go and so it did. Three nights ago he came round, very late, to my place and we made a bargain. When the boys were safely behind bars and we'd made suitable arrangements for his protection, he'd turn queen's evidence. But until that time he wanted all guns pointed at Lampier."

"Who was the cheese in the mousetrap."

"Exactly."

"Not a very comfortable role for him."

"Between you and me, I didn't give a brass farthing what happened to Lampier. He was a renegade policeman. In my book that means a lump of shit. If they'd succeeded in hanging him I shouldn't have lost five minutes' sleep over it."

Petrella was busy trying to work out the moves in the Machiavellian game of chess that Morrissey had been playing. He said, "Then you told Soltau and he told the boys where they could pick up Lampier. Practically invited them to do so."

"Right."

"And Soltau was your assistant stage manager for the grand finale in the Packstone Building. I take it he had persuaded Farmer to bring Hicks along."

"Had to have Hicks there. Once he was pegged we reckoned the West Indian gang would fall apart."

"And are you going to be able to bring these charges home?"

"Got a good chance of it. Can't say more. Soltau's our only witness to the murder of Flower. Unless we bring in your young friend Arnold who doesn't seem anxious to talk. Child witness. Always risky."

"Soltau's going to have to stand up to a raking cross-examination. And what's more, you haven't even got a body."

"No," said Morrissey with a grin. "But we've got all his teeth. Piggy was meant to throw them away, but he hung onto them. Most of them have been filled or capped or chipped in some way. His dentist will say that the chance of them belonging to another man is about a million to one."

"There'll be a lot of argument about that."

"Could go to the House of Lords. Our legal boys would love that. However, we're on firmer ground with the second charge. We can all say what we saw when we broke down the door. If you string someone up, you have to argue bloody hard to prove you weren't trying to kill him."

Petrella said, "I'm not a lawyer. But it seems to me you might be in some difficulty in bringing home a charge of attempted murder if it transpired that the attempt could never have succeeded, seeing that Lampier was being watched and protected by you and your men."

"How do you suggest that's going to come out? I'm not going to talk. And the team who were watching Lampier were picked men. Picked by me. Men I could rely on not to speak out of turn."

Petrella said, "I see." He was beginning to do so.

"One other thing. What do you intend to do about Kay?"

"He's retiring. As of now. At his own request."

"No disciplinary proceedings?"

"Difficulty is I could only convict him of treachery by admitting that I'd had Farmer's telephone bugged. At this stage in my career I wasn't prepared to put my head on the block."

Petrella again said, "I see." It seemed inadequate, but he could think of nothing more.

"Then if that's all, we'd better go along and make our mark with the legal eagles. I think, on the whole, the less you say the better. You could mention that you told us about the Packstone Building and the boy Arnold." At the door, he added, "One good result. I'm told that my daughter's dropped Lampier and transferred her maidenly affections to Sergeant Stark."

"A sound swap," said Petrella.

That, and the news of Morrissey's promotion, were the only things he had heard that morning which caused him any pleasure at all.

"Before reaching a final decision," said Lovell, "I wanted your own reaction to the idea of this cross-posting. You realise that it would mean promotion."

"It's attractive," said Petrella. "And there's no one I'd rather work under than John Anderson. But there's a piece of unfinished business that I feel I must wind up before handing over to my successor. I mean the matter which I set out in the memorandum I sent you last week."

"Yes," said Lovell, "we shall have to deal with that. I'd have answered it sooner, but I had to take it up to the Commissioner and there was one point in it which had to be referred to the Home Secretary. Let me lay out the facts, so that you can see whether I've got them straight."

Counsel for the defence, thought Petrella.

"You assert that there is an organisation headed by

certain City men – Seamark and Ringland are named – which arranges for video tapes to be shot involving boys. These were shot in Amsterdam and may now be shot in Morocco. When brought to England they go to a bookshop owner called Meinhold who sends them out to members of a club which has been formed to receive them. Club fees are paid to Meinhold in cash, which he passes on, less his commission, to his masters in the City. Right so far?"

"Perfectly right, sir."

"Now we come to something rather more difficult. Your identification of Seamark depends on the evidence of a nurse in the Central London Hospital. Evidence which is controverted by the doctor involved. Of Ringland, by his possible involvement with the operation in Amsterdam and by your father's success in identifying him with the man calling himself Harrington. He got this information informally, through friends in the Moroccan Immigration Service and he might be embarrassed if forced to produce it in court. Right?"

Petrella nodded. He knew, now, where they were going.

He said, "I did say, in my note, that the evidence against the City ring was slight and that is why I suggested how it could easily be strengthened, if not made conclusive."

"I considered that suggestion very carefully," said Lovell.

"My real point was, that this is an ongoing operation. And there's no easy way for them to stop it. The club members have paid their entrance fees and subscriptions, and are conditioned to getting their periodical doses of stimulation. If they stop the supply the City organisers will be in much the sort of trouble that other suppliers of drugs are in when they try to stop their operation. Particularly now that they no longer have the hired bullies to keep the club members in line."

"I've no doubt you're right about that."

"Then there are just two ways of breaking down the racket and getting onto the men at the top. Either pull in Meinhold on suspicion and frighten him into talking.

Or, simpler and even more effective, hold and inspect all mail going into and out of that shop. That would give you the names of the organisers *and* the club members and demonstrate the connection between them."

"I put both those points to the Commissioner and through him to the Home Secretary – whose authority would be needed to interfere with Meinhold's mail. His answer was, first, that the case against Meinhold was too inconclusive to justify either personal action against him, or interference with his mail. Secondly, that even if all that you have asserted was proved, legal action against the organisers would not necessarily succeed. Our advisers first considered proceedings under the Protection of Children Act, 1978. That's the Act that makes it an offence to take indecent pictures of children or to sell or distribute such pictures for gain. In this case the organisers don't take the pictures and there's no question of sale. The tapes are simply one of the perquisites of being a club member. At first sight, the Criminal Justice Act, 1988, looked more hopeful. Section 150 makes the mere fact of possessing such photographs an offence. It was considered, therefore, whether, by regarding Meinhold as an agent for the City men, a charge of conspiracy to possess the photographs might lie against them jointly. Unfortunately, this won't work. Section 150 only creates a summary offence and in such cases no charge of conspiracy can be framed without the consent of the Director of Public Prosecutions. A consent which, in the circumstances of this case, he was not willing to give."

"Because he was at school with one of them," suggested Petrella.

"On more sensible grounds than that," said Lovell. If the last comment had annoyed him, he was too experienced to show it. He said, "Think about my offer. Why don't you discuss it with your wife? We'll talk about it again when you've had a chance to do that."

*   *   *

The discussion started before supper and continued after supper, until Petrella applied the closure. He tried not to speak bitterly.

He said, "I'm sure the offer was a perfectly genuine one and it would be an interesting and worthwhile job, but I couldn't accept it at the price put on it. That I tear up my memorandum and forget all about Intriguing Publications and the paedo-porn outfit, which would presumably go quietly on, with tapes imported from Morocco or some other country. All right. I've learned my lesson. In police work, particularly if the establishment might be involved, what action you take doesn't depend on the rights and wrongs of the case. It depends on the nature of your quarry. If he is a member of the criminal class, anything goes. Telephones can be tapped, policemen can suppress evidence, one suspect can be chivvied until he changes sides. Another one can be manoeuvred into a position where he is scared out of his wits and then three-quarters strangled. Now turn over another page. This time the quarry is a respectable bookshop owner, acting for top men in the City. Now the situation is quite different. No one must be harassed, their privacy must be respected, their telephones and their mail are sacrosanct. Everyone must behave with decorum. And if it really does look – perish the thought – that they might be guilty, then you can always scratch around among a few Acts of Parliament to prove that you were completely justified in doing nothing."

Jane yawned, put away her mending and said, "No point in talking about it any more. You know what you've got to do."

When it got around that Petrella was leaving the police force and going to help his father run his fruit farm in Morocco, different people expressed different views on the matter.

Chief Superintendent Watterson said to Deputy Commissioner Lovell, "We've lost a lot of good men lately. I'd put him about top of the list."

Lovell said, "Yes. A great pity."

Chief Superintendent Roper said, "Just as well, perhaps, that he's got out. I've a feeling that we should have had to take official notice of some of the things he did."

Chief Superintendent – soon to be Commander – Morrissey said, "Stupid bugger!" but said it affectionately.

The editor of the *Sentinel* said, "Must be something behind it."

Bob Seamark said to Toby Ringland, "I'm having second thoughts about opening up in Morocco. Do you realise that there'll be *two* Petrellas there? Why don't we try Italy?"

Ringland said, "It's an idea. Cut the Mafia in on it. It'd cost money, but we'd be dead safe."

Detective Constable Peregrine Hoyland said nothing, which was wiser than saying what he thought.

The only person who was unreservedly in favour of the move was Donald.